His Name Was David Freeman

A Novel by
Ruth Kipnis

His Name Was David Freeman
Copyright ©2016 Ruth Kipnis

ISBN 978-1506-902-84-5 PRINT
ISBN 978-1506-902-85-2 EBOOK

LCCN 2016952279

August 2016

Published and Distributed by
First Edition Design Publishing, Inc.
P.O. Box 20217, Sarasota, FL 34276-3217
www.firsteditiondesignpublishing.com

ALL RIGHTS RESERVED. No part of this book publication may be reproduced, stored in a retrieval system, or transmitted in any form or by any means — electronic, mechanical, photo-copy, recording, or any other — except brief quotation in reviews, without the prior permission of the author or publisher.

Previous books,

Lane's End
A French Connection

*Keep, ancient lands your storied pomp," cries she
with silent lips. "Give me your tired, your poor,
your huddled masses yearning to breathe free,
The wretched refuse of your teaming shore.
Send these, the homeless, tempt-tost to me,
I lift my lamp beside the golden door.*

Emma Lazarus
The second verse of
"The New Colossus"
appears on the inner wall
of the Statue of Liberty

Author's note

Some years ago I wrote a family history hoping to put together something that could be passed on after my first cousins and I, the second generation, are gone. I was intrigued with the story my limited research revealed about my Grandparents journey to the United States. Their hardships and struggles to make a life for themselves in their adopted county.

When I decided to write a fictional story based on the period I expanded my research and so, 'His name was David Freeman,' was born. The fictional story of one man's journey, the trials he encountered, and the life he carved out for himself and his family told through the eyes of his granddaughter.

The book mirrors the stories of so many improvised poorly educated farmers who left the Ukraine in the late 1880's during the brutal reign of Czar Alexander the third. While some failed most, by sheer will and hard work, created a better richer life than they had ever know. Their children, benefiting from greater educational opportunities, contributed in great numbers to the growth and culture of the United States.

2.2 million Russian Jews came to the United States ending only when unlimited immigration ceased in 1924.

To the millions of immigrants who bravely left home and family to seek a better life in America, my thanks for the wonderful gifts of art, music, rituals, cuisine, and color you brought to our shores and enriched all our lives.

Acknowledgements

I've found a special bond of friendship between an author and the editor. The dedication, patience, understanding and good humor Sue Clark, my wonderful editor, put into this book deserves not just an acknowledgement, but my heartfelt thanks.

My thanks go out to my cousin Shirley Kirchoff, for her wonderful stories of growing up on a farm. I hope she finds the book enjoyable.

Prologue

The wooden stairs, their treads well-worn from years of footsteps, creaked as I climbed to the second floor. I paused in front of the closed door at the head of the stairs reluctant to enter. Taking a deep breath, I turned the glass knob and pushed open the door.

The sun shone through the branches of a large chestnut tree, casting rays of light through the dormer window. Everything in the room was as I remembered. The blanket had been pulled tight over the single bed, the hospital corners precise. The quilt my grandmother made years before was folded at the end of the bed.

The dresser, with a starched, white linen cloth spread across the top, held a fading picture of a young couple in wedding attire. The handsome male standing beside his bride was tall with military bearing, a full head of dark hair and dark piercing eyes. His slender bride looked no more than sixteen or seventeen. Her dark hair, hanging in curls, contrasted with her white, ankle-length wedding dress of satin, encrusted with tiny pearls. A short white Veil completed the picture.

The only other picture in the room depicted a tall man with a full head of grey hair and a grey mustache standing ramrod straight beside four middle-aged men.

In the center of the dresser top sat a shaving mug with brush, a straight razor, strop, and a tortoise shell-backed brush and comb.

As I looked around the room my eyes came to rest on the blue Wedgewood china teapot, sugar bowl, and two glasses resting on a Wedgewood tray on the window seat under the dormer. Tears began to roll down my cheeks as I sat in one of the two chairs at the small table along the back wall. Everything was just as Grandpa had left the room, and now he was gone forever. I'd lost my best friend.

I think I was eight or nine the first time Grandpa invited me for afternoon tea and honey cake in his room, and began telling me stories from what he called the olden days. The ritual went on almost every day but Saturday, until I was about sixteen.

Now, as a young married woman, I look back on those precious afternoons with a sense of sadness. My grandfather's life, and hence his story, ended last night with his death.

I knew my husband was waiting for me downstairs, but I had to take a few more minutes to remember. His stories played such an integral part in my life. I closed my eyes and pictured the afternoon it all began.

Part One

Chapter 1

The ritual started the day my mother sent me upstairs late one afternoon to bring Grandpa a letter the postman dropped off. I knocked on his bedroom door and heard his voice. "Come." He sat at the small wooden table across from the window with a glass in front of him.

He was dressed in starched denim work pants and a spotless white, starched, short-sleeved shirt. His iron-grey hair was slicked back, his mustache well-trimmed, as always.

"What brings you to visit, Maya?" he said, his voice, heavy with accent, reflecting his Eastern European birth.

"I have a letter for you, Grandpa."

"And who, might I ask, would be sending me a letter?"

"Mommy says it's from the State of Connecticut."

"Well, then, it must be important. But it can wait for later. You, my dear Maya, are more important than any letter from the State of Connecticut. Would you like to join me for tea and cake?"

"I've never had tea before, Grandpa."

"Well, then, today might be a good day to start."

Grandpa went to the window seat where his tea set rested and poured steaming tea from the pot into a medium sized glass, taking a sugar cube from a bowl on the tea tray, and cutting a small piece of honey cake, placing it on a napkin he brought to the table. "Sit, child," he said. "We will have a tea party."

I can still see Grandpa as he placed a sugar cube between his teeth and began to sip his tea.

"That looks silly, Grandpa. Mommy drinks her tea out of a cup."

"Ah, yes, but your Mama did not grow up in Russia or she would drink her tea as I do. Try it. Just hold the sugar cube between your front teeth and let the tea flow through."

Chapter 2

I don't recall how many tea parties Grandpa and I had before the conversation turned from my doings, and me to my quizzing Grandpa about what he did when he was my age. One afternoon, when I asked a question about where he grew up, his life story began to unfold, little by little, over the years.

"I had a wonderful childhood," Grandpa said. He closed his eyes, as the memories must have come flooding back.

"Sometimes remembering the past, Maya, makes it seem as if it happened yesterday, instead of so many decades ago. My father was the supervisor of the large estate of Count Fredric Von Zoransky, in what was then called Prussia, later Poland, not far from the Ukrainian border of Russia. My mother died when I was three or four years old. Strange as it seems, I have no memories of her. Being an only child I had no siblings to look after me, so my days were spent tagging alongside my father.

"We lived in a small two-room cottage, provided by Count Zoransky, close to the numerous horse barns housing all the workhorses and breeding stock as well as the Count's riding horses, and his many fine carriages. Remember, there was no such thing as an automobile in those days. Everything depended on the horse."

"Didn't you miss not having a mother, Grandpa?"

"No, not at all. My father was my hero and tagging along after him was always an adventure. The Count's estate," he continued, "was well over a thousand acres, largely tended by tenant farmers whose children were my playmates. We had fields to play in, trees to climb and a river for swimming. I remember the Count's stone and timber castle-like residence, which stood alone away from everything else, bigger and taller and grander than anything I had ever seen. As kids, we liked to peek through the iron gates looking at the big house and it's acres and acres of manicured gardens, all surrounded by high stone walls."

"That sounds like a wonderful place to grow up."

"Oh, it was, Maya. A very wonderful place and safe, unlike many places where young Jewish boys like myself grew up. I was happiest being in the barns and around the horses. Those special horses, I considered my friends, I gave my own names to. I would follow my father as he tended to the livestock, checking the horse's legs, applying strong smelling ointments to their strains, treating their injuries, and bandaging their wounds. All things he learned while serving in the Prussian cavalry.

"I would ask a million questions and my father would explain his actions with incredible patience. The grooms became my friends, as did the rest of the horseman. I was a novelty. It was rare for children to be allowed in the barns. On occasion, I would be allowed to ride atop the various carriages or wagons. The best times were when I got to exercise the ponies belonging to the Count's children.

"When I tired, I would climb the wooden ladder leading to the hayloft and would nap, cushioned by mounds of sweet-smelling straw."

Grandpa rose from his chair and walked to the window staring out at the fields of corn. "Child," he said. "Do you really want to hear more?"

"Oh, yes, Grandpa. I want to hear lots more. You're a really good storyteller. Did you ever get to see the Count?"

"I saw him and his son's on many occasions. The Count would come to the barn to speak with my father about the condition of his mounts, always treating my father with respect.

"I remember him well. He was about my father's age, a very distinguished looking gentleman, dressed in fancy riding clothes, or uniforms with gold braid and a chest full of medals. He had pale skin and rosy cheeks, deep blue eyes, and a bald head. I could not help but stare at his bushy brown, curly mustache. It went from his ear to his chin, then across his upper lip and across the other side of his face, to his other ear. I was fascinated watching him as he would stroke his mustache while he listened to my father speaking about the various horses."

"Did the Count have a wife, Grandpa?"

"Oh, yes. I had never seen anyone so beautiful. I saw the Countess only once when she came to dedicate a one-room wooden schoolhouse on the estate she had requested be built to educate the tenant's male children, but not all the boys went to the school. Some parents thought school was a waste of time thinking you didn't need to read and write to be a farmer. But my father thought differently and I was eager to learn.

"Our teacher, Herr Farber, oh, I remember him well, old and fat. He spoke only German, the language of that part of Prussia. He wore an old black suit, shiny with age, unlike any clothes I had seen before. His starched white shirt was yellowed at the collar and frayed. His belly was too big for a belt, so he wore suspenders that he would snap when he was speaking. Herr Farber thought we were all dullards. His impatience led to the swift usage of the large wooden pointer he possessed, not only to draw our attention to the blackboard, but also to whack us across our backside if we misbehaved.

"I spent six years in school learning to read and write German and mastered my numbers. When I was not in school, I was learning important lessons from my father, not only about horses, but about people, which would serve me well for the rest of my life."

Grandpa stopped and walked to the window to refill his glass with tea, asking if I would like more.

"No thanks, Grandpa. This is all a big surprised to me. Gee, I always thought you were born right here on the farm just like my daddy. If you were born in Prussia how did you get here? Isn't Prussia a really long way away, Grandpa? Please, please tell me all about it."

"Oh, Maya," he said. "It is a very long story as I've lived a very long time, but if you like, I will tell you all about it on another day."

Chapter 3

And so it went. Little by little Grandpa's story was revealed to me as the years went by. I would ask my father if he knew the things I was learning about our family and he would shake his head and say, "No, your Grandpa was never one for, as he put it, needless talk. You're the only one he has conversations with."

One afternoon, weeks later, over tea and honey cake, after my usual unmerciful begging, Grandpa continued the story.

"Everything you want to know happened so many years ago, dear Maya. We grew up faster in those days. One did not have the luxury of being a child for very long. In some ways I was not as fortunate as you and your brother. I had adult responsibilities at an early age. I learned to cook simple meals and keep a clean house. Our cottage had dirt floors. It was my job to keep them raked and to dust the furniture. The snowy winters were bitter cold for months on end, the fireplace being our only source of heat. The smoke the fireplace generated left a layer of black soot that covered everything. I had to dust every day.

"My father paid one of the tenant farmer's wives to wash our clothes, a job I wanted no part of. I did not mind the chores, as my father would always tell me what a good son I was. He would reward me with the raspberry flavored hard candy I loved. I considered myself lucky. Most boys my age worked long hours in factories, or like my friends, toiled in the fields.

"I had just turned seventeen when my father died, suddenly, of a heart attack. He had never had a sick day, as far as I knew. He just keeled over in the barn and was gone. I had no one else, no family. His loss was devastating. My only sense of security rested in the knowledge that outside of my father, I was the best horseman on the estate. What I lacked in years and in experience, I made up for by the careful attention I had paid to the lessons my father taught me, absorbing everything he showed me, committing it all to memory.

"I remember so well Josef, my father's assistant, storming into our cottage the day after father's burial, telling me I had three days to get out of the cottage and off the estate.

"Josef and my father never got along. Father always accused him of being lazy, of caring more for his vodka than his job. He told me many times, "Josef is not to be trusted." I did not think much of him as a horseman, either.

"I knew Josef hated my father and resented me. While I never imagined I could continue to live in the cottage with father gone, I never expected to be thrown off the estate. It was my home.

"I begged Josef to be allowed to stay and work with the horses, telling him I could live in the barn. I can see Josef now, dirty and disheveled, kicking at our dirt floor with his un-polished boot as he sneered at me. 'Out in three days, David. Be sure you take only what belongs to you.'

"For the first time in my life I cried...cried for the loss of my father and for the threatened loss of everything that was my life up until then.

"When I gathered my thoughts together, Maya, I washed up, put on clean clothes, brushed my hair, and left on the long walk to the castle to ask the Count to allow me to remain on his estate.

"When at last I arrived at the Castle gates, I found them locked. I had only one option, so I scaled the wall and started up the long tree-lined drive to the house. I had never been inside the gates before. I marveled at the manicured expanse of lawn, rows of green shrubs, the rose garden, and shade trees, grander than anything I had ever seen before.

"I brushed the dirt off my boots with my cap and ran my hand through my hair before I knocked on the huge oaken doors. Minutes went by before a livered footman appeared and looked at me with a 'What are you doing at the front door' stare.

'The tradesman entrance is in that direction.' He pointed to my right.

"I blurted out, 'I would like to speak with the Count.'

'Impossible. The Count and Countess are away.'

'It is very important. When will they be back?'

'Young man, I have no idea what you want, but under no circumstance will the Count receive you. Now, go before I turn the dogs on you.'

"He slammed the giant doors in my face.

"I stood there for the longest time not knowing what to do. With my head down, lost in thought I left following the path back to the cottage. A jackrabbit crossed my path and ran for cover. Birds were singing in the trees, a sound I usually enjoyed, but not that day.

"Entering the cottage, I sat at the carved oak wood table my father had crafted, wondering for the first time where would I go? I tried to figure out what to do next. It was not until my stomach started to growl that I got up.

"Opening the cupboard, I reached for the breadbox and tore off a hunk of stale bread, then brewed a pot of tea. I had not eaten since the day before. Finishing the last sip of tea I laid down on my bed and tried to sleep.

"I awoke at dawn. I did what I had done every morning since I was a child. I dressed in my work clothes, put on my boots and headed for the main barn. Josef stopped me before I got halfway there, asking what I was doing.

'Checking on the horses,' was my answer.

'You have no business here any longer. If you're not out of the cottage yet, remember you have only two days left before I throw you out bodily.' He poked his finger in my chest. I could smell the liquor on his breath. Turning, he staggered off leaving me no choice. I realized in that instant there was nothing for me to do but pack and leave. The question was, where would I go. What would I do?"

Chapter 4

I was always seeing myself in Grandpa's shoes. Sometimes I'd dream about the stories he told, leaving me to imagine how afraid he must have been. So I asked, "Were you scared Grandpa?"

"No, Maya, not scared. I was terrified. When I returned to the cottage I began to sort through the few things I possessed. What to put them in? I had no suitcase, so I laid my blanket on father's double bed and began to pile my things in the middle. My few pieces of clothing and my one pair of shoes took up most of the room. I found my father's warm winter jacket and his favorite sweater and folded them carefully before I added them to the pile. Then I gathered his shaving mug, tortoise shell brush and comb set, razor and strop, and wrapped them in my clothes. I didn't shave as yet, but was sure I would someday.

"I rummaged through my father's desk. He told me once that if anything happened to him, I was to go to his brother who lived in a village in the outskirts of Kiev in the Ukraine. I found his name and address in the strong box containing the money my father had saved over the years.

"No use putting it off. I would leave early in the morning. The village was a ten-kilometer walk. There, I could catch a train to Kiev.

"I hated to leave all the furniture my father had built over the years. Maybe I should take all the pieces outside and set them on fire so Josef could not use them. But I knew that was an act my father would never condone. Above all else, he was a very moral man. He had taught me to be the same.

"I arose the next morning before the sun, ate the last of the stale bread, and the last of the cheese, washing it down with tea. I tied the four corners of the grey blanket together, making a small bundle I could throw over my shoulder. Tucking the address of my uncle in my jacket pocket, I stuffed all but a handful of coins in my boots. It would be uncomfortable walking, but I did not want to get robbed.

"I glanced around the cottage for the last time, and then closed the door behind me. The pain I felt was overwhelming.

"I snuck into the barn to say goodbye to my favorite horses and a last goodbye to my childhood. I breathed in the sweet smell of horse sweat and hay, the aroma of freshly oiled harness and tack. I saw the ladder to the hayloft remembering the hours I spent sleeping in the straw, vowing someday I would have a big barn full of fine horses of my own. I started down the path to the village and a new chapter in my life."

Chapter 5

Grandpa was such a good storyteller. Even in the mind of a young girl, I could see the sights as he described them. I felt his sorrow and his concerns as if I was living his story myself. He wouldn't talk about his life every afternoon no matter how much I begged. I would have to prod him to tell me more, always reminding him of where he left off in the story.

He, in turn, was eager to hear all about the doings of my brother Billy and me. Grandpa saw little of us as the last few years he'd taken to eating most of his meals in his room. He'd put his breakfast on a tray and take it upstairs to his room after he finished his morning chores. My mother would bring him a tray at dinnertime and set it on his table. I asked him why he ate alone. He said it was a long story. I was too young to understand.

It had been raining too hard to go out of doors and play, and I was bored. Even though it was still too early for tea and cake, I knocked on Grandpa's door and asked if he would tell me what happened when he left home.

"Come in, Maya," he said.

"I can't imagine walking ten miles, Grandpa. If we have to go even a short distance we go by car. Tell me how you found your way to your uncle."

"First, Maya, it was not ten miles it was ten kilometers, a little over six miles." He seemed to think for a minute before he began to tell me of his journey. He put down the book he had been reading and began to speak.

"It took close to three hours to walk to the village, the grey bundle of my belongings thrown over my shoulder. My feet were beginning to hurt from the coins that kept moving around in my boots. The village was tiny, mainly a collection of small shops facing each other across a dirt road. The Count owned all the buildings and rented them to the various merchants who lived above their stores. I had been to the village only twice, and though small, I had no idea where the train stopped. I asked directions of a passerby, and following his instructions. I found the tiny station a short distance away. It looked more like a sentry box. I tried the handle but the door was locked. A chalked sign on the side said the next train would arrive at three o'clock.

"I sat on the small wooden bench in front of the station to wait. The clock high above the door read nine-thirty. The wait would be long.

"At about two forty-five, an old white bearded man arrived and unlocked the station door.

"I asked for a ticket to Kiev, but he told me I would have to buy my ticket on the train. 'Son,' he said. 'This train goes to Warsaw. You will have to change trains for Kiev at the Warsaw station.'

'How long will I have to wait for the train to Kiev?'

"The old man laughed. 'I have no idea. I've never left the village. My only duty is to stop the train if there is a passenger. Then I lock up and return to tend my sweet shop.'

"Seeing the white flag the old man had hung fluttering on a pole in front of the station, the engineer brought the train to a stop. I started to board the first car, but the uniformed man standing at the top of the steps looked at my blanket bundle and me with disrespect as he pointed to the car behind. I said I wanted to buy a ticket to Warsaw and was told, 'Sit down. Wait for the conductor to come round to collect the fares.'

"I walked back to the second car, third class seating, and opened the door to the compartment. Finding an empty place on a wooden bench I sat placing my bundle beneath my feet. The car was filled with men, Jewish, I guessed, as they were speaking Yiddish instead of Russian or German. They were loud, shouting over one another. The man seated next to me was telling a long story complete with hand gestures to several men surrounding him listing intently. No one paid any attention to me.

I settled in for the two-hour ride to Warsaw. I felt uncomfortable in this group of men and frightened at what lay before me. I watched as the train passed through several small villages, then through miles and miles of open spaces. All at once I realized there was a whole world outside the Count's estate I knew nothing about.

"The landscape began to change. Open fields gave way to factory buildings emitting clouds of dark-grey smoke, as the train approached the outskirts of Warsaw.

"Warsaw's population numbered well over two hundred thousand in those days, all under the rule of Tsar Alexander the second, of Russia. It had become an important railroad hub.

"The train pulled into the station, the engine belching smoke that blew back across my window obscuring my view I could barely make out the crowds of people milling about. More people than I'd ever seen before. When the train came to a complete stop, I stepped onto the platform. The people milling about were dressed in ways I had not seen before. The men dressed in dark suits of some fine material, with trimmed beards, hats, and fancy shoes. The ladies wore elaborate dresses that looked like they were going to a party, with large hats trimmed in plumes or flowers, and gloves. I'd only seen finery like that the day I saw the Countess. I felt out of place, frightened.

"The crowd noise was deafening, the language strange to my ear. The whole scene began to terrify me. I tried to ask for help, but I did not speak the language. People passed me by until a grandmotherly-looking lady approached asking in Yiddish if I was Jewish. She spoke the language of my father, a form of low German.

'Do you need help, young man,' she asked.

"I nodded yes. Taking me by the hand, she led me to a bank of cubicles with men sitting behind half-opened windows. She asked where I wanted to go, and then spoke with one of the clerks at the windows. Turning to me she asked for money.

"I took some change from my pocket and gave it to her. She turned back to the window and received my ticket, which she handed to me along with some coins.

"She showed me where to stand and what time the train would arrive. I thanked her.

'You remind me of my grandson,' she said. 'He's about your age.'

"She wished me good luck and went on her way leaving me to wait for the trains arrival.

"Arriving in Kiev fifteen hours later I was once again overwhelmed by the sight before me as I left the station. I had never imagined anything existed as grand and large as Kiev. Kiev was spectacular…wide streets with sidewalks, multi-storied buildings, block after block of shops. The sidewalks were crowded with people, the streets filled with fine horse drawn carriages. I stood on the sidewalk taking it all in, too much for a country boy to process all at once. The language was Russian, strange to my ears.

"Now I was scared my fears growing. How was I going to find my uncle if no one could understand me?

"I wandered for blocks looking in store windows, when as luck would have it, I overheard two men standing outside a tailor shop speaking Yiddish.

"I walked up to them, excused myself and said. "Please, sirs, can you help me find the house of my uncle?"

"They looked at me in a way that made me feel uncomfortable. 'Do you have an address for your Uncle,' the taller one asked.

"I handed him the paper with the information.

"The two men examined the paper, exchanged a few words and then nodded in agreement. 'You'll find this address in Grodov, a Shtetl, about twenty kilometers away. How do you plan to get to Grodov, young man?'

'The only way possible, sir. I'll walk.'

"They wished me good luck and pointed me in the right direction and went on with their conversation.

"On my way out of town, I spotted a bakery and realized how hungry I was. With the little money I had left in my pocket, the rest still safe in my boots, I bought a small loaf of bread and a pot of tea. I sat at one of the small tables doing my best to ignore the glares from the well-dressed people seated there. I knew I looked out of place in my work clothes, boots, and cap, carrying a knapsack.

"I let the hot tea warm my insides, the bread fill the hollow in my stomach.

"Finishing the last drop of tea, I put the remaining scrapes of bread in my pocket, hurried out the door and started to walk in the direction that would take me to Grodov.

"I had walked about a kilometer when a large wagon, drawn by two big bay workhorses, pulled alongside me. The wagon was loaded with an assortment of farm tools, sacks of flour, bolts of material, and assorted metal pots and pans. A large bearded man leaned down and said in Yiddish, 'Where are you going, son?'

'Grodov,' I said.

'You are in luck. I go past there on my way to Protov. Climb aboard. I could use some company.'

"We drove for miles as my benefactor asked questions about where I came from and what I was doing alone on the road. I told him my story and mentioned my uncle by name.

'I know him,' he said, a certain enthusiasm in his voice. 'A fine family man. He buys goods from me sometimes, but he doesn't live in Grodov, he lives beyond the town in a small Jewish farming village. I can take you to his door.'

"Suddenly I felt a sense of relief. There really was an uncle. Now I could relax and view the countryside as the wagon wheels turned, churning up dust along the way. The area looked barren. There was nothing except large copes of trees. Why I wondered was nothing growing along the road that followed the meandering river. If I were home, all the land would be cultivated. As the road took a turn, I could see roof tops in the distance.

'That's Grodov ahead,' the man told me.

"Soon we approached the large bustling Shtetl, shops and houses everywhere. We passed shops with painted signs overhead...butcher, tailor, bakery, jewelry. Then, as we drove past the various shops we came upon the blacksmith's open air space. Smoke from his fire billowed out onto the road. The sound, as he pounded on his anvil, rang in my ears. I saw carts and wagons everywhere piled high with trade goods. Some were stopped alongside the street, their drivers hawking their merchandise. The man, Moshe was his name, said Grodov served all the surrounding farming areas and today was market day. All the farmers came to town to sell their produce and to buy goods.

"We passed by rows of houses. Moshe explained as he pointed in different directions

'There are two separate districts in Grodov. One much nicer, where the Russians live, another for the Jews who are the shop keepers. Two different worlds.'

"As we left, hordes of beggars walked along the roadway headed to town, their dirty clothes in tatters. Some approached the wagon with hands out, asking for food...something I had never seen before.

'Who are these beggars?' I said.

'They're mostly Jews displaced from their farms and villages by the Russians. Finding employment,' Moshe said, 'is next to impossible so they're left to beg for food.'

"It didn't take long before we came to a small farming village of maybe thirty or forty wood-framed houses, some wider some taller, but they all resembled one another. The unpainted wood siding had turned an unattractive grey color. Rust stains showed where nails had been driven. Most houses had an animal shed attached. I saw fields planted with beets, carrots, cabbage, but mostly corn. In the distance were large fields of hay and oats.

"At last, we stopped in front of a house a little larger than those on either side. Moshe told me, 'This is where your uncle lives.'

"I thanked him for the ride and climbed down off the wagon, retrieving my bundle. 'Good luck,' Moshe called as he urged the horses forward.

"I walked through the gate into the fenced yard. Mature trees shaded the wide plank siding of the dwelling. Clothes and sheets were drying on the far side of the house on a line strung between two trees. The path led past a well and a vegetable garden free of weeds, to the front door. I took a deep breath and knocked."

Chapter 6

Grandpa's story was like a mystery. I didn't know what was going to happen next. I'm sure I pestered him until he'd tell me more. To this day I don't know if he was really interested in imparting his history to me or was I just an opportunity for him to relive the details of his life. Sometimes days or even weeks would pass before I'd hear another chapter. Then he'd put down his glass and begin.

"Maya, I remember how nervous I was as I waited for what seemed like ages for someone to answer, hoping for the best. A middle-aged woman opened the door, dressed in a long grey faded cotton skirt, a white muslin, long-sleeved blouse, and a head scarf.

"She looked me up and down. Before I could say a word, she said, 'We have no food to spare for beggars, but you're welcome to a glass of water or a cup of tea.'

'I am not a beggar,' I said in Yiddish. 'I am the son of Joseph, the brother of your husband.'

"She viewed me with suspicion. 'I know of no one by that name. You wait here. I will fetch my husband.'

"The woman shut the door behind her and walked past me to the shed calling, 'Jacob.' I could hear her talking to someone as she said. "There's a young man here who claims to be the son of your brother, Joseph. I've never heard you speak of a Joseph. Do you have such a brother?"

Moments later, a tall, stout, muscular man approached with a full red beard and a mass of red hair peeking out from under his cap. He wore a vest on top of his prayer shawl, the tassels hanging over his rough muslin shirt, his dirt-stained pants tucked into his dusty work boots. He gave me a long, hard look. 'What's your name?' he said, in a deep baritone voice that seemed to echo off the walls of the shed.

'David, sir,' I answered, my voice trembling. 'I'm your brother Joseph's son.'

'And what brings you here?'

'My father told me if anything happened to him I was to seek you out, that I might find a home with you.'

'And something has happened to your father?'

'Yes, sir. He died two weeks ago.'

"The big man standing before me let out a deep sigh *'Alav Ha-Sholom*, may he rest in peace. So let me look at you, David. You look a little like your father, tall, but oh, so skinny. He didn't feed you?' His hearty laugh filled the air around the shed. 'How old are you, David?'

'Just turned seventeen, Sir.'

'Well, Mama, take David to the house and give him something to eat. He can rest today. Tomorrow we put him to work. We can use an extra hand.'

"Tante Leah, Uncle's wife, led the way to a ladder that went up to the loft and pointed to a double bed, saying, 'You can sleep there with your cousins. I'll make space in the dresser for your things. Put them away then come below for a snack.'

"I feasted on fresh bread, still warm from the oven, cheese and tea.

'Supper is at sunset. Go up and take a rest,' Tante said, as she left the room.

"Taking off my boots, I rubbed my toes. Raw blisters had bled through my socks. I shook out the coins and put them on the top of the dresser. I would give them to Uncle Jacob that evening for my keep. I laid down on the bed and fell asleep.

"I was awakened by a hand tapping me on the shoulder, 'Wake up. I'm your cousin, Samuel. Everybody calls me Sammy. We're waiting supper for you. Hurry. I'm hungry.'

"I jumped up to see a figure descending the ladder.

'I'll be there in a minute,' I called. Putting on my boots was painful, but I couldn't go to supper barefoot. I placed the coins in my pocket and hurried below.

"Uncle Jacob was already sitting at the long rectangular oaken table, which took up most of the small room consisting of a sitting area and the kitchen with a tiny fireplace.

'Come, David,' Uncle Jacob said. 'Let me introduce the family. Sammy, you met.' He pointed as he said, 'this is Harry and the boy's sister Reba, the baby of the family. Children, this is your cousin, David. He is going to be living with us. Now sit, so we can eat.'

"I sat on the bench next to Reba as Uncle Jacob bowed his head and prayed.

'Ba-Ruch A-Tah A-Do-noi
Elo-HAI-NU Me-Lech HA-O-Lam
SHE-HA-Kol NI-H'YAH BI-D'VA-RO-D

Blessed are you, Lord our God, King of the Universe, by whose word all things come to be.'

"He raised his head and Tante Leah began to place ladles of hot beet soup in the bowls before us, what they call Borsht in Russia.

"I was starved. The broth was flavorful and the bowl was full of tasty slivers of beets. When we'd emptied our bowls she refilled them with a large potato and a small slice of beef. The board in the middle of the table held a whole loaf of fresh bread waiting to be eaten.

"I was the center of attention. The questions came fast and furious. Where did I come from? How did I get here? What were my chores at the Count's estate?

"The questions continued at a rapid pace until Uncle Jacob said, 'Stop,' in his booming voice. 'Let the poor boy eat. He needs to be fattened up.'

"Our meal ended with tea and cookies. Days had passed since my stomach had been so full.

"I offered to wash the bowls, telling Tante Leah I knew all about washing up and cleaning. She thanked me and said that was Reba's job. 'Go visit with your cousins. There's plenty of work for you to do tomorrow.'

"Uncle Jacob was in the process of lighting his pipe when he asked what I had been trained to do.

'I'm a very good horseman. My father taught me well and he was the best.'

'Well, David, we only have one old horse to pull the wagon and the plow, one cow to milk, a goat, a ewe, a few geese, and chickens. Don't worry. We will find work for you, just maybe not what you're used to. What kind of papers do you have, young David?'

'Papers?'

'Identity papers, of course.'

'None, sir. I've never had a need.'

'This is Russia. Everyone has to have papers, especially Jews. I can't imagine how you got this far without being stopped and questioned, but we'll take care of it at once, before it becomes a problem. Tomorrow we will visit the village head and register you. Now, out with you. Let me smoke my pipe in peace and quiet.'

"I went outside to find Sammy and Harry shooting marbles in the middle of the road with a group of boys about my age. I watched as they joked around noticing how different those boys were from the friends I left behind. They all wore prayer shawls and caps, and used words I did not understand.

"The game ended when it got dark and they all headed for home. I stayed behind as Sammy and Harry started up the ladder to their bedroom. I approached Uncle Jacob.

'I have these for you,' I said, as I reached into my pocket and pulled out the coins. 'This was my father's savings. It will help pay for my keep.'

'No, David, put the coins away. I cannot take your father's money. It was meant for you. Not to worry. You'll earn your keep while you are here, so say no more.'

"That night, when the three of us crawled into bed, I could tell my cousins were not too happy to share the cramped space with one more body, but I assured them they would be happy for the extra body heat when the cold of winter set in.

"The following morning, we all arose together. The boys and Uncle began their day with their morning prayers. A ritual I had not seen before.

"When the breakfast meal of bread, cheese, and tea was over, I followed Uncle Jacob to the rundown barn, looked at the old horse in a tie stall and started to feed and groom him. I could tell grooming was something that had not been done in a long time. I checked the harness and saw it too showed signs of neglect and a need to be repaired. I would make that my first job for that day.

"Looking around the fields, I thought this place was nothing like Count Zoransky's. Everywhere I looked, things seemed old, worn, tired. The fields were in poor shape. The sheds even worse. So different from where I grew up. It would take some getting used to.

"In late afternoon, Uncle Jacob came in from the fields telling me to clean up. We would be off to visit Mr. Mendelsohn about my papers.

"How was I to know, as we walked down the dirt path to the Mendelsohn house, that would be one of the most important days of my entire life. We were close to the end of the village when Uncle Jacob turned and opened a gate leading to the largest, best maintained house in the whole village.

I stopped short of the front door amazed at the bushes I saw growing along the front of the house. They were the same flowers I had seen for the first time in Count Zoransky's garden.

"Do you know what the beautiful flowers growing on those bushes are called, Uncle?"

"They're called roses. Why, David, you want to grow flowers?"

"No, just curious. I saw the very same bushes at the Count's estate."

"You're not likely to see them any place else in the village. Only a rich man can afford to plant flowers instead of potatoes."

'But why would he do that?'

'Too many questions, David. I don't know why. Something to do with his wife I think, but I don't have time to listen to the gossip of the village women. Come along, David. We have business to take care of. We've no time to waste on roses.'

"Uncle knocked on the door. The most beautiful girl I had ever seen, answered. She was almost as tall as me with auburn hair that glistened as it hung in a thick braid down her back. Her hazel eyes had flecks of gold and her warm smile showed perfect teeth.

'Good afternoon, Miriam. Is your father at home?'

'Please to come in, Reb Jacob. I'll tell Papa you're here.'

'May I introduce my nephew, David? He just arrived from Prussia and will be living with us."

"She smiled and executed a small curtsey. 'Welcome,' she said. Her sweet voice sent shivers down my spine. I was speechless. I'd never paid attention to girls before, but I could not take my eyes off Miriam, nor could I find words to speak.

"She excused herself. In short order her father appeared. He, like his daughter, was dressed in a different way from the rest of the villagers, more like the clothes I'd seen in Kiev. The house was much nicer than Uncle's. The rooms were larger, filled with fine furniture.

"My uncle explained my arrival from Prussia without papers of any sort.

'Well, Jacob, we'd better get him registered before the Russians come to do a body count and he has some explaining to do.'

"I was shown a large ledger resting on an ornate carved wooden desk and instructed to sign my name. Mr. Mendelsohn prepared a form that I was to carry with me when I left the village. He told me I would be required to show the form if Russian officials came to the village. He asked if I was running from trouble with the authorities at home.

'His father, my brother, died weeks ago. This is his son, my nephew.'

'I see. That explains his arrival. David, do you have any connections with the revolutionaries?'

"I shook my head. I had no idea what he was talking about.

'Fine, then. Everything is in order. I'm sure your uncle will explain the rules.' He showed us to the door. His daughter was nowhere in sight.

"I was curious as we started down the road. 'Why does Mr. Mendelsohn have a better house than the rest, Uncle?'

'He's the money lender. You borrow from him and pay high interest. Mr. Mendelsohn is a very rich man. He and his brother own the grain mill in Grodov. He also cooperates with the Russians. In many ways, he's a man to be feared.'

'His daughter is very pretty. How old is she?'

'I guess maybe thirteen or fourteen, but pay her no mind, David. She's never going to be promised to some poor boy like you.'

'Maybe I will not always be poor, Uncle,' I said as we approached home."

Chapter 7

I remember having conversations when Grandpa would ask about me and what went on in my life. I know I told him about Billy's girlfriend. It must have been in summer because I probably was complaining about Billy's never being home.

"I can hardly wait for school to begin, Grandpa. I miss my friends and my brother Billy is no fun anymore. He's either driving the new tractor or visiting his girlfriend. Her name's Emily and she's really stuck up and I don't like her very much because she makes fun of Billy something awful."

"I do not see much of young Billy anymore, either, just clouds of dust from the new tractor," Grandpa said. "Now I know why. But not to worry. Before he reaches manhood he will have many girlfriends besides Emily."

"You didn't, Grandpa. You only had Grandma for your girlfriend."

"True, but things were different in those days."

I don't remember when Grandpa told me about his time living with his uncle, only that he did.

"The year went by quickly, Maya. I learned to plow the fields, plant crops, milk cows and goats, and do rough carpentry. I worked hard, slept well, grew three inches and gained weight.

"The biggest change in my life was religion. I knew I was Jewish, but did not really know what that meant. My father didn't follow any of the rituals celebrated in Uncle's house. Unlike the Count's estate where my father and I were the only Jews, the whole village was made up of orthodox Jews. Their families had lived there for generations and they expected to live and die there like those before them.

"The countryside may have changed hands many times, governed by different rulers, but nothing changed in the village. The families were poor, but with hard work, somehow they got by. They lived, married, had children and died, forming a cycle that never changed. They never expected anything more out of life, so if tragedy did not befall them, they were happy in their meager existence. Much of that happiness came from their religion.

"I was slow to learn, slower yet to accept the religious rituals and it's tenets. Uncle was very patient with me. Maybe someday the prayers would be important, but to understand them I would have to learn Hebrew. I knew I'd never be as devoted as Uncle Jacob and Tante Leah. I found many of the rules silly and had no intention of following them, but I did enjoy the Bible stories Uncle Jacob told. He tried to teach me Hebrew, but I had little interest. I was a poor student.

"I wondered about Tante Leah and Reba. Females were not taught Hebrew, so how did they understand the prayers. Someday I would ask uncle.

"Almost every week a social event or religious celebration took place in the village, a chance for everyone to gather together. Marriages and births were community events as were the numerous Jewish holidays. Those events turned ugly at times. Long-held grudges would erupt into shouting matches. As everyone seemed to be related, one family's fight would soon involve many other families until one of the elders called for peace. I took advantage of every opportunity to seek out Miriam.

"By the end of the year, the attraction was mutual. We were eager to be together. Miriam would sneak out to meet with me whenever I could get away. Boys and girls of our age, Maya, were forbidden to spend time alone, so we were taking a big chance meeting as we did. I would wait for her, hidden from sight in a grove of trees, then we would walk down by the river having found a perfect spot where we had little chance of being seen. We would sit on the grass and talk for hours. I would tell her my dreams of owning a big farm with fine horses and she would listen, never questioning how I was going to make that happen. If I was not talking about the future, I was just as happy to spend the time looking at her. Her beauty made my heart race and my mind imagine all sorts of romantic notions.

"Miriam was about to celebrate her fifteenth birthday. More than anything in the world, I wanted to buy her a present. I talked Uncle into letting me ride along to Grodov with him when he took the plow to the blacksmith for repairs. While Uncle was busy overseeing the repairs and exchanging gossip with the smithy, I went looking for the jeweler. Finding his shop, I entered. A little bell over the door rang, but no one was in sight. I approached the jewelry case and looked through the glass top. There, resting on red velvet, I spotted a small, fine gold bracelet. The open work was so delicate. I lifted the top, reached in and picked it up. The bracelet weighed next to nothing. Set in the middle of the gold work was a small oval disc of gold holding a tiny red ruby. I put it back just as a white bearded, old gentlemen appeared from the back. He wore a black vest over a starched white shirt, his prayer shawl visible, a yarmaka on his head. He looked at me with suspicion.

'How much does that bracelet cost?' I said.

"The price he quoted was twice what I could pay, but nothing else would do.

'I'm sorry, sir, but I don't have that much money,' I said and headed for the door.

'Wait, wait, young man. How much money do you have?'

"I opened my hand and showed the jeweler my two gold coins.

"The old man scratched his long white beard, shook his head, and sighed. Minutes passed, he sighed again, then with a pained look on his face, the jeweler said, 'If that's all you have, then it will have to do.' He removed the bracelet from the case.

"I learned a big lesson that day, Maya. Never pay the first price.

"With Miriam's gift wrapped in silver paper, I left the store and looked for Uncle.

'Where were you off to in such a hurry? I looked all over for you, David.'

'I'm sorry, Uncle. I should have told you. I went to buy a birthday gift for Miriam.'

'That's very nice, but nothing has changed since the last time I told you not to set your heart on her. I'm sure her father already has plans for her future, none of which include you.'

"We drove home in silence, the only sound the clip-clop of the horse's hoofs, the squeak of the wagon wheels. I'll prove them all wrong, I decided. She will be mine.

"I hid the bracelet in the dresser underneath my clothes waiting for a moment when Miriam and I would be alone, which was getting harder and harder to accomplish. Her father and her aunt had begun to keep a more watchful eye on her, suspecting something was going on."

Chapter 8

Grandpa's story was beginning to be even more interesting to me. Especially as I'd reached that point when I was beginning to be interested in boys.

I wanted to know if Grandma liked him as a boyfriend as I told him about my first admirer, Bobby Graham, and the valentine he gave me. Bobby always followed me around even though I wasn't sure I liked him very much.

"Well, Maya, things were so different in my day. At fifteen, Mariam was no longer considered a child. She was of an age when girls married. Even if they knew the person they were promised to, they couldn't spend time alone before they were married. We knew what would happen if we were caught together. I didn't want to cause Uncle any trouble, but no way was I going to stop seeing Miriam.

"We planned to meet at our secret place on Saturday, mid-day, when everyone would be observing the Sabbath. I snuck out of the house, gift in hand, and waited for Miriam by the river. I had waited a very long time and was just about to leave when I heard a rustling of leaves. Miriam appeared. She was out of breath having run all the way from home, afraid, she said, I would be gone.

"We sat side-by-side on the grass. I reached out and held her hand. Touching was even a bigger evil than being alone, but I did not care and it seemed neither did she.

"I waited until she caught her breath, and then reached into my vest pocket, retrieving the gift and placing it in her hand. 'Happy birthday,' I said.

"I watched as she unwrapped the silver paper with care and looked at its contents. Her expression was one of awe and glee. Miriam let me fasten it on her wrist as tears began to run down her cheeks.

'David, it's so beautiful and I love that you thought so much of me you would buy such an expensive gift."

"After I'd fastened the bracelet on her wrist, Miriam said.

'This is so special because you are my first friend.'

'You mean your first boyfriend?'

'Oh, no my first and only friend.'

'How can that be. Aren't all the girls in the village friends?'

'Yes, but they treat me differently because my father is rich, but mostly because of my mother. She is different. A kind of sickness they talk about behind my back.'

"I sat down and motioned for Miriam to sit beside me.

'Do you want to tell me about your mother?'

'I've never spoken of her to anyone before.'

"I watched as she seemed to stare off into space. Then she began to speak.

'The story my auntie, my mother's younger sister, told me was that my mother was in love with a young man in her village. They wanted to marry, but her father disapproved and gave her instead to an older man, my father, who she'd never met. She was dragged to her wedding kicking and screaming, crying through the whole ceremony.'

Miriam stopped speaking for a minute. 'Maybe I shouldn't tell you the rest.'

'You can't stop now. I promise to keep anything you say a secret.'

'Well, Auntie said, on their wedding night my mother refused to perform her wifely duties. She screamed when my father touched her and ran from his bed. He caught her running barefoot down the path in her nightgown, carried her back to his bed and forced himself on her.

His anger grew as she behaved in the same manner the following night. He forced himself on her again despite her screams. This went on for a week until he decided to give her time to come to terms with what the Bible said was her duty.

He planted rose bushes in hopes of showing his love for her and as an apology for causing her pain.'

'Did it work?'

'She's never seen the garden. When he entered her room to tell her of the garden she began to scream. As he reached out his hand to her, she bit him.'

'So she's never seen the roses or forgiven him?'

'No. She spends her time alone in her room rarely uttering a word. Auntie says she's waiting for her lover to keep his promise to come and save her.'

'What happened to him?'

'I don't know. I don't even know his name.'

'That's such a sad story. I think you should be allowed to marry the one you love.'

'I do too, David. But that's not our custom.'

"Miriam smiled, tears forming in her eyes as she removed the bracelet from her wrist and tried to hand it back to me.

"I can't keep it,' she said as tears ran down her cheeks.

'Why not? I want you to have it.'

'I'm worried what my father will say. He suspects that we spend time together. If he saw the bracelet he'd know. He might even send me away.'

'Then keep it hidden until we are engaged.'

'Engaged? What do you mean?'

'When the time is right, when I'm old enough, and when I can support you, I'm going to make you my wife, no matter what your father or anyone else has to say. I love you, Miriam. You belong to me and to nobody else.'

"I took her in my arms and felt the warmth of her body, her heart beating, her sweet clean smell, the feel of her arms around me as she hugged me back. The embrace lasted only a few seconds before Miriam pulled away. If holding hands wasn't allowed, our embrace was clearly out of bounds.

'We mustn't," she said, as she moved further apart. 'I will keep your gift safely hidden. David, you know I love you, too. I would be happy to be your wife, but I'm not sure it can ever happen.' With that said, she turned and ran toward home.

"I heard the crunch of leaves under her feet, the rustle of her dress as she disappeared out of sight.

"I hoped to climb the large oak tree outside the loft window and not be seen returning home, but no such luck. Uncle was watching as I came down the path.

'Well, David, where have you been?'

'Walking, Uncle.'

'On the Sabbath? One should spend their time praying.'

'Walking and thinking.'

'Thinking about God on your day of rest? If this has anything to do with Miriam, I forbid it. Hear me. It must end now. I can't afford to have her father as my enemy. Soon I will need him to lend me money to buy a new horse. You know how lame and tired the old nag is.'

'But, Uncle.'

"He was quick to speak, 'No but's. As long as you live under my roof you will follow my rules. Rule number one...leave Miriam alone. Rules number two, three, and four...leave Miriam alone.'

"My eighteenth birthday passed with little notice. I'd been giving a great deal of thought to moving on. I felt restricted in the village. Too many senseless rules from century's past. Too little opportunity for a better life. My aunt and uncle had been very good to me, but I couldn't see spending anymore of my life under their roof. Only the thought of Mariam limited my options. I did not know fate would step in to dictate my future.

"By mid-April, winter was over and spring planting had begun. With the sun warming my back, I had been driving the old horse, his harness hooked to the plow, the long reins thrown over my shoulder, when I heard Tante Leah shouting for me to come at once.

"I unhooked the old horse from the plow and led him back to the shed. When I reached the cottage door, I saw two uniformed Russian soldiers. Tante Leah looked anxious, worried. Sammy was standing beside his mother, all the color had drained from his face.

"One of the soldiers handed me a paper. I looked at it, but could not read the words as it was in Russian.

'What's this?' I said.

'You're being conscripted into the Russian Army,' the soldier said.'

"So was Sammy it seemed, as he was holding the same official looking paper. We were to report to military headquarters in Grodov in one week. Failure to do so would mean the family would be removed from their house and not allowed to return to the village.

"That said, the soldiers turned, untied their horses from the fence posts, mounted, and rode away.

"Tante was crying, Sammy looked scared, and I had no idea what had just happened.

'Go, both of you,' Tante Leah said. 'Finish with the plowing. With only one week before you leave, there is much to be done.' She wiped her tears on her apron, went inside and closed the door behind her.

'So what does this mean, Sammy?'

'It means we better go find Papa.'

We found Uncle in the barn stripping corn seed from the dried cobs, ready for planting. He looked up. 'What are you two doing here? There is work to be done.'

'Didn't you see the soldiers come to the house?' Sammy said.

'No, what do they want now. I paid my taxes.'

'They want us,' Sammy said. 'We're to report for military service in one week.'

"Uncle's face turned ashen as he raised his hands to the sky.

'Why them, God,' he shouted, 'Why take them from me. Why? Why? Why?' He wrapped us in his arms. Moments went by before Sammy spoke again.

'What does this mean, Papa?'

'I don't know, exactly, son. Maybe it could be a good thing, maybe not. Thanks be to God, they no longer conscript children, that's a good thing. You could learn a trade, learn to speak Russian. Also a good thing. But you may be asked to shoot revolutionaries. Many are Jewish. That's a bad thing.'

'How long will we be gone?' I said.

'I don't know, maybe...two years, maybe eight, maybe

twenty-five. Its whatever the Russians want this year. Things change from year to year. To them you're only a bunch of third class citizens, cannon fodder, without any rights. Ever since Tsar Alexander the second was assassinated last year, the Russians feel a need to build a bigger army, fearing trouble from revolutionaries, so I hear from the gossip in Gordov. The Russians keep trying to blame the assassination on the Jews, but they know better.'

'Where will they send us, Papa?'

'Son, you ask me questions, but I don't have answers. In the past, if there were no wars, they let you serve near home. Maybe Kiev, who knows? Now, back to work. You have the whole spring planting to do in one week. We'll talk at supper.'

"Sammy and I headed off in different directions. We had a monumental task to accomplish. I couldn't stop thinking about what would come next. I knew I had to speak to Miriam. I needed to hear her promise to wait for me. Maybe after supper I'd clean up and make a formal call.

"Supper was unpleasant. Tante was either crying or praying. Reba spoke of being scared, spending most of the meal crying like her mother. Harry and Sammy, close in age, and devoted to one another, had never been apart. Uncle, somber, but stoic, worried about Sammy. He didn't trust the Russians. He had heard stories of their miserable treatment of Jewish soldiers. Uncle's concerns about managing the farm with only Harry to help were justified.

"I left the table as soon as I had finished eating, saying I had something to attend to and left before Uncle could ask me where I was going, although I'm sure he knew.

"Hurrying down the dirt road, I unlatched the gate to the Mendelsohn's house and walked to the door. It was not long before Miriam's aunt opened the door part way. 'Yes?' she said.

'Please, I would like to speak with Miriam.'

'She is visiting with her mother. Her father isn't here. Maybe some other time.' She started to close the door.

"I held the door ajar as I said, 'Please, I'm leaving in a few days for the Army and I must say goodbye.'

"I heard Miriam call from the back of the house, 'Who is it, Tante?'

'Its David, come to say goodbye.'

"I watched as Miriam ran down the hall, 'Goodbye. What does that mean? Please Tante, I must speak with him.'

'I'm sorry, Miriam, but your father isn't here and I'm too busy to sit with you two now. Maybe another time.'

'Go about your business, Tante. Mother can sit with us.'

"Before the older woman could say a word, Miriam motioned me to follow her. We reached a small room at the end of the hall. Miriam opened the door and I followed her inside. Only two tiny candles illuminated the small room, the sparse furnishings. A petite, frail woman sat in an overstuffed chair, covered from the waist down with a crocheted wool afghan of various colors.

'Mama, this is David, the boy I've been telling you about.'

"Miriam looked a lot like her mother, the same auburn colored hair, the same hazel eyes. Her mother must have been pretty in her day. She might be pretty, still, if she didn't have that dead look to her eyes.

'What was Tante saying about goodbye. Where are you going, David?'

'Bad news, I am afraid. I have been conscripted into the Army. I leave in a week.'

'No. That can't be. You can't leave. What will I do?'

"Taking her hand in mine, I said, 'You can promise to wait for me. They can't keep me forever.' I turned toward her mother, wondering if I was free to talk in front of her.

"Miriam, guessing my concern said, 'It's all right. I don't know what she hears and she rarely if ever speaks.'

'How long has she been like this?'

'As long as I can remember.'

"That being the case, I took Miriam in my arms saying, 'I love you. I will come back to take you as my bride. Promise you'll wait.'

'I want to promise, but what if father gives me to a man of his choosing? By tradition, I will be duty bound to marry him.'

"I stepped back a pace, and looking into her eyes said, 'Then you will tell him no. You love me and have promised yourself to me.'

'David, you know that's not how it's done, marriages are arranged by the families. I must do what my father says.'

'That's how it used to be done, but I'm changing the rules. You belong to me.'

'I don't know if I'm strong enough, or what father will do if I defy him.'

"I pointed to her mother. 'Is that how you want to spend the rest of your days? I remember the story you told me by the river, about how your mother was forced to marry your father, who was many years older than she. A man she had never met, who she saw for the first time at the ceremony. You told me how she loved someone else, a boy she'd grown up with. The bitter tears she wept for days before the wedding. How she had to be dragged screaming to the ceremony. You told me you were born before their first anniversary, but your mother never spoke after their wedding night, spending all her days and nights in this small room.

How her sister, your aunt, had come to care for her and for you. Do you want that sad story to be your story as well?'

"I walked over to the chair where Miriam's mother was sitting, her head bowed, and took her hand as I whispered, 'I love your daughter and she loves me. Give us your blessings and tell her to wait for me.'

"I watched in amazement as her mother raised her head high, smiled at Miriam and in a raspy voice whispered, 'My blessings, children.'

'You see, sweet Miriam, we have been blessed. You will be my bride. I should go now before your father returns and finds me here.' Putting my arms around her once more, I said, "I will try to see you before I leave. I will write to you as often as I can while I'm gone.'

'To what use, David? I cannot read.'

'Then I will send my letters to Harry and he can tell you what I wrote.'

"Miriam opened the door. I turned to her mother and said, 'Goodnight. I promise to take good care of your daughter.'

"I hurried to the front door and was on my way home undetected."

Chapter 9

I remember, even at my tender age, being amazed at how strange the traditions regarding marriage seemed. I kept thinking about Grandma not being allowed to marry who she wanted. I couldn't imagine wanting to marry someone and my father saying, "No, I've picked some rich old man for you to marry and I don't care whether you like him or not." I'd just run away, thinking how glad I was I didn't grow up in Russia as Grandpa began to tell me what happened next.

"The week passed all to quickly, Maya. No one spoke of our leaving, but it hung over the household like a dark cloud. I went about my chores eager to finish the plowing before the time came for us to go. I owed that to my uncle.

"Sammy and I arose early that Monday morning, still exhausted by the long hours we had worked to get as much done for Uncle as we could. Having packed my meager belongings the night before, I waited with Sammy outside the gate for Uncle to come driving the wagon for the trip to Grodov. Tante and Reba waited with us as Harry came rushing out the door. I watched the old horse pull the wagon out of the shed with Uncle holding the rains, stopping at the front gate. Uncle's booming voice called to us, 'Time to go.'

"Tante and Reba hugged me, wiping away their tears. Harry shook my hand, wished me luck, and promised to read my letters to Miriam. As we climbed aboard, Tante handed us fresh baked cookies wrapped in paper.

"I waved as the wagon began to move down the road. The year had turned out better than I had expected. I would miss my new family, but I would miss Miriam even more. What would come next I could not imagine. For the first time, there would be no one looking out for me. My father was gone and now I was leaving Uncle behind. Boyhood was over for me. The time had come to become a man.

"Uncle dropped us off in front of the small military outpost in Grodov. He had warned us during the drive to be careful how we acted, to always be respectful, to follow orders. The Russians could be cruel, especially to Jews who they had no love or respect for. I promised to write as Sammy and I climbed down off the wagon seat. I opened the side door alongside the big double gates in the high wooden enclosure that surrounded the outpost. Once inside, I surveyed the interior, noticing how precise the dirt had been raked and smoothed. A large green patch of lawn in the center of the parade ground boasted a tall flagpole replete with the Russian flag, it's vertical stripes of red, white, and blue rustling in the slight breeze.

"A sentry, rifle in hand, stopped us, examined our papers and directed us to a stone building to the right of the entrance. I stopped. Turning my head to the left having heard the sound of many marching feet. I saw a Russian Officer astride a handsome jet-black horse, wearing a dark blue tunic, white britches, and tall black boots. Troopers followed four abreast, marching in step. The officer signaled the sentry to open the large gates and the troop marched out of the compound heading where I did not know.

"Entering the building, we were stopped again. A soldier asked us to state our business. We showed him the conscription papers. After examining them he motioned us to follow, leading us to a room with about forty nervous men milling around. They looked to be about our age. All, I guessed by the prayer shawls, were Jewish.

"We were ordered to strip to be examined by a doctor, then given new grey uniforms...loose fitting pull-overs, belted in the middle, with stand-up collars, grey britches, caps, and boots. Those having prayer shawls were ordered to hand them over. I had no prayer shawl, as I'd never been a Bar Mitzvah. We waited, dressed in our ill-fitting uniforms, for what seemed like hours before a small group of soldiers, carrying rifles, entered the room and ordered us to follow them. They marched us to the train station where we boarded a train to Kiev, not in a passenger car like the one I had ridden in, but a boxcar that smelled of cow dung, where we stood, trying to balance ourselves during the bumpy ride. The armed soldiers guarded us as the train moved on.

"Arriving at the large Fort in Kiev, we were informed we would receive our training there.

"Soldiers ushered us into a large mess hall where we were given supper seated at row after row of long tables and benches. I watched as most of our group picked at their food. Not me. I was hungry. I had not eaten since the bread and tea at Uncles that morning. I was determined to make the best of it, but Sammy was having trouble coping with his new situation. Despite my pleading, he pushed his food aside, worried it was not kosher, voicing his concern that his prayer shawl would not be returned.

"After supper, a soldier marched us to a large barracks and assigned bunk beds. A mess kit, one blanket, a straw filled mattress, and a pillow were piled on each bunk. Sammy and I tried our best to stay together. I took the top bunk and he claimed the bottom one. I had no trouble sleeping despite the sounds of snoring and a muffled sound of crying.

"A bugle awakened us before dawn the following morning. We were ordered to dress. Beards and sideburns were to be shaved, and long hair cut over objections on religious grounds. We followed our sergeant to the mess hall for tea and bread. The next stop was a large room where we lined up to await our assignments. Before the sergeant in charge had gotten half way through questioning our group, the door opened. Our sergeant immediately came to attention clicking his heels, he saluted and shouted, 'Attention.' We stood, silent, as a tall, stately looking officer of high rank, based upon his uniform and medals, entered the room accompanied by two young officers.

Our sergeant introduced him as the commander of the fort, Colonel General Zoransky. I nearly fainted when I heard the name.

"The Colonel General made a short speech about what was expected of us, about our loyalty to the Tsar, and so on. As he was about to leave, I did the unthinkable. I shouted after him, 'Are you related to Count Zoransky, sir?'

"The sergeant, his hand ready to slap me across the mouth, stopped when the Colonel General turned and said, 'Who asked the question?'

"The sergeant started to apologize, saying the conscript would be punished severely for the outburst.

'Who asked?' the Colonel General said again, ignoring the sergeant.

"I stepped forward. 'I did, sir.'

'Why would you ask such a question, young man?'

'Sir, with all due respect, my father was the supervisor of the estate of a Count Zoransky. I grew up on the estate.'

"The two young officers with the Colonel General watched the exchange, ready to shoot me, if necessary.

'The supervisor. I see, and what was his name?'

'Joseph, sir.'

'Joseph? You mean the head horseman?'

'Yes, sir.'

'And you, who are you?'

'I am his son, David.'

'So,' he said. A slight smile crossed his face. 'You're the same little David who dusted off my boots after I mounted. The Count is my father'. Then, he turned to the sergeant. 'Place this man in the main stable and instruct the officer in charge David is to help with the care of my horses.' With that, the Colonel General turned and left the room, leaving me stunned.

"From that day forward, my life in the Army changed for the better although it meant I lost touch with Sammy. I was back caring for horses, a job I knew well. I was even happier helping with the care of the Colonel General's horses.

"The horse area consisted of work horses who pulled the wagons and cannons, and the officer's personal mounts which we grooms, like myself, were responsible for. The enlisted men were responsible for the care for their own mounts.

"Those of us in the horse detail had our own sleeping quarters and mess hall. As few if any beside myself attached to the horse unit were Jewish, the food was not kosher. I could have cared less. I was sure the food my father gave me had not been kosher and nothing terrible happened to me. It made little difference as now, under the reign of Alexander the Third, no kosher food would be served anywhere in the military.

"I saw Colonel Zoransky almost daily as I delivered his mount to him, saddled, bridled, and ready to go. He always commented on how fine his horses looked.

"I pretty much kept to myself, not complaining when I was called anti-sematic names or given all the dirty jobs beyond my regular responsibilities.

"I missed having anyone to talk to, so I did what I did as a child. I spoke to the horses. The Colonel General's horses knew all about Miriam and all about my dreams for a better life.

"Almost a year had passed since I had arrived at the fort. I had adapted easily to the discipline of Army life. The days were busy leaving little time for anything but work, but the nights were lonely. I lay in my bunk thinking of Uncle, hearing his booming voice, of Tante Leah always being sure I had enough to eat, and most of all of Miriam. I ached for her.

"So far there had been no talk about a leave. I longed to return home for a visit. I had received no letters from Harry even though I wrote regularly. I worried about Uncle and the family, and most of all about Miriam.

"One morning, as I was busy mucking out stalls, one of the Colonel General's aides came to get me. The Colonel General wished to speak with me. I started to clean up, but the aide said, 'No time for that. Come now.'

"As I entered the officer's headquarters, accompanied by the aide, the soldier behind the desk got up, saluted and walked down a long hall and rapped on a door, then opened it for the aide and me. I stepped inside the palatial office. The Russian flag in one corner, Pictures of Czar Alexander the Second and Third graced the wood paneled walls. The Colonel General was seated behind a large polished ornate desk.

'Ah, good to see you, David,' he said as he looked toward his aide. 'Leave us. I'll call when you're needed.'

"The aide clicked his heels, saluted, and left us alone in the room. I was concerned as to the reason for my being there. It must have shown on my face as Colonel General Zoransky said not to worry. He had a job for me.

"He explained that he wanted me to accompany him to look at an expensive horse he was interested in buying. He would see that I was left alone to examine the horse without anyone noticing. We were to leave at ten o'clock. I was to ride along with him to the farm located some miles outside of town. With that I was dismissed.

"His two aides accompanied the Colonel General, riding alongside him. I brought up the rear. As we approached the horse farm, about a forty minute ride from the fort, I saw large paddocks deep in green grass and a huge stone barn. I thought that was what a horse farm should look like. The paddocks were full of young horses prancing and playing, all of them jet-black with little or no white showing on their legs or face.

"We rode straight to the barn where an imposing looking gentlemen in britches and boots greeted us. The Colonel General dismounted, as did his aides. I took the Colonel General's horse and led him into the barn where I handed him off to a groom to place in a stall until we were ready to leave. I tied my horse to a post, trusting the aides would look after their own mounts.

"The imposing looking man led the Colonel General to an enclosed covered arena as I followed behind. He was shown to a front row seat while I stood off to the side, close enough to hear what was said. Though the conversation was in Russian, I had picked up a great deal of the language in the year since I had been at the fort where Russian was the only language spoken.

"Within a few minutes of our arrival, a rider, mounted aboard a handsome stallion, entered the ring. The horse, long and lean, stood about sixteen hands, jet-black with a thin stripe of white from mid-brow to his nostrils.

"As the horse began to walk around the ring, I was impressed by the overwhelming presence he had about him, an elegant carriage, his neck arched, his stride measured, his eyes alert, ears forward. The Colonel General inquired about the horses breeding. An Orlov-Rostopchin, was the answer. 'A unique breed developed on this farm. We produce only a small number of Orlov-Rostopchin foals every year, in addition to the many fine horses we produce for the Army, of course.'

"The rider began to put the horse through his paces as I watched his every move. I had never seen anything quite as spectacular. The horse took my breath away, the kind of mount one would expect the Commander of the fort to be riding.

"When the horse and rider exited, I ran to the barn to see if I could get a closer look at him while he was being cooled out.

"I made small talk with his groom offering to help as he bucket bathed the horse. While he soaped the horse's back with a large sponge, I bent down, as if to rub something off his hoof. I smelled his left front leg for I had noticed a few hairs curled as if the leg had been medicated and bandaged. When the groom had his back to me, soaping the big horse's hindquarters, I ran my hand down the flexor tendon, which seemed soft and tender to the touch in two spots.

"I began a conversation about the horse with the groom. 'Will you be sorry to see him go if my officer buys him?'

'Yes, in a way. He's a very nice horse to care for, but we have a better horse in the barn that is not for sale, so this one won't be missed.'

'A better one," I said. 'How is that possible? This one is as close to perfect as an animal can be. Could you show him to me? I find it hard to believe.'

'When I'm finished I will show you. Then you will see what I mean."

"The groom covered the horse with a light sheet and put him in his stall to dry, motioning me to follow. I walked into a stall occupied by another handsome individual. Almost a dead ringer for the horse the Colonel General hoped to buy. I ran my hand down his back, checked his legs -- tendons tight, legs cold. I checked his teeth, his eyes, his hoofs. All four were cold to the touch. He appeared sound and good natured as I inspected him. With his conformation, he had to be a good mover, but how good one couldn't tell until he had a rider on his back.

"I left as the groom continued his duties and waited in front of the barn for the Colonel General to return from his inspection tour of the farm.

"Colonel General Zoransky pulled me aside, asking if I found anything to worry about. He thought the animal was magnificent, the kind of mount befitting his rank.

"I told him my findings and suggested he look at the horse in the fifth stall on the right. 'They say he's the best horse in the barn. A dead ringer for the one you saw ridden. You might want to see how he moves.'

By the end of the day, the horse was the Colonel General's. The owner didn't want to let him go, but the Army bought most of what he produced, so he had no choice.

"We rode back to the fort. I again brought up the rear. The new horse would be delivered the next afternoon. I took the reins of the Colonel General's horse as he dismounted to return the horse to the barn. He thanked me saying, 'Your father taught you well. I won't forget the job you've done. I'll find a way to repay you. Until then, make sure my new horse is well taken care of.'

"My days continued to consist of routine duties. Most of the other grooms had stopped picking on me, but only a few exchanged words with me, and none became a friend. I had no time to think about anything other than work during the day, no time to be homesick. My nights, as the weeks and months dragged on, went beyond lonely. Even in sleep I dreamt of Miriam and the village.

"Rumors were circulating among the Jewish troops about the new edicts enacted by Alexander the Third, called the May Laws, changing the rules relating to all Jews, soldiers, and civilians alike. No new agricultural colonies could be established. From now on Jews were forbidden to settle outside of towns. Some villages were dismantled and its population moved to Kiev even though there were no jobs for the displaced villagers. Jews were forbidden to transact business on Sunday or on Christian holy days. Quotas would be enacted limiting the number of Jews admitted to high schools and universities on top of the already restrictive laws regarding the number of Jews that could be educated. Under the new law, it would be less than five percent.

"Some heard the second-class citizenship granted to Jewish soldiers would no longer apply. Soldiers would remain third class citizens and pensions would no longer be granted.

"The only positive feature of the new law was it set the time that constrictors were required to serve to six years with nine additional years on reserve, rather than the twenty-five years some had been forced to remain in the Army. The shorter conscriptions would allow the Tsar to have a trained military in reserve, without the cost of maintaining them after their training period was over.

"What the Czar had not taken into consideration with the enactment of new laws was the resentment building in the already oppressed Jewish population. The revolutionaries gained strength as the new laws incited more young men to join various forbidden underground organizations. Along with labor groups this was the beginning of what led later to the overthrow of the Czarist regime."

Chapter 10

It didn't surprise me, even as a child, that Grandpa had discovered a problem with the horse. Our town was too small to have a veterinarian. Many had discovered over the years what a knowledgeable horseman Grandpa was. They would come to the farm to ask his advice. Some sought him out to help with a purchase. We always had a few lame horses Grandpa was nursing back to health for their owners.

Grandpa even taught me to ride the old work horses when my mother wasn't looking. I liked the new one named Clipper, best.

But I begged to hear more about Grandpa's time with Grandma.

"Everything in its order, Maya," Grandpa said. "Be patient."

"Several months had passed since my visit to the horse farm when I received a message the Colonel General wanted to see me. I was ushered into his office as he was going over large maps spread out across his massive desk while his aides looked on. He looked up as I entered and saluted him. Turning to his aides, he said, 'we'll discuss this further in the afternoon. As for now, you're dismissed.'

"The two saluted, turned, and left the room as the Colonel General rolled up the maps with care, returning them to their cases.

"He opened his desk drawer and took out a form, which he signed with a flourish.

"I promised to reward you for your keen observation and ingenuity in ruling out the stallion and finding a better mount. I also feel obligated to you and your father for the many years of faithful service to my father, the Count. Therefore, I am taking a risk in giving you information, that at the moment, only my superiors and I have knowledge of.'

"He handed me the form he had signed, which I glanced at. It granted me two weeks leave. I started to speak, but he interrupted.

'Listen carefully to what I have to say and then forget you heard it. You are to go home and warn your family that they should be prepared for a massive raid in approximately two to three weeks. We suspect there are large numbers of revolutionaries active in Gordov and the surrounding villages. I cannot predict the outcome, as these things have a way of getting out of hand, but severe damage will be done if not to your family's village, then to one nearby to set an example. I'm giving you a chance to escape. The Austrian-German alliance will provide financial assistance for you to reach the Netherlands where ships are leaving for America. They consider it an inexpensive way to get rid of Russian soldiers who one day might be potential enemies. Gather your things, tell no one and leave for home immediately. Don't be foolish enough to stay in your village hoping to help. Neither you, nor your family can win a battle with armed Russian soldiers, or worse yet, drunken Cossacks bent on destruction. I'm taking a chance giving you this information, so take it seriously and be on the first boat to America.'

"I stood dumbfounded, not knowing what to say. Thank you seemed so inadequate.

'Now be gone,' Colonel General said, 'before I change my mind and have you arrested for something. And good luck.'

"Grasping the paper, I said thank you, saluted, and hurried out the door.

"I walked back to my quarters as fast as I could without drawing attention. Putting on a clean uniform, I gathered my few belongings, and headed for the front gate. I had enough rubles saved from my Army pay to take the train to our village.

"The guard at the gate examined my pass and let me exit. I hurried to the train station. I didn't stop rushing until I was seated in the third class section of the train on my way home.

"Somehow I would have to find a way to marry Miriam before I left for America, or take her with me and marry her in Amsterdam. Even if I had to kidnap her I was not going to America without her.

"I wished the train to go faster, and worried about all that needed to get done. When the train finally reached the village and came to a stop, I hopped off and started to walk to Uncle's house. Maybe, with luck, I might hitch a ride on a passing wagon. The late afternoon sun shone hot on my face as I hurried along the dusty road. Before long, the roof tops of the houses came into view. I remembered my arrival over two years before as a young lad. Now, I returned as a soon-to-be twenty year old, a grown man in my eyes, with the new world on the horizon... America where the streets were paved with gold, where people were free to live life however and wherever they pleased. Praise be to God, I hoped that was so.

"Everything seemed exactly the same as I walked by house after house. Time appeared to have stood still for the two years I had been away. Sheets still hung from lines being bleached by the sun, a slight breeze blew them to and fro. Men still worked in the fields and women still tended their vegetable gardens.

"I rushed to Uncle's door, knocked once and entered calling for Tante Leah. 'It's me, David. I'm home.'

"Tante pushed aside the drape that separated the living area from her bedroom, looking startled. She hesitated for a moment before she rushed toward me, her arms open, greeting me with a hug. 'David, I'm so glad you're home. It's good to see you. Jacob will be so pleased. But where is Sammy? Is he with you?'

'No, Tante, I'm alone. Sorry to say I have not seen Sammy in many months. I must find Uncle at once. It is important.'

'He's been helping Levi repair his roof all day.'

'I'll find him,' I said, as I rushed out the door.

"Levi lived in the neighboring house. As I approached, I could see two men on ladders hammering rough wooden shingles in place. Neither one looked up as I neared. One learned to pay as little attention to Russian soldiers as possible.

'Uncle,' I shouted, 'It's me, David. We need to speak at once. It's urgent.'

"Uncle looked down. It took a moment for him to recognize me in my uniform. A broad grin appeared on his face as he scrambled down off the ladder. Wiping his hands on his pants, he embraced me, and said, 'David, my boy, you have grown taller. Let me look at you. In the three years since the skinny boy arrived on my doorstep, he has turned into a strong handsome man. What are you doing here? Is Sammy with you?'

'Uncle, it's important that we talk at once, in private. Not only important for you, but for the whole village.'

'So come, we will go home and talk.' He called up to Levi. 'If you need more help, I'll come tomorrow.'

"Uncle started back toward the house. I suggested we talk in the shed. I didn't want Tante to hear. I proceeded to tell him that the village might be a target for a *pogrom* in the next two weeks. The very word *pogrom* struck fear in all who heard it, for in Russia, it meant an organized destruction of property, looting, rape, and the massacre of Jews. I told him he wasn't to tell anyone where he heard the information, but he must help the village to get ready for the worst.

'So how do you know this for a fact and not just another rumor, David?'

'I can't tell you how, Uncle, but believe me, it's true. Grodov is the main objective of the Russian's attack, the Jews their target. They think the Jews are harboring revolutionaries responsible for the murder of Tsar Alexander the Second. Some even joining the movement. They plan to attack the surrounding villages as well.'

"The color drained from Uncle's face. 'I must meet with the men of the village to make plans, but I do not know what we can do to protect ourselves. Will you stay and help us prepare or do you have to return to Kiev.'

'I can't stay. I'd be shot if they found me here, probably taken for a revolutionary or a traitor. But I am not returning to Kiev. I won't be part of an attack on my own people. I am going to America. We'll talk of that later. For now, I have to change out of my uniform and find Miriam. Tell me, Uncle, is she still here? Not married?'

'Yes, she's here and not yet promised. Go, David. I have some thinking to do. We will talk later.'

'I'll leave my uniform in the shed. Burn it. The Russians must not suspect I've been here.'

"I approached the door to Miriam's house with a mixture of joy and trepidation. Would she leave her family and come with me? We'd not seen each other for two whole years. Well, I thought, as I rapped on the door, only one way to find out and that's to ask.

"Miriam opened the door. We starred at each other, speechless. She was surprised to see me and I became aware of the changes two years had made. Miriam had grown into womanhood. If I thought she was pretty before, I was unprepared for the beauty I saw before me. Her bosoms, now apparent, contrasted with her slim waist. Her hair no longer hung in curls, but was pinned back off her face and piled high on her head. We looked at each other like strangers for what seemed an eternity before she said, 'David, is it really you? Are you home to stay?'

'No. I'm here for only a week or ten days at most, then I'm off to America.'

'Come in. America? What are you talking about?'

'It's a long story, but the only thing that's important is I've come home to marry you and take you to America with me.'

'Come, sit down, David.'

"She seemed nervous. Confused by my sudden appearance.

'This is all too much for me to understand. Let me look at you, David. You've changed.' She smiled. 'You're quite handsome.'

'As have you. You're more beautiful than I remember. Miriam, tell me, do you still love me?'

'Of course, why would you ask?'

'If you love me, then the only thing you have to understand is we're going to make a new life together in America. If your father agrees, we can marry this week. If not, we will run away together and marry in Amsterdam before we board a boat for America.'

'Wait, David, go slow. I still don't understand. It's been two years since you left and now you come home to say we're leaving for America in a week. No, I need time to think. It's all too sudden. I'd never ever imagined I'd live any place but here. This is my home, David. How can I leave my mother? What will my father say? So many questions.'

'I'll ask your father today. He'll understand why it's important for you to come with me. The only thing that matters is, are you willing to come with me? If I leave without you, the likelihood is we will never see each other again. Can you live with that? Can you live with your father marrying you off to some wealthy old man when I'm gone?'

'Oh, David, I've wanted nothing else but your return. I waited for your letters, eager to hear from you, but America and in a week? Stay longer. Give me time to get used to your return. We can make plans together.'

'I can't stay. I can't return to the fort, and if I'm found here I will be shot.'

'My God. Shot? No that can't happen. It's just the idea of leaving everything and everyone, of traveling to America. I'm not very brave.'

'I'm brave enough for the two of us. Just say yes and I'll speak with your father this very minute.'

"Tears rolled down her cheeks.

'I'm frightened, David, but I'm more frightened of losing you. Never seeing you again. Yes, I'll come to America with you. Father is in his office. Come, we'll see him together.'

"Miriam knocked on the office door.

'Father, David has returned, he and I wish to speak to you.'

'Come in.' Mr. Mendelsohn looked surprised. 'You've changed. I almost didn't recognize you. So, David, when did you get home? Is your time in the Army over?'

'I came home today, Mr. Mendelsohn, and you might say, in some ways, my time in the Army is over.'

'What do you want to talk to me about? Are you here to borrow money?'

"I took a moment, gathered my thoughts and answered. 'Mr. Mendelsohn, I'm leaving for America in the next week or ten days. I'm planning on marrying Miriam and taking her with me. I'm asking for your blessing.'

"Miriam's father looked at me as if I was crazy. Then, in a dismissive tone, he said, 'You must know, young man, this isn't how marriages are arranged. There are rules to be followed, and America? What makes you think for one minute I'd allow Miriam to go to America, let alone marry a penniless villager like you. No it will not happen. Miriam will be promised to someone able to provide for her in the same manner as I have. Someone older, settled. A man of means.'

'Sir, I don't intend to follow your rules. I love Miriam and she loves me. I will find a way to marry her with or without your permission, if not here, then somewhere along the way. I'd think you'd be happier to be part of our ceremony.'

'Miriam,' her father said. 'I know you wouldn't think of going off to a foreign land leaving you family behind. Let alone disobey me by marrying without my permission. David, get out of my house. I will never bless nor will I ever allow you two to marry. You are no longer children. It's time to put an end to your seeing each other. I forbid Miriam to see you again. Do you understand? Miriam my word is final. You are not to see David again.'

'But, Father, I want to go with David.'

'What you want, Miriam, is of no importance. I know what's best for you. Now David, I've asked you to go.'

"I looked at Miriam and asked her to leave the room. 'I have something important to say to your father.'

"She looked confused by my request, but walked out the door closing it behind her.

"When we were alone I spoke of the coming *pogrom*. Mr. Mendelsohn was well aware of what that might mean. Homes destroyed, people killed and worse yet, young women raped. The *pogrom* in Kiev, after Czar Alexander the Second was assassinated, lasted for three days destroying not only Jewish homes, but their places of business. Seventeen Jewish women died while being raped, another two hundred and twenty-five rape victims survived. Every Jew had bitter memories of that event.

"I asked, 'Don't you think Miriam would be safer with me. As beautiful as she is, she would be a prime target for gang rapes. At least in America,' I said, '*pogroms* don't exist. I promise to take care of her always, to protect her, and provide for her as best I can.'

"Minutes passed before he spoke. The color had left his face, his brow furrowed. I knew he was digesting what I'd told him. He knew he couldn't protect her. There was nowhere he could send her where she'd be safe. I heard him sigh before he spoke.

'You, David, it seems, are the lesser of two evils. You would never be my choice as a husband for Miriam, but there is much about you to be admired. Your stubbornness to not let anything stand in the way of what you want will get you far. With great reluctance, you have my blessing if for no other reason but to be sure she's safe from harm.'

'Thank you Sir. The wedding must take place this week. Miriam and I must be out of the area before the trouble begins. My leave papers should see us safely out of Russia, but they expire in two weeks. You mustn't tell her what I've told you. Only Uncle knows what's to come. I'm sure he will call a meeting soon. Now, I must go and tell Miriam the news.'

I left Miriam's father a disheartened man, his shoulders sagging, his color ashen. His daughter was all he had in the world.

Chapter 11

I didn't want Grandpa to stop the story just when they were going to get married. Romance, love, and weddings were becoming more interesting now that I'd entered my teen years. I remember asking if I could bring my boyfriend, Tommy Anderson, to meet him.

"Of course, Maya, but what happened to the other boy, Bobby something?"

"He's not my boyfriend anymore. Not since he tried to kiss me."

"And Tommy, he hasn't tried?"

"Oh, no, Grandpa. He's much nicer. That's why I like him. He says he likes me a lot and he walks me home from school almost every day."

"Anderson, I do not know an Anderson. Where is his family's farm?"

"Oh, he doesn't live on a farm. His father's a doctor and they live in town."

"So, Maya, this young man walks almost a mile with you to the farm and then a mile back home." Grandpa smiled, a twinkle in his eye, 'Yes, I would say he likes you a lot. Bring him for tea and cake if your mother says it is all right."

"That's nifty. Maybe we can show him around the farm. He doesn't know anything about horses, or cows, or farms, but I guess that's okay because he's going to be a doctor just like his father. If I pour you more tea, will you tell me all about the wedding?"

It took a while before he spoke, sipping his tea while his mind seemed to be in another place.

'Maya,' he said, 'I cannot begin to describe the frenzy that was occurring among the villagers. They hurried preparations for the wedding at the same time they were readying for a possible raid by Russian soldiers. Everything of value had to be hidden. Vegetable plants were carefully dug up and family silver, heirlooms, money, as well as anything they held dear was hidden deep in the soil before the plants were replaced.

"Everyone in the village planned to take part in our joyous celebration. For those who were aware of the horror that might befall them, the wedding might be the last time the villagers would celebrate together.

"How all the festivities came together was a mystery to me, but Saturday evening, when the Sabbath ended at sunset, the last minute preparations were completed and the crowd began to assemble for the wedding ceremony.

"The wedding contract had been signed and was ready to be read aloud at the end of the ceremony. I waited, nervous, beneath the canopy erected outside under the stars for my bride to appear on the arm of her father. The white robe worn on Yom Kippur felt uncomfortable as it covered my new black suit. I can see it all now, Maya. I feel my heart skipping a beat just as it did that evening as I saw my Miriam approaching. She wore the pearl incrusted white satin wedding gown that had been her mother's, her face covered by a veil. Her father handed her off and she circled me seven times according to some ancient custom I did not understand.

"We joined hands as the Rabbi began the ritual, offering us a sip of wine when the blessing was completed. I was so worried I would forget the words I was to say before I placed the wedding ring.

Grandpa closed his eyes. Maybe he was reliving the ceremony. He just seemed to forget I was there. After a while he opened his eyes, then spoke the words he'd said that night.

"Behold you are betrothed unto me with this ring according to the law of Moses and Israel."

"Then, Maya, I placed the gold band on the forefinger of her right hand. The contract was read aloud, the Rabbi gave his seven blessings followed again by a sip of wine. A glass was placed under my right foot to be broken. The ceremony was over. Now, whatever happened, we were husband and wife.

"The banquet began, none too soon as I was starved having been obligated to fast all day. There was singing, and men dancing, and shouts of mazel tov. Uncle was drinking more and singing louder than almost anyone. Sensing what was to happen, the celebration was larger, and more elaborate than usual. The adults resigned to whatever was to come, knowing their worldly possessions were buried underneath the vegetables in their gardens, their safety in the hands of God.

"We were to leave before dawn the next morning for the train station in Kiev, on our way to Hamburg where Miriam's father believed it could be reached safely. Hamburg had a port with more opportunities for passage to America.

"As we had no house of our own, much to my dismay, Miriam and I returned to our houses alone. Consummating our marriage would have to wait as would our first kiss. Harry was laughing so hard, the tears were rolling down his cheeks as I crawled into bed beside him.

'So David, you have a beautiful bride and you choose to sleep with me? I'm flattered, but no kissing.'

Having asked Grandpa if Grandma was a beautiful bride, he was quick to reply. "Let me show you."

I watched as Grandpa got up from his chair and walked to the dresser, his steps short, but his back straight as an arrow.

"See," Grandpa said, handing me their wedding picture. "She was the most beautiful bride in the whole world. Have you ever seen a bride more beautiful?"

"I'm so sorry Grandmother died before I was old enough to remember her."

"Ah, Maya, she waited for your birth with such excitement, looking forward to her time with you, but God had other plans and my Miriam died before she could watch you grow up."

"Grandpa, can I ask you a question?"

"Ask what you wish my child."

"Do you love me because I look like her?" I pointed to my Grandmother in the wedding picture I was holding.

"Maya, I'm pleased you look like my beloved Miriam. I find joy in seeing her every time I look at you, but I love you because you're you."

"I like that, Grandpa. I love you because you're you, too."

Chapter 12

I don't remember when I met with Grandpa next, but it couldn't have been too much later as I wasn't about to let him stop. Once again I reminded him of where he left off. This time he was about to leave on his to journey to America.

"Leaving Uncle, Tante Leah, Reba, and Harry was difficult, Maya. Knowing I would never see them again was only part of my distress. What was to befall them made the parting even harder.

"I had drawn a plan for the village to defend itself and presented it to Uncle to share with the men of the village, but much to my surprise, Uncle just laughed at me and tore the plan to shreds.

'I don't know why God brings such pain upon us,' Uncle said. 'But it is ours to endure. We cannot fight the Russian Army nor will we leave. This has been the home of my family and the others in our village for many generations. If they destroy the village we will rebuild. I trust in God's promise never to forsake us.'

"Uncle put his arms around me, a knowing look on his face. 'Oh, David, you don't understand how we survive. Some will run, some will hide,' he said. 'The rest will stand and watch, hoping their home will be spared. If someday, David, you have land and a home of your own, you will understand why we must continue to stay on at any cost. God must have a reason why he puts us to such a test. It's not my job to question God.'

'I guess I don't share your faith in God, Uncle. So far He hasn't done a very good job of taking care of the Jews. I believe in taking care of myself and if God wants to help, fine by me.'

"I promised to write to Harry, and when I could, send money to bring Reba to America. Earlier, I had placed the few things I owned in the large wooden trunk that held Miriam's possessions. The rest would go in a small suitcase I would carry.

"I walked to Miriam's house, glimpsing the village for the last time. The horse and carriage waited by the gate. As I approached the door, Miriam's aunt pushed it open, tears streaming down her cheeks.

'She's saying goodbye to her mother,' her aunt said.

"Miriam's father appeared and handed me an envelope. 'I can't give you furniture, or chickens, or a cow as part of Miriam's dowry, so I give you money, instead." He called to his daughter. 'Miriam, we need to leave.'

"Moments later, Miriam walked down the hall dressed in a dark blue ankle length wool skirt, a high-necked, long sleeved silk top and a wool jacket that matched her skirt. She wore a large blue wool shawl draped around her shoulders and an oversized-brimmed hat, its silk tassels tied under her chin. She looked beautiful. As she neared, I could see she had been crying.

'Time to go, my bride.' I held out my hand and she placed her gloved hand in mine. I noticed she was wearing the bracelet I had given her years before. We walked down the path in silence. I knew leaving her family, and the only home she'd ever known for all her seventeen years, was a challenge.

"After the buggy ride to the village, Miriam and I waited alongside her father as we watched for the train. I could hear it coming. I smelled the black smoke, and felt the tracks vibrate. The sound of the rails were almost like music as the train came to a screeching halt alongside us.

"With the help of the station master, I lifted the trunk aboard as Marian clung to her father saying their goodbyes. While neither put it into words, they knew they would probably never see each other again. I hadn't told Miriam of the dangers that were likely to befall the village. Someday I would explain the reasons behind her father's strange behavior in consenting to our marriage and sending her off so quickly.

"We boarded the train in the second class section and found seats together. Miriam's father had provided the extra money to purchase second class tickets. He wanted to spare her the trauma of the third class car. I suggested she sit by the window to see the wonders that were before us, but she seemed too overcome with sadness to be interested in the view.

'Miriam, my love, be joyful. We are starting on an exciting adventure. We are going to build a new life together, and you will not be without family. Your father is telegraphing your aunt and uncle in Brooklyn that we are coming.'

We had to change trains in Kiev. I held tight to Miriam's hand. The station was crowded. Miriam seemed nervous in such a large mix of people. I wouldn't let on how nervous I was as I watched Russian military guards surveying the crowd, pulling people aside to check their papers. The last thing I wanted was to be questioned by the guards. Thankfully we boarded the train without incident.

"We spoke very little as we traveled to Hamburg. I hoped we would avoid any future trouble with the Russian authorities, as Jews were not permitted to travel without special permission. My leave papers would be my permission, maybe applying to Miriam as well, but it was against the law for Jews to leave the country without the proper exit papers. Those papers we did not possess. With any luck, the Germans would let us steal across the border. That's what crossing into Germany without papers was called.

"After two days, we reached Hamburg. Both of us were tired and hungry. The food we'd brought with us was long gone and sitting for days on the uncomfortable train seats left every bone in my body crying out in pain. Miriam had spoken little. A certain sadness reflected on her face.

"I took Miriam's hand, helping her step onto the platform after the train stopped, holding on tight to the baggage claim I'd been given. The station was crowded. I followed the signs in German that led to the street exit. We pushed past dozens of aggressive vendors trying to sell ships passage or rooms at boarding houses, each vendor trying to outdo the other for our business. I pushed on, asking directions to the offices of Hamburg-Amerika shipping company. I was not about to buy passage from some stranger in a train station.

"Exiting the station, the city of Hamburg lay before us, a sight to behold...parks and canals along the Elba River, cobblestoned streets, and beautiful structures. The clock tower of the church of Saint Michael was visible above all the buildings.

"We found the main office of the shipping company with little trouble. Miriam sat while I spoke with the clerk behind the long counter whose top was covered in brightly colored brochures depicting the various steamships and their destinations.

"In answer to my question the clerk said, 'There will be a steamship leaving for America in five days.' He seemed surprised that we arrived by train and were not immediately taken to the holding area. 'Maybe you were overlooked because you didn't look like peasants. Persons seeking passage to America aren't allowed to set foot in the city of Hamburg ever since the cholera outbreak which killed many townspeople a few years ago,' the clerk informed me.

"I studied the brochure he handed me listing the various accommodations and their price for passage. First class was not a consideration. The decision was between a private cabin in second class or third class, better known as steerage, which was in the hold of the ship with no private accommodations.

"I looked at my bride, knowing she had never known hardship and thought hard before making my decision. Much as I'd like second class, the price for our passage would be double that of third class. It would take too big a bite out of our money. If we arrived in America penniless, we would be turned back. I had no choice. We would sail in third class.

'Is there room for us on the next vessel to leave for America?'

"I was assured there would be room. I questioned the clerk about someplace to stay and was told that the company had a village for passengers awaiting passage called *Auswanderer-Hallen at Viddel* on the outskirts of Hamburg. Our stay there was mandatory. I could purchase our tickets at the compound. He took the baggage claim for our trunk, saying the company would retrieve it from the train station and put it aboard ship.

'Wait here,' he told us, 'While I arrange transportation to *Viddel.*'

"I was sorry we would not have a chance to explore the beautiful city of Hamburg. The ride took only about fifteen minutes providing the only glimpse of the city we would see. As we approached the village I was alarmed to see a high stonewall surrounding the compound. German soldiers were guarding the entrance. This gave me cause for concern. Why the walls and why the armed guards?

The gates were opened to reveal a long series of garden plots with trees and flowers, and about thirty new, very attractive buildings. The area seemed neat, clean, and attractive. It looked safe. Not foreboding. I could see people were milling about in the distance.

"A gentleman, dressed in dark blue pants and a white shirt with Hamburg-Amerika embroidered on the pocket, met us. He led us to the administration building where we were informed fumigation was required before we could proceed to the rest of the compound. Daily medical examinations would take place. Passage could be arranged and money converted into American dollars at a fair exchange.

'Beds are provided free in the dormitory,' he said. 'For a small fee, you can stay in a boarding house with private rooms. You will be required to stay within the compound until embarkation. Under no circumstances can you leave the village.'

"It sounded ominous. I chose the private room and paid the fee. Minutes later, another man arrived, wearing the same uniform, and asked us to follow him as he led us to the fumigation station. I tried to explain to Miriam what was going to happen and that it was necessary that everybody be clean and free of parasites. She was horrified, screaming, as the foul smelling spray was applied, voicing concern that her clothes would be ruined. 'Why are you doing this? I am clean. I am clean.'

"Before I could calm her down and stop her hysterical sobbing, we were led to the hospital for our medical examination. I'd been through this in the Army, but I doubted Miriam had ever been examined by a doctor. She was trembling, terrified that a strange male was touching her, unhappier by the minute with her decision to come with me. That was not the joyous, happy start to our married life I'd hoped for or promised her.

"The doctor spoke of the outbreak of cholera, how it was blamed on the emigrants, which was why we wouldn't be allowed to leave the village until time to board the ship. All passengers, we were told, had to pass a rigorous physical and mental examination before being allowed passage. Anyone arriving in America sick or feeble-minded would be sent back.

"We received a ticket to be punched after our daily medical examination, and handed a map of the village with x's marking the boarding house where we would be staying, the kosher kitchen, and the synagogue, all surrounded by green lawns and trees with a scattering of benches. No matter how uncomfortable, each step was bringing us closer to my dream.

"We spent our first night together. The room was small, but tidy. We had a bed and a dresser. The pitcher of water standing in a bowl on top of the dresser was the only item in the room. The bed smelled sweet. Much as I wanted her, this was not the perfect time. I held Miriam in my arms and tried to comfort her until she dropped off to sleep.

"We awoke late in the morning feeling better having had a good night's rest.

"After our medical examination, we were free to wander the grounds or just sit on one of the many benches in the sun resting up for the long journey ahead."

Grandpa stood saying, "Now, dear Maya, that's enough for one day. Go and find your friends. I'm sure you have better things to do than listen to an old man ramble on about the past."

"I love your story, Grandpa. I'll go if you promise to tell me about the sea voyage next time."

"I promise. Now run along."

Chapter 13

I went looking for Grandpa and found him in the barn tending to a lame horse he had in a stall. He looked up surprised to see me.

"What brings you here, Maya? You are early for storytelling."

"I came to tell you I can't come today. I have to leave this very minute for town with my mother and we won't be home until late, but I promise I'll come tomorrow afternoon instead."

"It is alright, child. We will talk tomorrow. Now run along. Don't keep your mother waiting I don't want her upset with me."

"Okay, Grandpa, but don't forget you were going to tell me more about your trip to America."

"Ah, yes, more about the trip."

I left Grandpa sitting on a bale of hay alone with his thoughts.

I sat back on the hay bale, closed my eyes recalling that time clearly. Thinking I couldn't tell Maya all that happened next. She was too young and it wouldn't be proper.

Some things are better left unsaid, but I wanted to relive that night, the night we made love for the first time. Letting my mind drift, I remembered as if it was yesterday the joy of our first mating. Every detail was clear in my memory of that night.

We had wine with our dinner, a first for both of us, as we enjoyed the company of a couple from Lithuania, older by far, childless. Our conversation lasted long past the meal, continuing over coffee, each discussing what we hoped to find in America.

As we parted company, I took Miriam by the hand and suggested we stroll through the gardens before bed. I was excited and scared about taking Miriam to bed that evening. We'd walked for some time. I was carefully planning my actions when Miriam interrupted my thoughts. I remember she asked why was I so quiet. Of course I couldn't tell her the truth, so I started talking about the ship as I guided her back to our quarters.

I shut the door to our room and took her in my arms. I kissed her for the first time and felt a stirring in my loins. "I want to take you as a wife, Miriam" and I kissed her again. My heart was beating so fast, a ringing in my ears. I didn't think I could have said another word.

I led her to the bed and began to unbutton her blouse. I don't know what I expected, but I found no resistance. When her breasts were exposed all I could do was stare. I told her how beautiful she was as I continued to stare. I'd never seen a woman's breasts before.

Miriam rose from the bed, touched her lips to my forehead and lifted her delicate white linen nightgown, trimmed with pink satin bows, from our suitcase. I can see her now as she turned her back to me and removed all her clothes. The beauty of her naked form sent a rush of blood to my head, a swelling between my legs. Pulling the gown over her head, Miriam turned and smiled as she crawled into bed beside my naked body.

We were both virgins, but nature does have a way of taking over. To my surprise and delight, I found a passionate and willing partner that night. Ah, yes, and for all our life together. But that first night, as I touched every bit of her beautiful body, we shared the ultimate expression of our love. That experience was something I hold special to this day. I think no two people ever loved each other more than we did.

I can see her now as I saw her that night, the most beautiful woman on earth and she was mine. We awoke from sleep to see the morning sun shining in the window. We lay in each other's arms basking in the afterglow of our love, eager to recapture the feeling.

I can feel the warmth of that morning's sun even now and smell the sweet aroma of her body, the feel of her lips on mine, such beautiful memories. I miss her every minute of every day.

I stood. Well, time to finish my chores. No time for an old man to daydream, no matter how pleasant, when there is work to be done.

Chapter 14

I was anxious to hear about the trip to America. "Grandpa," I remember saying, as I settled into my chair at the table, the next afternoon. "I bet it was exciting sailing on a big ship. Someday I'd like to go on an ocean voyage. Weren't you scared? I know I would be."

"Yes, Maya. Mostly excited, but a little scared. I'd heard stories about terrible things that happened on the ocean."

Grandpa drank the last drop of tea and began to describe the passage.

"There were notices posted in many different languages throughout the compound telling of the ship's sailing in two days. We were expected at the compound's dock at eight in the morning with our luggage and medical records. A tender would ferry us to the ship.

"The time had come to make Miriam aware of what was about to happen. I sat with her in the garden after breakfast and took her hand in mine as I tried to describe the journey. My assumption fell far sort of the ordeal that lay before us.

"The morning of our departure we were herded aboard the tender like cattle, packed in elbow-to-elbow with our fellow passengers. We looked different than most of our traveling companions. Miriam's high fashion dress and my wedding suit set us apart from their peasant attires. That was how we managed to exit the train and enter the city of Hamburg. We didn't look like immigrants.

"We debarked at the passenger hall to be greeted by the sight of hundreds upon hundreds of people. Single men and women, families with children, all dressed in as many different styles as there were people, everything from peasant attire, to ethnic costumes, to high fashion. They had an assortment of possessions in every conceivable manner of transport from trunks, to suitcases, to cloth bundles, to heavy paper bundles wrapped and tied, to blankets...everything to represent our fellow passengers meager possessions. Many of the infants and small children seemed poorly dressed for the cold breezes of the ocean.

"First and second class passengers were few in number, and formed a separate line from steerage, cordoned off by heavy chains strung between two poles.

"We lined up, medical reports and tickets in hand, ready for our final health inspection. This time the doctor was accompanied by a representative of the American government. Anyone considered feeble minded, ill, or judged unfit by the way they moved weren't allowed to board, as they would be turned back when the ship docked in America.

The shipping company would be fined and the passengers returned to their various countries at the shipping company's expense.

"Having passed our final inspection, they herded us back to the tender to take us to the ship.

"We boarded the steamship and walked past the cabins on the main deck. Sailors directed us to a ladder leading down to what had originally been the cargo hold. I went ahead, Miriam close behind. A few open portholes let in light and a limited amount of ventilation. I hoped they'd remain open as we got underway. The air smelled dank, a strong odor of mold, stuffy even though we were among the first to board. The ship was not due to sail until morning.

"Single men were housed in a forward compartment with two tiers of bunks. Single women had a similar compartment aft. The married couples occupied either side of the hold. The families with children were housed in the space between. The bunks took up every bit of available space leaving little room to walk or stand. The best bunks, a sailor told me, were those on the top tier as we would be safe from the vomit of seasick passengers. I didn't share this information with Miriam, but it was a clue to what we could expect. There was one bathroom for women and one for men, neither proved adequate for the number of passengers. First and second-class passengers were limited by the number of cabins, but there was no limit to the number of passengers they could pack into the hold.

"We claimed a space for ourselves, and found a mattress stuffed with straw, a blanket and two mess kits in the middle of the bunk, which was barely big enough for two skinny people to lie down. A burlap curtain on a metal rod could be pulled closed for privacy. That small cubicle would be our home for at least twelve days.

"I tried to be upbeat, but failed. Better to be honest with Miriam and tell her this would be twelve to fifteen days of hell, but there would be a rainbow waiting for us at the end of the voyage. I could say nothing else.

"The hold began to fill. The final count was somewhere between eight hundred to a thousand passengers with only two bathrooms.

"By morning, the last of the passengers were scrambling to find a place to settle as the ship left port.

"The ship's movement was slow and steady as we steamed down the Elba River to the North Sea. A sense of excitement in the air even though the foul smelling smoke from the engines was drifting in through the open portholes.

"A member of the crew came below to announce breakfast would be served in what was jokingly called the dining salon at eight o'clock.

"After the tea and bread that was breakfast, I suggested we go up on deck. I thought it would be better to spend as much time outside as possible, away from the large number of people crowded into such a small space.

"Lunch, the big meal of the day was at one o'clock. We went below again, taking our tin plates and cups with us. A long line was beginning to form outside the door of the salon, a salon in name only. Just another dingy part of the hold where long tables and benches had been set as well as shelves along the walls. We ate in shifts, as there wasn't enough room for everyone. Once the tables filled those without seats stood elbow to elbow eating off the shelves. Crew members ladled hot soup into our cups from the large buckets they carried, followed by a potato, a small slice of beef, and a slice of bread put on our plates. Some of the men clamored for more to no avail. The sailors kept yelling to eat faster. They had many more to feed.

"If we couldn't push our way into the first seating, we had to eat cold food at dirty tables. The whole thing became a nightmare. People began lining up after breakfast to be first in line for lunch. As the days dragged on, tempers grew short and arguments over places in line were settled with fist fights.

"Miriam wasn't happy with the ugly scenes that took place at mealtime. She couldn't understand how people could act that way and began to resist leaving our bunk. I had to coax her to come with me to the salon. I begged her to eat, telling her she'd be sick if she didn't put food in her stomach. Only hours into our voyage and the situation was miserable at best. Twelve days was going to be very difficult.

"We rinsed our dishes in a barrel of salty seawater and returned to the deck. Supper, served at seven, consisted of tea, sugar and bread.

"By bedtime we crawled into our bunk and laid down together, unable to undress. I took Miriam in my arms and kissed her good night, doing my best to quiet her fears. One of the crew closed the portholes and the hatch for the night. It didn't take long for the hold to become a sweatbox. The heat from the steam engines had no place to go, nor could the body heat of the mass of people in the closed hold.

"Time hung heavy on our hands. Each day was worse than the last. In the beginning, people who'd brought musical instruments, violins, accordions, and harmonicas would play. There was singing and dancing on deck for those lucky enough to squeeze into the limited space. The festive feeling didn't last very long.

"Soon, many of the passengers began to suffer from sea sickness and tempers grew even shorter as the days dragged on. The stink below was overpowering and getting worse everyday. A combination of sweat, unwashed bodies, and vomit as well as the stench from the overflowing bathrooms seeped into the living quarters and made breathing unbearable. Hell couldn't have been any worse. I was having a hard time coping, but Miriam shut down completely. She'd shed her outer garments and laid in our bunk all day, drenched in sweat. She refused to go for meals. She wouldn't talk to me. She cried herself to sleep every night. She loved me and hated me at the same time. I felt guilty bringing her to this hell hole.

"The rough seas we were experiencing didn't make the going any easier. No one was allowed on deck. The crew shut the hatch, locking us in the hold. Hard as I tried, there was no way to shut out the sounds of crying babies or the screams of unhappy women and children. Grumbling and fighting could be heard among adults yelling in a mix of languages. We had no control over anything. We simply existed. We had no place to go.

Racial and religious differences began to boil over. I spent most of my day in our bunk alongside Miriam. As the arguments became uglier, fights broke out among the men, while women sobbed as an ever-increasing number of people began to die. Much to the horror of everyone, their bodies were tossed overboard after the doctor had indicated the reason for their death in his record book. I'll never forget the heartbreaking screams of one woman as the doctor took her dead child by force from her arms and handed him to a crew member who tossed the body in the ocean. One more thing to worry about. If someone died because of a contagious disease, the whole ship could be quarantined and wouldn't be allowed to dock.

"As if the journey hadn't been bad enough, a horrific storm occurred on the tenth day of the voyage. The hatch had been secured and locked. We were prisoners in the hold. The wind howled and the ship's hull creaked as she rolled from side-to-side, then pitched up and down like a seesaw. When the ship dipped deep into the bottom of a trough, everything that was not strapped down began to slide toward the bow then slide back as the ship reached for the crest of the wave, some as high as fourteen feet the crew said. Most people had taken to their bunks as standing was almost impossible. The sounds of sobbing women and terrified children, the howling wind, and the waves crashing over the decks made me think we might not make it.

"I overheard the sailors nervously talking of killer waves sinking ships. took her to the bottom in an instant", one of the crew said.

"I kept thinking of the stories I'd read about the Atlantic that sank with over five hundred passengers in eighteen seventy-three, and the Princess Alice that went down in eighteen seventy-eight with over six hundred passengers aboard. What a horrible death to be thrown into the ocean to die, but there was no turning back even if I wanted to.

"I was beginning to worry Miriam wouldn't survive the trip. I'd tried bringing back whatever food I could, but liquids were impossible to carry with the movement of the ship. She refused anything I tried to tempt her with. She'd given up eating. I stayed close to her, wiping her brow of sweat, telling her it was just a few more days, but I got no response. The thought of her dying and being thrown overboard like a piece of trash was tearing me apart. I did the only thing I knew how to do. I prayed even though I didn't know the Hebrew words. I promised God I'd be a better Jew if he just let us survive.

The storm made it impossible to reach the dining salon so we had no food. Probably just as well. It would be difficult to hold anything down with the pounding motions of the ship.

Twenty-four hours of gale force winds seemed like an eternity.

"With dawn came a welcomed change in the weather and once again we were allowed topside. I dressed Miriam as best I could, noticing how her clothes were hanging loose she'd lost so much weight. I wrapped our blanket around her on top of her shawl and carried her topside. We were going to spend the day in the fresh air no matter how cold it got. I could stand the cold, not the foul odors. The monotony was beginning to get to me as well. Just one hellish day after another.

"When I began to think we could not hold out much longer, one of the crew announced we'd be arriving in the New York harbor in the morning. The roar from our shipmates was deafening. People began to sing and dance again. The mood changed to one of excitement. We'd made it. Nothing we would encounter in America could be worse than the journey. We had survived.

"I woke Miriam early so we could find a place on deck to watch the New York shoreline come into view. Her spirits were lifted with the news of the journey's end, that at last we would reach land. I watched the shore line came into to view then, all of a sudden there she was, the Statue of Liberty, glowing golden in the morning sun. I had one arm around Miriam, the other waving at the statue, well aware of the tears streaming down my face. I was so excited I couldn't find the proper words to say, so I just keep repeating, 'God Bless America.'"

"Stop, Stop, Grandpa. I think you made a mistake. The Statue of Liberty is green."

"You are correct, Maya, the statue appears green now. She is coated in a thin layer of copper that has oxidized over the years to a green patina, but when Grandma and I arrived in New York's harbor, the statue had only recently been installed on Liberty Island. She was golden."

"Wow, Grandpa, I had no idea. Wait 'til I tell my history class. I bet my teacher doesn't even know that. We talked about Ellis Island in class this year. Is that where you landed?"

"It is where we were processed. What did you learn about Ellis Island?"

"Not much, only that that's where all the immigrants from Europe entered the country."

"That is true. The original Ellis Island building doesn't exist anymore. It was a large structure at least three stories high, built of wood. It burned to the ground five years later and the new building is the one on the island today. Ellis Island, dear Maya, is the place where the hopes and dreams of twenty-two million immigrants, like your grandmother and me, saw our dreams of living in America, living in freedom come true. I can't explain what it means to be free, because you have never known anything else, but Maya, believe me, freedom is the ultimate gift from God. Every day I pray, 'God Bless America.'

Chapter 15

"Grandpa, I found a picture of Ellis Island in a history book in the school library. I wanted to bring it home to show you, but the librarian said I couldn't check out a reference book. Ellis Island looked huge and kind of scary. Tell me what was it like."

"Ah, yes, Ellis Island, our last hurdle. I remember my feelings as we docked. I was relieved the monstrous trip was over. I swore I'd never board an ocean-going ship again. But for the first time, I was coming to grips with what lay ahead. Beginning to understand that getting here was the easy part. I needed to find work before our dollars ran out. I had a wife to support. Responsibilities. For the first time I wondered how I'd find work. I didn't speak the language. In all my dreams and the excitement, that was something I'd not thought about before.

"The ship landed at the port of New York as all those things were spinning around in my head. I watched the first and second-class passengers walk down the gang plank and enter the cheering crowd awaiting their arrival. Those of us in steerage would not be allowed to leave with the rest of the passengers. Miriam and I, along with the rest of those who traveled in the hold, were marched across the pier holding on to our luggage, baskets, bundles, and screaming children to a large waiting area. It seemed, if you were rich enough to arrive in first or second class, America didn't care if you were feeble minded or ill. All that mattered was you were rich.

Each of us wore a name tag with our manifest number written on it in large black figures. In groups of about thirty, we were led to a barge and packed again like cattle onto the upper deck while our baggage was loaded into the hold. I looked at the rest of the group and wondered if I appeared as disheveled and smelled as bad as they did. Nervous apprehension of what was coming next showed on their faces. I had to admit I was scared. One cough, one false step by either Miriam or myself, and we could be deemed unfit to enter the country.

"The barge docked at Ellis Island leaving us to walk the length of the pier as the ground swayed like giant waves beneath our feet, the water lapping at the pilings. We were met by an interpreter and led through the main doorway to a steep stairway leading up to the enormous registry room. Miriam held tight to my hand looking like a lost child. I could only imagine what was going through her head at that moment.

"A doctor, dressed in a white coat, a stethoscope round his neck, stood at the top of the stairs looking for signs of illness, lameness, or trouble breathing as we climbed the steep stairs. We were examined once again, this time with special care to our face, throat, hair, neck, and hands. The eye examination was the most crucial. I cringed as they rolled back my eyelid with a metal buttonhook to look for signs of trachoma. They asked my name to determine if I was deaf or could speak. If there was concern, the doctor marked the name tag with chalk, as he did to the man in front of us. He was detained for further examination, then depending on the findings, he'd either spend time in the island's hospital where he could be deemed cured and released, or deported.

"Everyone was exhausted from the trip and tempers were hard to control as we were poked and demeaned once again. Those had to be the longest minutes of my life. I passed the medical examination. I waited, nervous and stressed, as Miriam's examination was completed.

"Together, we approached the final step. A primary line of inspectors, seated on high stools, had the ship's manifest on the desk in front of them, an interpreter at their sides. The men were placed in one line, the women and children in another. Miriam looked frightened as she was forced to leave my side. It took about two minutes for twenty or thirty questions to be asked and answered. The inspector asked my name, which I had given earlier to the steamship company as David Freeman. If I made it to America I'd be a free man. I didn't use my real name as I couldn't chance being identified as an Army deserter. I was asked if I was traveling alone, where had I come from, where was I going, could I read and write, how much money did I have? The inspector looked me over, and in a split second, made his decision…an admittance card.

We left the building relieved it was over and in awe of what we saw as we walked out the door into the sunshine and the mass of people holding up signs with their names and the names of new arrivals they were there to meet. I was excited about the future, but Miriam seemed apprehensive.

"I scanned the area wondering what I would do if no one was there to meet us. Off to the left, I saw a well-dressed grey haired man waving a sign with Miriam's name written on it. We walked up to him and Miriam asked if he was Nathan Goldberg, her mother's brother.

"He nodded as he reached for Miriam and wrapped his arms around her. 'Welcome to America, children. Let me have a look at you, Miriam. Ah, yes, you look just like your mother did at about your age. Give me your name tag and baggage claim and I'll arrange for your things to be delivered to my house, then we can be on our way. Wait here, I'll be back.'

'If you don't mind, sir,' I said, 'we'll come with you. I don't want to get separated.'

Chapter 16

"I can't imagine coming to a country where you didn't even speak the language, Grandpa. You and Grandma were really brave. What was Grandma's uncle like? I really want to hear the rest of the story, but when do we get to the part about the farm and Billy and me?"

"I know, Maya it's a very long story, but remember it's my whole lifetime. I can't tell you everything all at once. Try to be patient. I promise to get to you and Billy in good time. Enough of my story telling for today, so now tell me what is happening in your life?"

"Okay. Let me think. School's fine. I got all A's, and I bet you can't guess where I'm going on Saturday?"

"I could not even begin to guess."

"I'm going to the movies to see Snow White and The Seven Dwarfs. It's the biggest movie of nineteen hundred thirty- seven. Isn't that cool?"

"Cool? I guess. So, Maya, who is Snow White?"

"Oh, Grandpa, you really don't know who Snow White is?"

"Really, I do not know."

"She's the beautiful princess in my favorite fairy tale, even if thirteen is a little old to still like fairy tales. It's all about her wicked stepmother and a handsome prince who falls in love with her and the dwarf's she lives with. The dwarf's sing "Ho, Ho, It's Off To Work We Go" and Snow White sings "Someday My Prince Will Come." and it's all cartoons they call animation and I'm so excited I can hardly wait until Saturday."

"Well, Saturday will be here before you know it. No story I could tell could be as exciting as Snow White."

"Oh, no, Grandpa, you're wrong. Snow White is make believe. Your story is much more exciting because its real."

"So run along, Maya. You can tell me about the movie when we have tea again."

At thirteen I was old enough to appreciate what my grandparents had gone throughand surprised by what I thought had always existed, like bathrooms, electric lights, and telephones. I do remember asking what it was like to see America for the first time, fascinated as Grandpa started telling me about leaving Ellis Island.

"After Miriam's, Uncle Nathan, who everyone called Nate, made arrangements for a drayage company to deliver our trunk to his house, we made our way to the dock and a ferry boat tied up at the end of a long pier. Miriam looked at me as if to say, not another boat.

Uncle Nate bought three tickets and we boarded. Everything was different this time. There was plenty of room with ample places to sit, vendors were roaming the aisles selling food and drinks. It took about twenty minutes for all the ferry passengers to board and then our trip to Battery Park in Brooklyn began as we watched the skyline. I couldn't believe we were here in America. It still felt like a dream.

"Uncle Nate asked if we were fine walking the short distance to the Brooklyn Bridge where we could, if we tired, board a train to take us across to South Brooklyn. We were both so glad to be on solid ground, we were happy to walk across the bridge. We were beyond tired.

"I looked in wonder as we approached the long suspension bridge spanning the East River. I'd never seen anything so spectacular in all my life. The bridge was so wide rail passage, horse and buggies, and people were walking across all at the same time.

"When we reached the far side, Uncle Nate hired a horse drawn carriage to take us to his home. He instructed the driver to go the long way, down Fulton Street, so we could glimpse Brooklyn Heights. As the carriage proceeded, Uncle pointed out Hoyt and Teale Clothiers, AC Flatley's Furniture store, the St. George Hotel, and Holy Trinity Church. We saw one fine building after another until we turned onto Ramsen Street and stopped in front of a block-long series of three story brownstone houses on the tree lined street. All the houses had common walls and steep stairs to the front door. Uncle Nate called them row houses, grander than anything I'd ever seen in the Ukraine. Even nicer, newer I thought than the European cities I'd glimpsed. I could tell, by the look of wonder on Miriam's face, she was beginning to feel better about the whole journey.

"Neither the sidewalk nor the street was paved with gold, but they looked golden to me. We climbed the steep steps and watched as Uncle Nate placed his key in the lock and opened the door beckoning us to come in, calling, 'Mama, we're here.'

From the back of the long narrow house, a heavy-set woman in her forties approached, well dressed, with greying hair pulled back off her face and fashioned into a bun.

"Children, come,' she said, greeting us. 'You must be exhausted. Have some tea and cake, and then you can clean up and rest before dinner. Our whole family is coming to meet their newly arrived relatives.'

"She led us to a dining room with a table whose top was so smooth and highly polished I could almost see my reflection. Nothing like the rough wooden tables I was used to.

'Sit, children,' she said, and called to someone in the kitchen to bring tea. While Miriam's upbringing was more cultured than mine, I was sure she'd never seen anything like this before.

"We answered questions about conditions at home, and Uncle Nate asked after his younger sister who'd he not seen since she was ten, his having lived in America almost twenty-five years.

"He wasn't happy with what he heard, but pleased she was well taken care of.

"When we'd finished tea and cake, Mama, whose name was Rebecca, took Miriam by the hand and beckoned me to follow. We climbed a steep, narrow flight of stairs to the second floor and shown a bedroom she said would be ours.

'Come Miriam, I'll show you the bathroom. I'm sure you'd enjoy a hot bath.' Aunt Rebecca led Miriam down the hall to a sight neither one of us had seen before, indoor plumbing. A large cast iron tub sat above the wood floor on four claw-shaped feet. Hot and cold water faucets rose on metal pipes above the tub. Auntie closed the door leaving me standing in the hall listening to the sound of running water.

"Later that evening, bathed and dressed in clean clothes, we entered the well-lit living room and scanned the crowd. The adults, a little older than me, were surrounded by small children.

"Uncle Nate hushed the group as we entered and he started to speak. 'Children, these are your cousins, Miriam and David Freeman, newlyweds, just arrived today after a long and very difficult trip from the Ukraine. Let's welcome them to America.' "One-by-one we were introduced to Uncle and Auntie's three sons, their wives and children, as well as their daughter and her husband, also newlyweds.

"With the introductions over, we all entered the dining room as the children were spirited away by a maid. The large table was set with a lace tablecloth, matching china and crystal glasses. A silver bowl filled with flowers sat in the middle of the table, silver candle holders on either side. Gas lamps, attached to the walls, held glass chimneys rising above brass fixtures, the effect different from the candlelight or kerosene lanterns we were used to. The room was brighter, more cheerful.

"Uncle bowed his head and prayed, thanking God for our good fortune and for the meal we were about to eat, the same prayer Uncle Jacob said everynight. The food was delicious. Though anything would taste good after the slop we were given on the ship. No soup bowl containing a potato and a slice of meat at that table. We were served on a fine china dinner plate with an assortment of silverware at our place, rather than the one spoon I was used to. I was wrong in thinking everyone in America lived and dined like this. I would find out in a very short time, Uncle was the exception, a wealthy immigrant, who owned three garment factories, rather than what the large number of poor immigrants owned who worked in his factories. Which was next to nothing.

"Questions from Uncle about the conditions of Jews in the Ukraine, and our trip were interspersed with laughter and large amounts of the sweet red wine consumed by the men. Uncle's son's were all born in America and had little understanding or interest in the plight of those remaining in the Pale. As my telling of the conditions in the Pale continued, one son said,

'What is this pail of which you speak? The only pail I ever heard of is something like a small bucket.'

'I will try to explain, but it's difficult to comprehend if you haven't experienced it. It's called the Pale of Settlement, a part of imperial Russia, designated by Catherine the Great as the area where Jews were permitted to live. They can't live outside its boundaries. Can't even travel outside without permission. They live under very poor conditions most in poverty. A small number of Jews, maybe five percent at most are permitted to be educated. A few become merchants, doctors, nurses, midwives, and educators, leading a better life. The rest farm small patches of land barely producing enough to feed their families.

'Why do they live under those conditions? Why not just leave,' one of the sons said.

'That's what I'd do,' another son said.

'Some did, like your father, David said. 'Others were not so lucky. They either had no money for transport or had a family they couldn't leave behind. But it wasn't until the assassination of Alexander the Second that things went from bad to worse.'

'How could they get any worse?' the first son added with a laugh.

'Oh, they did. The few rights the Jews had were taken away by the Czars who followed. Every Jew, regardless of education, was regarded as a third class citizen, with no rights at all. The status some had earned as second-class citizen was taken away. *Pogroms* began in earnest, killing, raping, burning villages and shops. That's why Jews by the thousands, like Miriam and me, are finding a way to come to America.'

"The expressions on the faces of those at the table reflected their disbelief that such conditions existed, but I knew they couldn't possibly understand the circumstances under which the Jews in Russia lived, seeing how well they lived in America, so I changed the subject.

"We excused ourselves after dinner. It had been a long and exciting day, and we were beyond tired. We left with the promise from the various cousins of invitations to meet again.

"I couldn't wait to fall into bed, tired, full of rich food, and feeling the effects of too much wine, with no interest in thinking about the Pale.

"The feel of a real bed was a joy unto itself. Tomorrow would be soon enough to deal with the future. That night my bride and I would enjoy, for the first time, the privacy and joy of a comfortable bed in a beautiful room, safe in America.

"I awoke with the morning sun, not sure where I was, then I heard Miriam's steady breathing. We were safe. I rolled over and fell back asleep.

"We got up at mid-day after lounging in bed, having a long conversation about our good fortune. Miriam was pleased to find such a large family eager to welcome her, relishing their home and lifestyle. She admitted that as of that day, it had all been worth it, wishing her mother and father could make the journey, too. She realized, of course, her mother was too fragile to travel, and I was not prepared to tell her of the raid.

"Auntie was about to leave as we came downstairs. 'Children,' she said, as she greeted us with a smile. 'I hope you slept well. I'll be home early as will Nathan. The hired girl will see to your breakfast. Rest. We'll visit later.'

"The maid served cream cheese and lox filled bagels, filling our cups with steaming coffee the likes of which I'd never tasted. I ate with gusto. It had been too long since we had a decent breakfast, the stale bread and weak tea aboard ship still fresh in my mind. We spoke of our next move as we awaited Uncle Nate's arrival.

"I heard the front door open in early afternoon. Uncle entered leaving his hat and walking stick on the table in the entrance hall. He inquired about our health and comfort as he joined us in the living room.

'Everything is wonderful, Sir. I can't thank you enough for your hospitality, but can we have a few minutes of your time for a serious discussion?'

"Settled in comfortable chairs in the living room, I spoke of my need to find work and a place for us to live. Uncle seemed concerned, when in response to his questions, I related my work experience and my time in the Army.

'There is little need for an experienced horseman like yourself in the city. The carriage drivers take care of their own horses.'

"I listened as he spoke of his factories, which produced women's clothing. 'I, too, have no use for a horseman, David, but I'm sure you could learn to operate a sewing machine or master other duties in one of my factories. Maybe, in time, if you work hard, learn the trade, you could earn management responsibility, but there would be better opportunities if you spoke English.'

"When I mentioned the need of a place to live, Uncle seemed concerned by the small amount of money I had. The exchange of our Russian rubles hadn't resulted in a lot of American dollars.

"Factory jobs you will find, David, don't pay well. I'll speak with Mama. Maybe she might have an idea where to find a rental you could afford. Best you stay in Brooklyn. The immigrant living conditions in New York are dismal at best.'

'I need to find work at once, Uncle. If you're offering a factory job, that will do for a start. When can I begin?'

"Auntie found a rental for us in a different section of Brooklyn, miles from their house. Miriam and I moved into two furnished rooms on the top floor of a brownstone row house owned by an older, widowed German woman. It had been converted from a single family home into three residences. The rental brought the extra money the widow needed to make ends meet. She occupied the first floor. The second floor was rented to a young Jewish family, a mother, father, and two small children who'd been in America three years from Lithuania.

"Our rental, at four dollars a month, was the part of the third floor that was no longer attic space. The rent was cheaper because of the number of flights of stairs. The two rooms included a few pieces of furniture in the living area and curtains on the two small windows that overlooked the back of the buildings on the next street. The bedroom's sloped ceiling left little space to stand without being hunched over. It held a double bed and dresser. Since the attic had no kitchen the second floor family shared their kitchen with us.

"The contents of Miriam's trunk provided welcome comforts. We had large pillows stuffed with goose down, a goose down comforter sufficient to keep us warm on cold nights, bed linens, towels, an assortment of dishes and pots, enough to start housekeeping.

"The neighborhood was made up of blue-collar, poor working class German, Irish, Italian, and a sprinkling of Jewish immigrants. The row house was old and tired, the outside steps cracked, the siding missing bricks. The inside was clean, but the row house and the neighborhood looked nothing like Uncle's house. Here and there, on the treeless street, were flowers in discarded tin cans sitting on the steps providing the only bright spot in the rundown area. I realized few Americans lived like Uncle Nate, but this was far safer than how Jews lived in the Pale. We were lucky to have settled in Brooklyn rather than the lower eastside of New

York where most of the Jewish immigrants ended up. The living conditions in the tenement houses were horrible.

If Miriam was disappointed, she never complained. Being together was all that was important. She enjoyed having her own house as she set about cleaning and scrubbing every inch until it met with her satisfaction.

"I walked the fifteen long blocks to Uncle's factory every morning and home again at night, saving commute fare. The factory was located in a grimy old building, smoke and soot from nearby factories filled the air. The building itself was a hellhole. Every inch of the three floors was packed with row after row of young immigrant women bent over sewing machines. Here and there men such as myself sat at sewing machines as well. The days were ten-hours long, six days a week for three dollars a week. I could see why they called the factories sweatshops. With the doors and windows closed and locked, there wasn't a breath of fresh air. Floor managers walked up and down the rows of workers, smoking foul smelling cigars, making sure no one was slacking off. Quotas had to be met. The floor managers were cruel, foul mouthed, abusive men who delighted in bringing tears to the eyes of the young women. One of Uncle's sons managed the factory, but I had no contact with him. As family, I was paid four dollars a week, one dollar more than usual, as long as I met my quota.

"From my first day on the job, I vowed to save every penny I could to buy the farm I'd promised myself as a boy. I wasn't cut out for the city, nor was I meant to be a factory worker. I needed the sweet smell of soil under my feet, crops growing, farm animals to tend, fresh air. Being locked up ten hours a day was like prison.

"I came home at night exhausted, my back sore from bending over my machine. The only thing that made life bearable was a smiling wife happy to see me with a hot meal waiting for me. To my surprise, Miriam was turning out to be a good cook. Olga, our second floor neighbor, took Miriam under her wing and taught her the fine art of cooking, shopping, and keeping house. That made up for the things she hadn't learned growing up in a rich Jewish family, rich by Ukraine standards.

"After dinner, if it was a warm night, we'd sit on the stoop and visit with the neighbors. The lifestyle was so different than anything we'd ever known. No gardens, no fields, no cows or geese, just grimy windows on row after row of brick dwellings, and noise. Nothing was ever quiet or peaceful. If a family argued, the whole neighborhood could hear their shouts. If you listened carefully you could learn to swear in many languages.

"Other nights we sat side-by side on the old lumpy horsehair sofa while I would tell Miriam of my plans for our future much as I did years before as we sat by the river. There was no way I was going to spend my life working in a factory or living in that sea of concrete. More often than not, we took to our bed to enjoy our newfound pleasures.

"One night a week, I went to classes held by the Jewish Immigrant Society, learning to read, write, and speak English. Miriam refused to come with me. She felt that reading and writing were not for women. I insisted we try to speak English all the time. We were not Russian or Ukrainian anymore, we were Americans. 'I didn't come all this way to continue the old country ways,' I said. I vowed we would live and act like Americans, whatever that meant.

"We were invited to Sunday dinners at Uncle Nate's house, but after a few visits we stopped going. The distance was too far to walk, and I couldn't spare the money for the horse drawn streetcars. I tried to explain to Miriam we couldn't continue to arrive empty handed, that we had no extra money for gifts. She was disappointed, but she understood. I promised we would try to stay in touch as best we could.

"Fall came and went, and winter set in. Our rooms were cold. The only heat in the attic rose from the floors below, but at least the sweltering heat and humidity of summer was gone. By February, Miriam knew she was pregnant. We were both excited and scared. I was worried about the responsibility and the added money it would cost. We would wait until the baby was born to wire her parents the good news. I hoped they were still alive.

"We became friends with Olga and Victor, the second floor tenants. Olga was not only company for Miriam, but a good role model as well. The two of them went shopping together, did their laundry together in washtubs on the concrete pad behind the row house, as well as shared the cooking. For me it was a comfort to know Miriam wasn't alone all day. We began to share our evening meals at Olga's kitchen table. Cooking for four was cheaper than cooking for two.

"Victor was a finished carpenter working for a construction company in Brooklyn that built multi-story buildings, stores on the bottom floor and small apartments above. The influx of immigrants was creating a need for cheap housing and more shops. One evening over dinner, Victor asked if I'd be interested in a construction job. With the onset of spring weather, the company was looking for good workers.

'The work is hard manual labor,' Victor said. 'But the pay is better than the factory.'

I jumped at the chance. I was strong, used to manual labor. Not only would it mean more money, but I would be working outside. No more would I be imprisoned inside the factory. With a baby coming I would need more money.

"Aaron Samuel Freeman, an American citizen, was born August twelfth, eighteen hundred ninety-four. The best and most nerve racking day of my life.

"There was nothing I could do to help Miriam through her long hours of labor. The midwife kept telling me everything was all right, first babies take longer, but that was of little help as I paced hour after hour.

"I guess Olga could hear the sound of my feet overhead. The old floors creaked. She called to me to come downstairs and offered a plate of food while telling me, 'Eighteen hours is about how long it took my first baby to be born. So you shouldn't worry. It will be awhile.'

'How can I stop worrying? My wife is in pain, I hear her moaning, crying out and no one, including me is of any help.'

"Victor opened a cabinet above the sink and took down a bottle of brandy, offering me a drink. I downed the liquor hoping it would calm my nerves, thanked Olga for dinner, and hurried upstairs.

"I couldn't bring myself to sleep. I stretched out as best I could on the sofa, my feet hanging over the arm, and tried to calm myself all the while hearing screams coming from our bedroom. When morning came the baby still hadn't been born. I had to leave for work. I stayed home the day before waiting for the midwife to arrive, not wanting to leave Miriam alone, but I couldn't afford to lose my job or another day's pay.

"The midwife, a heavy set older Jewish lady, with piercing dark eyes and an ill temper, stood with her arms folded barring the bedroom door. She wasn't going to allow me to see my wife. I'd have none of that. I pushed her aside and went to Miriam. She looked so small lying there, so pale, so weak. I wiped the sweat from her brow and told her how much I loved her. I'd watched enough foals being born to know all the terrible things that could happen. I prayed to God to protect my wife and baby, and left for work with the terrifying sounds of Miriam's screams ringing in my ears.

"I hurried home that evening running up the flights of stairs and throwing open the door finding a darkened room and no sounds. Miriam, I called. No answer. I was beginning to fear the worst as I opened the bedroom door to find my wife asleep in our bed, a baby wrapped in a blanket by her side. I crept to the side of the bed and looked at the two of them peaceful in sleep. Tears of joy ran down my cheeks. I thanked God for the gift of a child, not knowing whether it was a boy or girl.

"I must have dozed off on the sofa when I was awaken by a gentle tap on the door. Opening it, I found Olga standing there, a big grin on her face, offering me a plate of food. Such good friends.

'Mazel Tov, David. He's a fine baby boy. How is Miriam feeling?'

'A boy. I had no idea. A boy. I have a son. I am blessed.'

'And Miriam, how is she?'

'She's sleeping. Should I wake her? What's a father supposed to do?'

'I watched as she nursed the baby before you came home. Let her sleep, she needs her rest. She'll tell you if she needs anything and the baby will cry when he needs to be feed. I'll come by during the day and keep an eye on both of them while you're at work. Try and get some rest yourself. Come get me if you need help.' She turned and closed the door.

"I finished eating and stretched out on the sofa. The last thing I remember, before I fell asleep, was thinking what a lucky man I was."

Chapter 17

As I grew older maybe a little smarter, a little less impatient, I began to understand that it wasn't a good idea to ask too many questions. Most of the answers came as Grandpa told more and more of his story. Maybe there were some things Grandpa didn't want to talk about. I could always ask my father. So I came for tea and cake, and let Grandpa tell his story in his own time and in his own way.

"The years flew by, Maya, but my routine remained the same, leaving home before dawn and returning after dark. I'd saved enough money, with what Miriam's father had given us, to add up to almost five hundred dollars. I continued going to class and by now I could speak English quite well. My reading and writing were improving, but I found it harder and harder to study in our small quarters since Benjamin, son number two, was born in eighteen hundred ninety-six.

"Miriam was a wonderful mother, devoted to the children and to me, who she referred to as her number one child. She never complained as I scrimped and saved every penny I could, denying her small pleasures, always promising her a better life soon, which I'm sure by then she didn't believe. She'd made many Jewish friends in the neighborhood. They did laundry together in the small spaces behind the houses with clothes lines strung between opposite buildings. Small children played between the lines of clothes hung to dry. I knew Miriam spoke Yiddish with them, but English was what we spoke at home, though sometimes it was hard to understand each other, so a Yiddish word or two crept into our conversations.

"I'd read about something called the Jewish Agricultural Society in the day-old newspapers I took out of a trash can I walked by everyday on my way to work. The long article told of the society, founded by some German Jew named Baron Maurice de Hirsch, who among other things, was lending money to Russian Jews to purchase farms.

"I tore out the article and put it in my pants pocket. I couldn't wait to show Miriam. After the babies were asleep, I read the article to her saying maybe this was our way out of the city and into a place of our own.

'Miriam, just think, a place where we could put down roots and raise our boys. Give them security we never had. Owning land,' I said, 'made you rich, made you important. That's why Jews were never allowed to own land in Russia, but here in America, my dreams could come true. What a wonderful place this is. God bless America.'

"Miriam wasn't so sure. She was happy where she was. She had friends and family. Moving away to a strange place, just when she was getting used to life in Brooklyn, was not something she was excited about or even interested in.

'How will my father find us if we move again? I can't be lost to my family. Maybe we could find a bigger rental in the neighborhood. You have money saved.'

"Was that the time to tell her about the letter Cousin Harry sent years ago, addressed to Uncle Nate's house?

'Mama,' my new name of endearment for Miriam. 'Sit. I have sad news I've been putting off telling you for far too long. Maybe now you should hear it.' I took her hand in mine.

'Do you remember when I came back to the village to find you?'

"Miriam nodded yes, a worried look on her face.

'Well, the reason I came home was because I knew the village would probably be raided by Russian soldiers. When I asked you to leave the room, I told your father what I'd already told Uncle Jacob. That's why your father agreed to let you marry, why the wedding took place so quickly. Your father wanted me to take you away where you would be safe.'

'David, why didn't you tell me the real reason why we left in such a hurry?' Miriam raised her voice in anger. 'You lied to me. You said it was because you would be shot. How could you do such a thing?'

'I didn't lie. I would have been shot if the Russians found me in the village. I just didn't tell you the whole story, knowing you wouldn't leave.'

'So what aren't you telling me, now?'

'Two years ago, I got a letter from cousin Harry with news of the village. I'm so sorry. I couldn't bring myself to make you unhappy with the sad news.'

'David, what are you saying? What sad news? Tell me now.'

I put my arm around Miriam and slowly began to tell her the news. 'Your father is dead. He was shot trying to protect your mother from Russian Cossacks on a drunken rampage. They burned your house to the ground. Your aunt's body was never found.'

"I watched as she began to understand what my words meant. Grief stricken, the tears flowed as she shook without control.

"Miriam jabbed her fist into my chest. 'Why didn't you tell me? I would never have left my mother. She needed me. Now two years later you're telling me my mother's gone and my father, too? How selfish of me to have left.'

"I took her in my arms, holding her close, trying to comfort her. 'If anyone was selfish it was me. But tell me what good would it have done if we stayed in the village and died as well. I love you. I couldn't stand by and see you killed or worse, raped by a gang of hoodlums. I had the opportunity to keep you safe and I took it.'

'My God, David, everyone in the village was so happy celebrating our wedding. Did they know?'

'Your father knew of course. Uncle and many of the women knew. They were making preparations along with the men in the village to save what they could and try to protect their families, so yes, almost all of them knew.'

"It took a while for her tears to stop as I held her tight. She asked about my family.

'I'm afraid only Uncle and Harry survived. Both Tante and Reba were dragged off and found dead in the fields days later. The village was burned to the ground. Cousin Sammy was so distraught when he heard the news of what had happened to his mother and sister, he went on a rampage shooting several soldiers at the fort before he was shot and killed.'

'David, tell me. How do I live with this?'

'You thank God, every day, for being safe in America where such things don't happen. That was what your parents wanted. You have two fine boys you can tell stories to about your parents so they will never be forgotten.'"

Chapter 18

"Grandpa, that's terrible. Russian soldiers really killed all Grandma's family, most of your family, and burned the village? Don't they have any laws in Russia?"

"Oh, yes, dear Maya. The Russians have many laws, but they are not meant to protect the Jews. As third class citizens, they have no rights and no protection."

"Wow, it's a good thing you left or I wouldn't be born."

"If Grandma and I had stayed behind in our village, you are right. We would be dead and there would be no you."

"What happened next?"

"The next day, Maya, instead of going to work. I took the train to New York to find the office of the Jewish Agricultural Society. I'd never been to Manhattan before. If I thought Brooklyn was a busy modern city, New York City was beyond description. For a country boy, the financial district of the city was magical. I entered The Agricultural Society's office on Maiden Lane and stepped up to the counter where a clerk, looking very official in a dark suit, starched white shirt and tie, asked if he could help me.

'Yes,' I said. 'I'm a Jewish immigrant from Russia. I read the article about your society in the newspaper, and I want to borrow money to buy a farm.'

'Well, that says it all. Have you any experience farming?'

'I grew up taking care of horses and watched my father, the overseer of a large estate. I took care of horses in the Army as well, and farmed alongside my uncle for two years, planting fields of hay and corn, milking cows, and everything else that needs to be done on a farm.'

'I see. Are you married, young man?'

'Yes, Sir,' I said with pride. 'I have a wife and two sons.'

'Do you know where you would like to farm? Do you have any money?'

'No and Yes. I have saved five hundred dollars, but I don't know where people farm in America.'

'That's a lot of money. How long have you been in the United States?'

'Four years.'

'Quite a lot of money, I must say, for such a short period of time in America, and you speak English very well. Can you read and write?'

'Yes Sir. I've been going to classes at the Educational Alliance.'

'Very good. Do you speak any other languages besides Russian?'

'I speak German and read and write the language as well, and I speak Yiddish and Russian.'

'Well, young man, you seem intelligent, responsible, and knowledgeable. First things first. Take these forms over to the desk in the corner and when you've finished filling them out, bring them back to me. What did you say your name was?'

'David, Sir. David Freeman.'

"I took the stack of papers the gentleman handed me and sat at the desk. The forms were printed in three languages. The first page asked for information about me, the second and third pages were yes or no, or multiple choice questions. I was so excited, my hand holding the pen shook, afraid I'd stain the paper by spills from the ink well.

"When I'd finished filling out the forms, I took them back to the counter, impatient while the clerk spoke with another man. I could hear only a small part of the conversation, but I was surprised the man had come to the office looking like he had come right out of the fields. My father taught me to be clean and polished at all times. Something the Army required as well. Something I have carried out my whole life.

"When it was my turn, the clerk said they would search the files for available farms and would mail information along with the terms and conditions of the loans. He explained that most farms came with houses, some furnished. The farms were fifteen acres, thirty-five acres, sixty acres and a few about one hundred acres. He asked me if I knew what size farm I was looking for.

"I didn't hesitate. 'One hundred acres, Sir, would be just fine.'

'Not surprising,' he said. 'The information on the available farms will arrive by mail in a week or two. Goodbye, Mr. Freeman.'

"I left the office on cloud nine, my head held high, my step more buoyant. I knew it was going to happen, but a week or two for information seemed like forever. I couldn't think of anything but having a farm of my own. I went right home. It was not the time for sightseeing, no matter how magical the city was.

"I thought I'd wait to tell Mama of the events of the day until the information arrived. She'd asked why I was dressed in my best clothes when I left in the morning. I told her I had business to attend to. Not a lie, just not the whole truth.

"The days dragged by. Every evening, when I arrived home, the first thing I asked was, 'Is there a letter for me?' and every day the answer was the same. No.

"I was beginning to give up hope when one evening, as I climbed the three flights of stairs, bone tired after a long day's work in the hot sun, a large envelope waited for me on the table in the sitting room, which now doubled as Aaron's bedroom. Benjamin slept in our room.

"I tore the envelope open and pulled out the contents, which consisted of a large group of pictures and descriptions of available farms. Glancing at one after another, I discarded them as I went along. Almost half way through the stack, I saw a picture of a farm in Connecticut.

"The description read, 'One hundred acres of prime farmland located along a river. The nearest city was Hartford.' I read on. 'Ninety flat bottomland acres and ten hilly acres of hardwood.' The picture showed a three-story, wood framed farmhouse, painted white, with large trees all around the perimeter to provide shade from the summer heat. A large front porch ran the length of the house. A cow barn and shed made up the rest of the buildings. I didn't need to look at the rest of the farms. I knew this was the one. Now, if I only had enough money to make it happen.

"I read the pages slowly, carefully studying the requirements for the foundation to provide funds. First, I needed one third of the price of the farm as a down payment. The balance would be in monthly payments of principal and interest at five percent. If I made all the payments, the farm would be mine at the end of five years. The last line of the letter set a date and time for me to come to their office to discuss the terms if I found a property to my liking.

"Was it time to tell Mama of my decision? Or should I wait to see if the Connecticut farm was possible? I thought about it for a long time and decided to wait until the deal was done, if there was to be a deal. I was the man of the family. I decided what was best for us.

Chapter 19

"Grandpa, were you nervous about buying the farm? Isn't that what you always wanted?"

"Yes, such a farm was what I had always dreamed about, Maya. Could I make my dream come true was a different situation. I was nervous about what the terms might be and if I could I meet them. The only thing I had ever purchased in my whole life was the bracelet I gave your Grandmother for her fifteenth birthday and train and steamship tickets. I had never borrowed money before. I had no idea what to expect."

"Quick, tell me what happened. I'm on pins and needles."

"On the proper date and time, I arrived at the Society's office, nervous, excited, and with high hopes all at the same time, waiting to be ushered into the big windowless room with the large picture of Baron de Hirsch on the wall. A group of eight gentlemen sat around a large table with one empty chair. The gentleman at the head of the table invited me to take the empty seat.

"He was mustached, coatless, wearing a vest over a starched white shirt and fancy silk tie. He was the first to speak. `

'Mr. Freeman, we understand you wish the foundation to extend a loan for the purchase of a farm. Is that correct?'

'Yes, Sir,' I said, my voice cracking, my hands shaking, uncomfortable in my suit which I was fast outgrowing.

'Of the available properties we own, which one have you chosen?'

'Yes, Sir. The hundred acres in Connecticut. Here,' I said, as I handed him the information.

"He scanned the sheet, then pulling out a sliding drawer in a nearby cabinet he sorted through numerous folders and withdrew a file.

'You do understand,' he said, 'you've picked the most expensive property we have. Fifteen dollars an acre is the usual price for our farms, but the Connecticut property is twenty dollars an acre. How do you plan to repay a loan of two thousand dollars? I trust you have the one third required as a down payment, which would be,' he paused as he scratched some numbers on a pad of paper, 'six hundred sixty-six dollars.'

'I have a little over five hundred dollars saved, but I wish to put only two hundred and fifty dollars down.' I saw the skeptical looks on the men's faces at the table. One man shook his head in disbelief. But the more I spoke the more confident I became.

'Sirs, I need one hundred acres. It takes a lot of farmland to make money. The property has acres of trees I can cut for new fences and a new barn if needed. The farm is bottomland that I won't have to clear, not rocky soil that's hard for crops to grow on, and it's next to the river, so there will be plenty of water. I need the extra money to buy any equipment I might need, seed for planting and livestock, and I need the extra money to see me through the winter when there will be no income to pay the loan. With hard work and some luck, I'll be fine after the first harvest.'

The men exchanged glances and a whispered word here and there until the mustached man spoke again.

'One more thing you should take into consideration, Mr. Freeman, there are no Jewish families in the village, nor any Jewish farmers we know of in the area. We have other smaller farms available where there is a community made up of a large number of Jewish families. Wouldn't you be happier there?'

"I thought for a long moment before I answered, then I spoke from my heart as I said, 'I've traveled a long way and worked hard to save money for my American dream of being a landowner. I want to take care of my family, to farm on land of my own, to become an American citizen. I can do all that whether I have Jewish neighbors or I don't. My fate is in God's hands and in my hard work.'

"Silence filled the room. Maybe I was too outspoken. I began to feel concern about the outcome. Moments passed before the mustached gentleman glanced around the table. He whispered something to the gentlemen sitting next to him, receiving a nod, then he spoke.

'Mr. Freeman, please leave the room while we discuss your request. We'll call you back when we've reached our decision.'

"I paced up and down the hallway waiting. What would I do if they turned me down? The other farms were nothing special, nothing like I'd dreamed about. The time passed slowly, it felt like an eternity before I was asked to return.

"I walked into the office, glancing at the faces staring at me. Their stern looks led me to believe I'd been refused the loan. I hadn't met their terms. I felt lost. I'd worked so hard, struggled to save, jeopardized my family's comfort and well-being for my dream. Could it all be slipping away? Was I destined to live in the attic and labor for others my whole life?

"The gentleman with the moustache spoke.

'Well, Mr. Freeman, it's been a difficult decision as you have requested changes in our normal procedure regarding down payments. However, we've been impressed by your passion and the strides you've made so far, your clear understanding of what the first year would entail.

Therefore, we are making an exception in your case and we are prepared to grant the loan. Congratulations. I'm sure you will be successful.'

"It took a moment for the words to sink in. When they did, I began to wipe away the mist forming in my eyes. All I could say was thank you. My mind was racing between excitement and the challenge that lay ahead.

'If you will wait at the front desk, they will prepare the paperwork for you to sign. Good luck.'

"I waited while the papers were prepared for signing. I unfastened the pouch I'd hidden in my waistband and retrieved cash for the down payment. Having signed all the documents, I was handed the keys to the house and a map showing the location of the farm, as well as a book of coupons to be mailed with each month's loan payment of thirty-three dollars and two cents. A far cry from the four dollars a month I paid for the attic and now I would have no job and no income.

"Returning home earlier than normal, emotionally exhausted, I was concerned how Miriam would react when I told her what I'd done, how I had decided our future without speaking with her first. Well, I thought, isn't that what men do? They make decisions and their women follow. At least I hoped that's how it would turn out.

"Her response to my announcement was not what I'd hoped for. Miriam cried and then in a tone I'd never heard before, she berated me for making such a decision without asking her first. She had never spoken to me like that before. She always accepted what I said or did without question. How would I deal with her new attitude?

"I listened as Miriam told me, through her tears, over and over again, how she didn't want to leave the city, didn't want to leave her friends, didn't want to live on a farm somewhere, didn't want to be miles from a town. I'd torn her from her family, and now that she had finally found friends and had adjusted to her new life I wanted to tear her away again. Though her tears continued, she never said she wasn't coming, so I decided to just be quiet and continue to make arrangements to move. The sooner I saw what was needed at the farm, the sooner I could plan for the future.

"My plan was to go ahead to check out the house and buy whatever we needed, then I'd come back to get my family.

Chapter 20

"This is getting really exciting, Grandpa. What did the farm look like when you first saw it? Did it look like it does now?"

"Slow down, Maya. I'll answer all your questions in due time."

"Good, because now it gets to be about me and Billy."

"Not for a long time, child. Your father wasn't even born yet."

"Gee, I didn't know it was that long ago."

"Maya, how could I ever forget that day? I took the train to Hartford and transferred to the short rail to Trinity. I walked the short distance from where the train stopped to Chester Avenue, the main road through town, really a village. A two-story inn was the first building in town. Several long blocks of fine houses were set back off the street, their green lawns and flower gardens painted a pretty picture on that warm fall day. A boarding house with a vacancy sign in front stood on the corner. A church, its white clapboard exterior and bell tower, was across the street. A little further on, taking up almost the whole block, was the general store and post office. The small schoolhouse stood on the town's last block.

"My heart pounded as I continued down Chester Avenue, holding the map of the area in my hand, checking the addresses on the mailboxes. I'd walked almost a mile when I spotted a silver mailbox with the number one five six painted in black on its side.

"I stopped. Looking down the long dirt road. I could see a white farmhouse. It looked just like the picture. I stood there unable to move, my mind trying to process what my eyes were seeing. Could this really be the place? It looked too good to be true.

'Thank you, God,' I said, as I walked down the tree-lined dirt road and approached the house. I saw rows of mature fruit trees growing along the south side of the building...apple, peach, and cherry, in need of pruning. Huge chestnut trees stood in front of the house to provide needed summer shade. What was once a green lawn had turned brown from lack of water, no doubt.

"This is all mine, I thought, as I walked the fields picking up handfuls of dirt and letting it run through my fingers. Fine topsoil with a fresh smell, ready for planting.

"I neared the old barn and found two thin horses in a small grassy paddock off one side of the structure. Climbing through the bottom rail of the fence, I walked up to them. Even at a glance I could tell one horse was blind in his left eye and the other was dead lame.

"I checked the big pasture on the other side of the barn and found four old dry cows munching on the sparse grass. There'd be no milk from them until they were bred and delivered, but at least I could slaughter one cow to provide meat for the winter. I tried not to be disappointed. After all, I hadn't expected to find any animals.

"I walked part of the back section looking at what had been a large field of corn, the old stalks waiting to be cleared. I had more than enough land to feed us, but I needed to sell crops in order to pay the loan. I'd ask around in the next few days to see what cash crops the farmers were planting.

"Walking back to the house, I took the key from my pocket and unlocked the front door. The first thing I noticed was a musty smell. The house needed a good airing. It smelled as if the house had been closed up for some time. The staircase to the second floor faced me as I stepped inside. The long hall to the left led to the parlor with a big fireplace, and much to my surprise, a sofa and chairs, a few wooden tables, window drapes, and a worn Persian rug covering part of the hardwood floors.

"Further down the hall was a big family kitchen. A long rectangular wooden table and benches sat in the middle of the room. Against one wall was a large wood-burning stove. The sink at the kitchen window overlooked what must have been a vegetable garden at one time. A pump was set in the wooden counter adjacent to the sink, meaning there was running water in the house. No need to fetch water in buckets. A mudroom off the kitchen led to the outside. Opening a door on the left, I saw a long flight of stairs leading to the cellar, the cellar air rose to meet my nostrils. I'd need a lantern to see what was down there. I closed the door and headed upstairs.

"There I found one large bedroom and two smaller rooms heated by a franklin stove in the hallway. Another set of stairs led to the third floor, which consisted of three small bedrooms and some attic space. What a fine big house to raise our family. Finer than any place I had ever lived. Every room had windows that looked out on trees, or green fields, or blue skies. No more living in the crowded third floor rental with only one window that overlooked the building next door. With time, I could make the house even finer. If I closed in the front porch with fine wire mesh, to keep out the bugs, it would be a wonderful place to sit on summer evenings. I was full of ideas, eager to start. Convinced it had all been worth the struggle, I never in my wildest dreams expected anything so grand.

"I'd eaten at the train station in Hartford, so I could do without an evening meal. Besides I was too excited to be hungry. I thought I'd check out the barn and then try to sleep on one of the beds left behind by the former owners. The next day would be busy. If all went well, I planned to return to Brooklyn the following day and bring the family to the farm before the next month's rent was due on our Brooklyn rental. There were so many things to do before winter set in, I didn't want to waste a day or a dollar.

Chapter 21

"Grandpa, you must have made a mistake. There isn't a train station in town."

"No mistake, child. There was a train to all the villages, like Trinity, until the automobile became popular. Now, we have the bus to take us to Hartford."

"I'm sorry, Grandpa. I should have known you wouldn't make a mistake. Tell me more. I want to hear what Grandma said when she saw the farm for the first time."

"The train was about to pull out of the station as I ran and jumped aboard. I took a minute to catch my breath as I settled into the first empty seat. No first, second or third class sections on those trains. It had taken longer than I'd expected to find suitable horses for sale. I paid fifty dollars for a pair of Belgium Greys, much more than I'd planned, but I was pleased with my purchase. The two were young, well matched in size, sound, and well conformed. I couldn't take a chance with anything less, as they would be working hard. The owner of the livery stable, not far from the railroad station, agreed to keep the horses, along with the harness and wagon I bought. until my return in two or three days.

The horses and wagon were the last items on my list, but I still needed to put in supplies for the winter. Before leaving the farm, I watered the lawn and the remains of the vegetable garden, hoping to coax some plants back to life. I had cut dead limbs off the fruit trees and chopped them into pieces small enough to fit into the stove, and made a list of things I'd still need to purchase. It was too late in the year to plant forage, oats or corn. That would have to wait until spring.

"My biggest job lay ahead. Moving the family.

"I bounded up the stairs two at a time calling, 'Mama, I'm home.' Opening the door to our apartment, I found Miriam sitting on the floor playing with young Benjamin. Taking her arm, I lifted her up, wrapped my arms around her, swinging her in circles as she pleaded with me to stop. I kissed her on both cheeks and placed her feet back on the floor.

"Mama, the farm is wonderful. The house is big. The town is nice. We will be so happy there, I promise. Now, this very minute, we have to pack our things and be ready to leave tomorrow or the next day at the latest.'

"The look Miriam gave me was one of surprise and shock, 'Not so soon, David. I'm not ready to leave so soon. Later, we can go.' She paused. 'Maybe in the spring.'

'No, Mama, we have to go now. Spring is too late. There is much to get ready before planting time. I'll fetch your trunk so you can start packing.'

"With tears in her eyes, she handed me the baby, ran out the door and down the stairs to Olga's apartment.

"I tired of waiting for her return, so I put Benjamin in his crib and followed her downstairs. Olga and Victor were just finishing dinner. Miriam was sitting at their table, a cup of tea in front of her. Tears ran down her cheeks.

'Mazel tov,' Victor said as he stood and slapped me on the back. 'This calls for a celebration. Sit, I'll get the vodka. So,' he said as he filled two glasses, 'you're going to be a farmer on your own land.'

'On my own land as long as I do not miss a payment on the loan.'

'Well, we will miss you, but I'm happy for you. When do you leave?'

'Tomorrow or the next day.'

"Victor and I lifted our glasses in a toast as Olga and Miriam held on to one another, tears still flowing. Victor and I shared two more glasses of Vodka, more liquor than I had had at any one time in my life. The glow felt good. Nothing Miriam would say could spoil my happiness. I knew sooner or later she would come around. I fell into bed and slept like the dead.

"Somehow we managed to pack our belongings, gather the children, and after tearful goodbyes, left for the train station in a hired wagon with the trunk and our many bundles piled high. Aaron was excited about the train ride. Benjamin was just happy to be going somewhere.

"I managed to get the family settled once we got aboard, hoping the boys would be still for the long ride. The motion of the train was calming enough to put Benjamin to sleep. Aaron remained quiet fascinated by the whole experience.

"Miriam hadn't said a word. She was filled with a combination of sadness and anxiety. She'd be happy, I hoped, when she saw her new house.

"We ate the lunch Miriam had carried on the train, but we would need to buy more food for the evening, and for breakfast when we reached Hartford.

"The livery stable was a short walk from the station. Miriam choose to remain in the station's waiting room with the children and all our belongings, until I returned.

"With the help of the stable owner, I harnessed the horses and hitched them to the wagon, then climbed up took the reins, and headed for the railroad station. It felt wonderful to have reins in my hands again. My dreams were coming true. God bless America.

"With all our possessions aboard, we headed for the three-hour trip to our new home. I hoped to be there before dark.

"After we left the bustling city, I let Aaron sit on my lap and hold the reins as we traveled down the country road. I'd make a fine horseman out of him in time, just like my father did with me.

"Miriam, exhausted by all the preparations, had fallen asleep. As we came to the farm entrance, I tapped her on the shoulder, 'Wake up Mama,' I said. 'Were here.'

"I watched as she caught a glimpse of the house. I thought she looked surprised, even pleased.

"I helped her down off the wagon, then lifted Aaron down telling him this was his new home, and then little Benjamin. After tying the horses to the hitching post, I opened the front door. 'Well, Mama, what do you think? Isn't this a fine house?'

"I watched as Miriam looked around. 'Yes, David,' she said. 'A fine house.'

'You and the boys explore while I tend to the horses. Then I'll get us settled for the night.'

"Somehow we got the boys to bed. Aaron was worried about being in his new room all by himself. Maybe it was time to move Benjamin into Aaron's room. They could keep each other company and we could have our bedroom all to ourselves. Our love making depended on how soundly Benjamin was sleeping. I would be happy when that arrangement was over.

"The following morning, after breakfast, I took Miriam and the boys on a tour of the farm. The vegetable garden had begun to look a little better after only one watering. I'd water again later that day.

"Miriam's expression was one of surprise as she kept asking, 'Is all this ours,' leading me to think we'd be fine.

'I know you had a dream, David. You've talked of nothing else since we first met, but I thought it was just that, a dream. I never imagined you could make it come true.'

'It may be hard for a few more years, Mama, but I promise you I will make the house the fine home you deserve and our children will have a wonderful place to grow up. We will be people of property.'

"I was more than a little concerned when Aaron appeared afraid of the cows. He cried when they approached him. 'They smell bad, Papa,' he said. He would have to get over that. Milking cows would be part of his growing up. Benjamin, on the other hand, laughed, and wanted to pet the horses as well as the cows.

"Having shown my family the farm, I hitched up the wagon for a trip to town to buy supplies. I asked Aaron if he'd like to help groom and harness the horses, feeling disappointed when he said, 'No' and ran back to the house and his mother.

"I watched the disappointment on Miriam's face as we stopped in front of the general store. That was not Brooklyn. No push carts overflowed with fresh food stuffs, no vendors peddled their wares, and no housewives chattered in Yiddish.

"The storeowner, Mr. Henderson, welcomed us. 'I hope you have much success in your new home,' he said. 'I know the farm well. It's a fine property.'

'What happened to the prior owners?' I said.

'The McDougal's? A fine family of Scotch decent. The family had lived in these parts for generations, but after old Conon McDougal's wife died, and all his sons left home, McDougal decided to move to the city where jobs were more plentiful and where his boys had settled. That's when some New York agricultural society bought the farm, and I guess sold it to you.'

"Miriam walked the length of the store looking at the stock of canned goods on the shelves, disappointed there was no cheese, or fresh fruits, and vegetables.

"I purchased flour, sugar, kerosene for the lamps, and checked them off my list. Miriam picked out some canned goods to add to the meager supply of food we brought with us. Mr. Henderson handed the children a sweet as I paid for the supplies. 'I will come back in a few days. I have some questions,' I said, as I loaded the supplies in the wagon.

"Noticing the disappointment Miriam exhibited, Mr. Henderson called after us. 'If you or the misses want something special, I can order it. Takes 'bout two weeks. Thanks for the business, folks. Hope you'll be happy here.'

"It must have been a week or two later when I looked up to see a middle-aged man on horseback come riding down our road. He stopped at the house and dismounted. 'I'm your neighbor, John Harris, come to welcome you and invite you and your family to tea this afternoon.'

"I stopped stacking the wood I'd chopped, and stepped down off the porch to shake his hand. 'David Freeman. Glad to meet you. My wife and I would be most happy to have tea with you.'

"That was the start of a lifelong friendship. Through the years we helped each other build new barns, and repair old ones. We fixed leaky roofs and built additions to our houses. He was free with advise on crops and a willing teacher who showed me ways to make a farm pay. Our wives were friendly, but Mary Harris, even though she helped deliver three of our babies, could never replace Olga.

There was a lot to do to prepare for winter and when it came it arrived early and with all the forces of nature, the coldest, snowiest winter in decades. Had the road not been so rutted that it was impassible, I would have packed up the family and left. Was God telling me there was a price to pay for my good fortune?

"For days on end we were snowed in, huddled in the kitchen, wearing layers of clothes. The wood-burning stove provided barely enough heat to keep us warm. The four of us shared one bed, piling on all the quilts and using our body heat against the cold.

"The chimney in the parlor needed repair, making it unusable and the old Franklin stove in the hall wasn't adequate to heat the house. Snow piled up at the front door and the windows making all but the kitchen feel like an icebox.

"The stores of potatoes, corn, carrots, and turnips that were in the cellar were about gone. I did not blame Miriam for her sense of despair. Once more I had taken her from her comfortable existence with a promise of a better life. Nothing I could say would make a difference, so I said nothing. I was sure she'd had enough of my promises.

"I hoped and prayed for an early spring. Thank God, my prayers were answered. By February the snow began to melt. By April the sun was shining. Hard work and long hours were in front of me. I repaired the hen house during the winter and purchased one hundred chickens when the snow melted. I could sell their eggs for ten cents a dozen. I purchased two milk cows. They'd provide enough milk to make butter and cheese for the family. I increased the herd in the fall when I had enough hay stored to feed them over the winter.

"I planted ten acres of tobacco seeds on John Harris' advice. He told me it was a good cash crop that the farmers referred to as the mortgage payer. I planted a vegetable garden for Miriam to tend. By late spring, fruit trees were in full bloom. Life was looking better. I didn't mind the hard work or the twelve-to-fourteen hour days. Everything I accomplished was for a better life for my family.

"Somehow I had to build a tobacco barn before the end of growing season in order to dry the tobacco leaves after I picked them. John helped me draw a rough design and I leveled a space. I began to fell some chestnut trees on the back of the property, hoping to find the time to start the barn, when early one morning a rough looking man carrying an old leather suitcase, speaking Russian, showed up at the barn asking for work. I said I wasn't looking for help, but when I found out he was an experienced carpenter, I thought he would be a big help in building the tobacco barn.

'I cannot pay much. I have little money until the tobacco crop sells, but you can have a room in the attic and three meals a day.'

'Any small bit you can pay is fine,' he said. 'I have little need for money, just a place to stay and a large bottle of vodka once a week. I can fix some space there,' he said, as he pointed in the direction of the end of the barn. 'I like to be by myself. When your new barn is finished, I'll probably move on. I don't stay long in any one place.'

"He said his name was Serge. We shook hands on the deal, and he went to work. I soon discovered he was good at a great many things. He was an experienced horseman.

"Miriam wasn't happy at the thought of Serge eating his meals with us, not only was it one more mouth to feed, but she wasn't looking forward to having a stranger at our table.

"The problem soon became a non-problem. Serge would sit down, clean his plate in a hurry and leave. The only word he uttered was *'Spasibo'* as he left the table. Thank you, in Russian.

"To get back in Miriam's good graces, I cleared a spot at the side of the house, outside our bedroom window, for a rose garden. Serge and I fashioned a picket fence surrounding the plot and painted it white. Then I waited for the rose bushes I ordered from the general store to arrive.

The rose bushes were in the back of the wagon hidden from view by an old horse blanket. I arose earlier than usual the next morning, and planted the bushes before Mama was awake. Then I went about my chores. After breakfast, I took Mama by the hand and led her to her new garden.

"Was she surprised, Grandpa?"

"Oh, yes. I stood there not knowing what to say. I am not very good with words, but I was sure she would she understood their meaning as she kissed me with tears running down her cheeks. She knew they were meant to show how much I loved her, and how I was sorry for any pain I caused just as the garden her father had planted for her mother.

I hadn't spoken Yiddish in years, but I wanted to be sure Miriam understood my wish that she would see every flower as an expression of my love for her. She lovingly tended her rose garden for the rest of her life.

"Oh, Grandpa, that's the most beautiful story I've every heard. I think when I grow up and get married I want to have a rose garden of my own."

"Serge and I worked late each evening hoping to finish the tobacco barn by September in time for picking the leaves. Many the night I fell into bed after dark, exhausted, glad Miriam and I no longer shared our bed with the boys. They moved into their own bedroom with the coming of the warm spring weather.

"Somehow we got the barn up and ready just in time. Serge was indeed a master carpenter. The barn was built without a single nail, only round pegs that would last as long as the barn itself.

"I planted the fields in corn, grain, and hay. Serge and I added on to the old horse barn, making it suitable for milking the cows I planned to buy.

"Though Serge and I worked side-by-side, he never spoke of anything other than the job at hand. He never complained about the long hours we put in, seeming to be happy to have a place to stay and a sense of being needed.

"By summer, with the pasture green in deep forage, I was ready to buy dairy cows. I could join the cooperative in town where farmers sold their milk to a local creamery for six cents a gallon.

"Miriam's pregnancy was one unexpected result of our having our bedroom free of children. She was happier with the change in weather and resigned to the fact that the farm was to be her home. She still was not happy to have given up the city-way of life with its paved streets, ease of shopping, and her friends...all she'd known from the day we arrived in America. But little by little she put her own touches on the house while waiting for all the things I'd promised her.

"I'd never worked harder in my life and had never been happier."

Chapter 22

And so it went. I'd climb the stairs to Grandpa's room, sometimes after school or on a Sunday afternoon. I'd listen for hours as his life story unfolded. My parents were busy. My father running the farm, my mother caring for the house. They had little time for me and less time for storytelling. My routine was pretty much the same. I'd remind Grandpa where he left off and after a minute or two, he'd begin. As I look back, I think he was enjoying the telling as much as I was enjoying the listening.

"I woke every morning, Maya, to hear the sounds of cows mooing, roosters crowing, birds singing, all music to my ears. The sky was clear, a beautiful shade of blue. No foul smelling smoke, only a few clouds here and there. I was up and about my chores before the first rays of the sun, long before the rest of the house was awake. There were cows to milk, horses and chickens to feed before I could think of breakfast. Aaron was getting old enough to start doing some small chores just as my father taught me when I was his age. I vowed to teach him to feed the chickens. He would soon start school so feeding the chickens was something he could do before his school day started.

"I was concerned about Aaron. He was having a hard time adjusting to farm life. He didn't like getting dirty and seemed uncomfortable around the animals. He complained about everything. I had already given up any hope of his becoming a horseman. I thought he spent too much time with his mother who catered to his every wish. That was all wrong. Not the way I was raised. Boys needed to work alongside their fathers. That's how they grew to be men.

Benjamin, on the other hand, was hard to keep track of. He was always following after Serge or me, asking a million questions or happily chasing after the horses or following after the cows. Dirty was a word that had no meaning for Benjamin.

"Mama's work was never ending. She tended to her vegetable garden, saw to the children, a full time job in itself, and did all the cooking. No longer could she walk down the steps of our row house to find groceries and food on carts, nor share the chores with Olga, but she'd made my dream hers and never complained.

"We were better prepared for winter the following year. I repaired the fireplace in the parlor so we had adequate heat downstairs. I moved the old franklin stove to the boys bedroom and installed a new stove in ours. The cows had shelter in the addition Serge and I built on the barn. Now they could be milked indoors. We stocked the cellar with home grow potatoes, vegetables, and the fruit from our trees Mama canned.

"Serge decided to stay for the winter. I welcomed the help as well as his company. Milking twice a day was a full time job. In his spare time, Serge built a beautiful one-horse sleigh that would make it easier to get to town on those days when the snow was too deep for the wagon.

"On the first day, sufficient snow had fallen for a sleigh ride, we took blankets from the barn, and with sleigh bells tinkling on the horse's harness, the family rode to town. The sleigh caused quite a stir. The townspeople had never seen anything like it, although it was typical of the Russian sleighs I'd seen in the Ukraine belonging to the wealthy upper class Russians.

"Winter brought a wonderful gift. With the help of Mary Harris, Irving was born in March, another fine, healthy American boy. He was followed two years later by Jacob and five years after that by Daniel. The farm was making enough money to hire an immigrant woman to help Mama with the chores. Laundry for our growing brood was a big job. I purchased a new gadget called a wringer from the Sears catalog. I attached the wringer to the sink in the mudroom to squeeze the water out of the washed clothes. The catalog was full of amazing things. Mama and I turned the pages together on many a night.

"I managed to make all my loan payments on time and with the sale of milk, eggs, and tobacco, I had a little money to spare. We always had a chicken available to be slaughtered for dinner. I butchered one old cow past her prime as soon as it was cold enough for the meat to freeze. We had meat to eat all winter.

"Aaron started school in the fall. The one room schoolhouse was a little over half a mile from the farm. Aaron groused about the walk every morning and seldom found time to feed the chickens. Little Benjamin usually did Aaron's job for him. He loved roaming the area around the hen house with a basket looking for eggs from hens that preferred to lay them outside under bushes or in other hiding places. Miriam would help him collect the eggs in the hen house as some hens were unwilling to give them up. Before long, Benjamin would take over that job, too. While Aaron complained about how the chickens smelled, Benjamin made pets of them.

"I guessed Serge would leave when he was ready. I couldn't figure him out. He spoke Russian like an educated man, not a peasant. He could do so many things so well, I stopped being surprised at his accomplishments, but still he never said a word that was not about a project we were working on. I supplied him with his bottle of Vodka every week, but I never knew if he bought more in town. He never took a drop during the day, nor did he ever appear drunk. He called me, Sir, even though he was much older than I.

"Serge seemed to have great patience with the children. They were the only one's he spoke to, whittling toys for them out of wood scrapes, building racing sleds for winter play as they grew older. He suggested we flood the front field in the winter and let it freeze over so the boys and all the neighbor's children could have a skating rink. It started a tradition that lasted until all our boys were grown. Whatever he choose to keep secret from his past was his business. I welcomed his help and his companionship for as long as he wanted to stay.

"Word had spread that I was a knowledgeable horseman and I was called upon to treat lame horses or help with new purchases. I didn't charge for any of my services. I figured it was part of a being a good neighbor. Whoever I helped would drop by our house with a home baked pie or preserves or some fancy foodstuff to show their appreciation. I was happy to be making friends among the area's Yankee farmers, Maya. Their families had settled here before the Declaration of Independence, their ancestors coming to America from Great Britain when an English King ruled America.

"A great deal of suspicion and resentment began to build among the townsfolk with the coming of large numbers of Polish and Italian immigrants. Many of the immigrants made the mistake of living as they had in the old country, not adopting to American ways, or learning the language. The immigrants stayed to themselves making no attempt to make friends, while I was gaining the communities respect. The merchants who were growing in number as the population increased called on me to act as a translator.

I was happy in my new country and my town, never feeling I was unwelcome, but now a great deal of ugly anti-Semitism was apparent among the Poles and Italians who brought their old world resentments and hatreds with them. There had been a few Russian Jews, over the years, who had tried and failed to farm in the area. Now we were the only Jewish family in the two neighboring towns so we felt the brunt of all the hatred. It was all directed at my family and me.

"The boys had no idea what anti-Semitism was all about. They'd never had any problems in school. The children in town skated on our ice every winter, so they had a hard time dealing with the ugliness and abuse thrown at them. More than once they came home from school dirty and bloody having been a part of fist fights they didn't start. Miriam was upset and asked me to speak with the parents. I knew that wouldn't help. Besides it was good the boys protected one another that they learned to stand up for themselves.

Chapter 23

"Grandpa what does anti-Semitism mean? Were my uncles the only ones who got into fights?"

"That is not a question I'm sure I can answer for you, but I will try. Many nations had persecuted Jews for numerous reasons since the beginning of time. I am sure you know the story of Moses leading the Jews out of Egypt and the Spanish inquisition, but it was the Jews religious beliefs, no matter how untrue. The Catholic Church as well as other Christian Churches preached that the Jews were responsible for the Romans crucifying Jesus. That was the cause of the problems, the fights, for my sons. Jews were considered Semites and anti means against. Does that answer your question?"

"So if I called somebody a Semite, why would they want to fight?"

"Because they did not call your uncles Semites, they called them Christ killers. They accused them of drinking the blood of Christians at Passover, and taunting them about being an inferior race.

"Now I think I understand, Grandpa. But wait, not really. Why would anyone think those things are true. I don't want to hear about such awful things. I want to hear your story. Tell me what happens next."

"Life continued much the same. The seasons came and went, but the work never stopped. Your grandmother was growing happier with her life as a farmer's wife. The only thing she wished for was not to be. As much as Miriam loved her five boys she yearned for a daughter. We hoped and prayed, but we were not blessed with any more babies.

"One day she received a letter that brought joy to her heart. Olga and Victor, and their children, planned to spend a few days with us. She busied herself with preparations for their visit, cooking, cleaning. She could not stop fussing.

Miriam was so happy to be with her old friend. Their visit was such a success they came every summer for years afterwards, staying for a week or more.

"I was proud of the way my boys were growing, each one quite different from the others. They brought joy to my life. I was not a demonstrative man nor was I long on conversation. I raised my sons the only way I knew how, as my father had raised me, with hard work and praise for a job well done. I loved my father, but I wondered if my sons loved me. I would like to be more like Uncle, full of laughs, and hugs, and stories. A more warm hearted outgoing man, but I could not.

"My boys each treated me with respect, except for Aaron. Why he hated me was a mystery, but it showed in all his various forms of disrespect. The only reason I could find was his resentment that his mother's love for me came first. I treated him no differently than his brothers, but work of any kind was hard to get out of him. He was clever enough to either talk his way of his chores or get his brothers to do his jobs for him. Aaron was a handsome boy, very intelligent. I was sure he would find, in time, a place for his talents.

"I made the last payment on the farm and the deed was signed over to me. We made a big party with special treats for everyone. At last the farm was finally ours. Now I could hold my head up high and celebrate. All the hard work had paid off. My dream had come to pass. I was a wealthy man, a landowner, someone to be looked up to. I had a beautiful wife and five healthy sons and now an extra thirty-three dollars and two cents a month to spend. God Bless America.

"But it was not always easy. There were good years and bad years. Too much rain or not enough rain, too much early snow, spring late in coming, crop prices rising, crop prices falling. There was the year lightning struck the hen house killing at least half our chickens. I had to sell a good cow for less than she was worth just to get enough money to make the mortgage payments.

"Only Aaron got new clothes and new shoes. Everything he out grew was handed down to his brothers. It was a good thing Daniel grew so tall or he would never have had a new pair of shoes or new clothes that weren't worn thin. But I'm proud to say my family always had plenty of food on the table, a roof over their heads, and a warm bed to sleep in.

"Without mortgage payments I had money for improvements. Serge and I screened in the front porch and built a porch swing we hung from two chains attached to the ceiling. We built an addition to the house for the indoor bathroom I had promised Miriam when the loan was paid off. I took Miriam to Hartford for the weekend to buy the new furniture she wanted and to celebrate our tenth anniversary, the first time we spent time alone together since Aaron was born.

"Electricity came to our town in the spring of that year and I had enough money to wire the house. No more oil lamps.

"The years flew by with only minor setbacks. That was the year Aaron was to start high school. A suit and tie were the required dress. He was never the same after that. He still hated the farm and anything to do with work, but once he put on a suit and tie, he considered himself a city boy. He refused to help with the morning milking, telling his brothers, 'I can't get my suit dirty.'

"During Aaron's junior year in high school, his teacher sent a note home asking me to visit her. While the elementary school had grown to two rooms with the influx of new students, the high school was in the neighboring town, a large brick structure serving all the surrounding villages. Besides the classrooms, the school had an auditorium and playing fields. Benjamin loved sports and played baseball and basketball. Aaron, complained. He didn't like to be near all the sweaty bodies and took no part in sports. His sport was girls.

"I had long ago outgrown my wedding suit and had no need for fancy clothes those past years, but my work clothes were clean and starched, and my boots polished as I entered the school building.

"I knocked on the classroom door and a pleasant voice said, 'Enter.'

"Opening the door, I saw a pretty woman, her brown hair pulled back in a bun, wearing a long black skirt and a white, long sleeved blouse, sitting behind a wooden desk. I introduced myself.

'I'm Miss Richards, Aaron's teacher. Thank you for coming, Mr. Freeman. Please sit down.' She pointed to a chair alongside her desk. 'I'd like to speak to you about your son.'

"I took a seat as she handed me a stack of papers. I noticed a large map of the United States on one wall of the schoolroom, a globe resting on a stand in one corner, and a copy of the Bill of Rights tacked to the blackboard, nothing like the small school on Count Zoransky's estate. I hoped my son appreciated his opportunity to get an education, but somehow, I thought he would never appreciate anything he was given.

'Mr. Freeman, do you read English? I note that you speak the language very well.'

'Yes, Ma'am. I studied reading and writing at night school in Brooklyn when I first came to America.'

'That's wonderful. Then you will see, in looking at your son's homework papers, they are incomplete or at best not up to the standards of an intelligent young man. Aaron is lazy, always looking for the easy way out. I've caught him cheating on more than one occasion. That I will not tolerate. If I catch him cheating again or refusing to do the assigned work, I will see that he is expelled. I have no time for students who aren't interested in learning.'

"I could feel my blood boil. I was embarrassed and ashamed that I was called to school to hear such words from his teacher. I thanked her. 'I will speak with him tonight. I do not tolerate cheating.'

'Before you leave, I have one more incident I wish to speak about. Although I have no proof, one of my students, a rather small boy for his age, told me Aaron has been bullying him, demanding money. As I said I have no proof, but I can't believe the young man would lie to me.'

"I felt my face turn red. I felt disgust gnaw at my stomach. 'If my son is stupid enough to give up a chance at an education', I said, 'That's one thing, but stealing, no. No son of mine will get away with being a thief. It will stop now.' My voice rose. I was so mad, so disappointed. 'This is not how Aaron or my other sons were raised,' I said, as I left the classroom.

"All the way home, after meeting with Aaron's teacher, I tried to figure out whether I'd been too strict with Aaron or not strict enough. Maybe his problem was he didn't get to know me as a young child. During the Brooklyn years, I worked long hours. Aaron was asleep by the time I got home, not awake when I left in the morning. He spent all of his time with his mother who doted on him, giving in to his every wish. But now it was time he and I have a long overdue talk.

"I washed up before dinner and went looking for Aaron. I found him in the tobacco barn stretched out in the old sleigh smoking a cigarette. I snuck up alongside, reached in and pulled him free, throwing him to the ground.

"Aaron, a startled look on his face, yelled, 'Hey, watch it, Pop. What're you doing?'

'Stand up. Put out that cigarette, and watch how you speak to me. I am your father and still strong enough to knock some sense into you.'

'Hold it, old man. What's the big deal. Everybody smokes nowadays.'

'I'm not talking about smoking. I'm talking about a visit I had today with your teacher. She knows what I know. You are a lazy, good for nothing. Your brothers do your chores as well as theirs, while you sit here like a king, smoking cigarettes. Your brothers are doing their part for the family, learning to be good farmers while you do nothing.'

'Yeah, well, I don't need to know how to farm because as soon as I graduate I'm out of here. I don't intend to be a dumb, poor, hard-working farmer all my life. I intend to be rich.'

'Well, if you do not intend to farm, you had better learn to do something else well if you expect to be rich. Your teacher said you're not going to graduate if you keep on cheating. She will have you expelled if you do no more than take up space in her class.'

"My words seemed to have little impact on Aaron. I slowly slid the heavy leather belt, feeding it through the loops in my trousers as I said, 'From now on, as long as you are under my roof and eating my food, you will help with the chores. No work, no food. Understand. You are not so big that I can not whip you. Now, get out of here before I decide to use the belt right now. Go help your brothers, and oh, yes, how much money did you take from the young boy you bullied?'

"The look he gave me was pure evil. 'Why? What business is it of yours?'

'It is my business to see you pay every penny back. If you want money, earn it. Do not steal it. I will not tolerate a thief in my house. You have disgraced yourself and our family. I will be happy to beat you to a bloody pulp if you give me or anyone else any more trouble. Now, get out of here and help your brothers or don't bother to come for supper.'

I tried to calm down. I could feel the sweat dripping from my brow. How was it possible that I could have raised such a son.

"I had no problems with the younger boys. If they hated doing chores, they did not complain. Aaron was the only one who was disrespectful toward me. Children do not speak to their fathers the way he did. How had I failed? I could no longer hide my feelings.

"I didn't know I had an Uncle Aaron, Grandpa. Daddy never mentions him."

"It is a long story, Maya. Aaron doesn't keep in touch with his brothers, and I washed my hands of him a very long time ago."

"Well, I don't think I'd like him very much, either."

Chapter 24

"Sorry I haven't been to see you in a few days, Grandpa, but I've been busy getting ready for school to end for the summer. There's a dance for freshman and sophomores at the high school on Friday night and I have a date with Tommy. It's my very first date and I'm really excited. I'll bring him upstairs before we leave and you can see me all dressed up, if that's okay."

"Very much okay, Maya. I have not seen young Tommy in a few years. Is he still your boyfriend?"

"Yes, Grandpa. He's very smart. He's been helping me with geometry, and Grandpa, I'll have more time to spend with you now that summer's almost here."

I still remember my pale blue party dress, my first real grown up dress. I felt like Cinderella. I was so excited when Tommy gave me a gardenia corsage. He looked very nice in a sport coat, slacks, and a shirt and tie.

He really didn't want to visit with my grandfather, but I dragged him upstairs, anyway. I remember how surprised Grandpa looked when he saw me all dressed up.

"Every day you look more like your grandmother," he said. '"You are turning out to be a very pretty young lady, Maya.'

Grandpa and Tommy talked for a minute or two and then we left for the dance.

"See you tomorrow, Grandpa, for the next chapter in your story."

I remember I couldn't wait to tell Grandpa all about the dance so I rushed upstairs before my breakfast and knocked on his door.

"Come." Grandpa was reading the morning newspaper, the breakfast tray still on the table in front of him.

"Good morning, Miss Maya. You are early today."

"Can I ask you a question, Grandpa?" as I looked at the tray full of Grandpa's breakfast dishes.

"Ask."

"Well, why do you have your meals in your room? Why not eat at the table with us like you used to?"

"It's hard to explain, Maya, but for many years I sat at the head of the table. I was the man of the house, Papa to my sons. Then they all grew up and went their separate ways, except your father. Now, he is the head of his family. He doesn't need an old man butting in when he should not. Hard as I try, I cannot keep quiet when I know I should, and being the good son, your father would never tell his Papa to mind his own business. So better I eat alone, reading my books, and keeping peace in the family."

"Well, Grandpa, if you ever get lonesome I'll come and eat with you."

"Thank you, child. I don't get lonesome. I have my memories."

"Then will you tell me more?"

"Of course. Just let me remember where I left off," Grandpa said.

"I bought my first automobile in nineteen hundred and twelve, a model T Ford for five hundred and ninety dollars. It made the trip to Hartford faster and easier than our horse drawn carriage. As Aaron was the eldest, he was the one Mama picked to drive her to the city. She loved riding in the Ford and felt proud to be one of the first in Trinity to have an automobile.

"Once a month, the Synagogue in Hartford held a dance on Saturday evening for the young singles, a chance for the Jewish young men and women of Hartford and all the outlying communities to meet and get to know one another. Aaron talked Benjamin into going along with him to the dances and one-by-one as the boys got old enough to be interested in girls, they went along as well. The boys weren't allowed to interact with the Polish or Italian girls. Their brothers kept them away from my sons. There were still plenty of name-calling and fistfights between their communities and my boys. It was probably not going to end, if it ended at all, for at least a generation.

"Aaron's graduation was in May. I did not expect him to be around much after that. I was sure as soon as he could find a job in Hartford, he would be gone. Good riddance. Life would be simpler when he left. I spent too much of my time and energy chasing after him to do his chores. He resented me, but knew what would happen if I caught him cheating.

"As I expected, it took less than a month for Aaron to find work. One night at dinner, Aaron announced he would be leaving in a week to start his new life in the city. The boys were full of questions, and with an air of importance, Aaron spoke of his job at a men's clothing store and how he could buy clothes at a discount, and the boarding house where he would live. He thought he might come home on Sundays, if he didn't have a date with a city girl.

"I saw the look of sadness on Mama's face. Her baby was leaving home. The chatter was so loud I am sure I was the only one who heard Serge utter, 'Good' in a tone just above a whisper.

"When the day came for Aaron to leave, Mama packed all his freshly washed and ironed clothes in our old suitcase. With tears in her eyes, she kissed him and wished him well, shouting concerns about eating well, getting plenty of sleep as Benjamin drove off at the wheel of the black Ford with Aaron seated beside him. He said not a word of goodbye to me.

Chapter 25

"The farm continued to prosper. The boys grew into men. Benjamin graduated two years after Aaron and enrolled in the Connecticut Agricultural College at Storrs. Now they call it the University of Connecticut. He met a girl at one of the dances in Hartford and fell in love. Her name was Leah. Her father owned a drug store in Hartford. Benjamin, being the clever boy he was, decided to become a pharmacist, a four-year course of study, but he returned home every summer, always willing to help on the farm. Mama was happy to have him home though we saw little of him. When chores were over, he would take the Ford, drive to town and spend his evenings with Leah.

"His second summer at home, he asked if he could bring Leah to our home. He wanted us to meet her. Poor Mama was a nervous wreck making sure everything was perfect, worrying that she was dressed well, and that I behaved.

"They arrived early on a Sunday afternoon in July. I watched as a slim, dark-haired young lady in a white cotton frock, white gloves and a white straw hat stepped out of the car holding on to Benjamin's hand. He was beaming as they walked up the steps to the front porch. 'Mama, Papa,' he said. 'I'd like to introduce Leah Cohn.'

"I took her hand and wished her welcome. Mama invited her into the house where she had set lemonade and small cakes in the parlor.

"Leah was a fine looking young lady and I liked the way she looked me straight in the eye. She seemed happy to meet us, not the least bit nervous.

"The meeting went well, I thought. Leah and Mama seemed to find conversation easy. They chatted about her parents and her two sisters. Benjamin had little to say. He just kept looking at Leah with a silly grin on is face. I recognized the look. He was in love.

"Irving, Jacob, and Daniel joined us. They seemed ill at ease not knowing what to say. Although I heard Daniel whisper to Jacob, 'She's really pretty.'

"We drank our lemonade and the younger boys devoured the cakes.

"Leah and Benjamin stayed about an hour, then Benjamin said they had to leave. They were expected at Leah's house for dinner.

"Mama and I stood on the front porch, hand-in-hand, watching the Ford drive down the road. 'Well, Mama,' I said. 'I think you have just met your first daughter-in-law. What do you think?'

'I think I am growing old and all my babies are growing up. Soon they will all be gone.'

"Then you and I can be alone at last. We can sit in rocking chairs on the front porch all day long, hold hands, and count our blessings and our grandchildren."

'I don't think you would know how to sit in a rocking chair all day long,' She said with a smile.

"June nineteen hundred and sixteen, what a special year. Benjamin graduated from the University, something no one in either of our families had ever done. The whole family attended the ceremony. Mama cried, but I felt such pride in the tall, handsome dark-haired man who was my son, as he walked on stage in his cap and gown to receive his diploma. Under my breath, I said, "God Bless America," as I took Mama's hand. Irving, in his second year at the college whispered in my ear, 'I'll be next, Papa.'

"Leah sat with us, as well. She and Benjamin announced their engagement the next fall at a party at her parent's home."

Chapter 26

"Why don't I know Uncle Benjamin or Uncle Irving, Grandpa?"

"Patience, Maya. I will tell you more stories when the time comes. Everything in order, child, or none of it will make sense."

"I'm sorry. I'll try hard to be patient if you tell me about the party."

"The excitement about the engagement disrupted the whole household for weeks with shopping trips to Hartford, trips to the barber shop, and Mama lecturing about manners. I bought a new suit for the engagement party, and Mama fussed over her new dress wanting to look her best. I thought we still made a handsome couple. Irving, Jacob, and Daniel were dressed in their best, as well.

"Look how handsome our boys are, Mama, Maybe we should have a few more." Miriam didn't have to answer me. The look she gave me said it all.

"Irving was driving as Jacob gave him directions. We stopped in front of a two-story brick house with a large lawn and shrubbery in front. Such a fine house. By the look on Mama's face, I could tell it was the kind of house she would like to live in. The nice neighborhood of tree-lined streets spoke of wealth.

"I heard voices and laughter as I knocked on the door. A mid-sized, grey-haired man opened the door wearing a well-tailored, dark blue suit. 'Please come in,' he said. 'You're Benjamin's family, yes?'

"I nodded.

'Harry Cohn,' he said as he put out his hand. 'I'm so glad to meet you at last. Your Benjamin is a wonderful boy. We're so happy to have him join our family. Come, let me introduce you to my wife and the rest of our family.'

"Leah's mother, Rose, and Leah's two sisters, Sarah and Bella came forward to greet us as we entered the formal parlor crowded with important looking, well-dressed people. We met aunts and uncles, nieces and nephews, family friends, and friends of Leah and Benjamin's.

"Benjamin, a glass of champagne in his hand, walked toward us. He kissed Mama on the cheek, shook my hand and patted his brothers on the back. 'I'm glad you're here. I'm like a fish out of water. I need a familiar face.' Looking at his brothers, he said, 'Aaron didn't come with you?'

'Aaron, Aaron who?' I said. 'If you mean your older brother, we have not seen or heard from him in over a year.'

'I spoke with him a couple of weeks ago and he said he'd come. I guess I just expected he'd come with you. No matter. Did you meet everybody?'

"I spoke with many of Leah's relatives, all business men, but none from the Ukraine. They were all German most having come to America many years ago. They'd done well having had the benefit of a good education in Germany. They had no use for the Ukrainians. They considered us ignorant peasants.

I noticed Irving in the corner, deep in conversation with Leah's sister, Sarah. Just as we were about to sit down for dinner, the door opened and in walked Aaron, dressed in a fancy outfit more suitable to a sporting event than an engagement party, with a female on his arm wearing a glitzy satin dress and too much makeup. They both looked out of place in the rather reserved group of people.

"Benjamin hurried to speak to him. I could tell the conversation was getting rather heated. Benjamin took Aaron's arm, and guided him to Leah's parents, leaving the girl friend standing at the door. After a short conversation, Aaron approached.

'I guess I'm not staying. I congratulated the happy couple, met her parents, so now having been uninvited, Nora and I are on our way. Good to see you, Mama. You look very nice.'

"Aaron did not speak to me or to his brothers as he turned and walked toward the door. He took the young woman by the hand and they were gone as the guests watched their departure with dismay. He had managed to bring shame on the family once again.

"I saw Benjamin speak in hushed tones with Leah as dinner was announced. We were treated to a wonderful formal meal with many speeches and toasts to the young couple as their wedding the following June was formally announced.

"I looked around at the setting and the guests. I knew Leah would make a good home for our son. He would be entering a part of a society where we could never fit in. But isn't that what parents want, their children to have a better life than their parents? I'm happy with my life, which is better than my father's. Isn't that what America is all about?

"The wedding was to take place the last week in June at the synagogue in Hartford. Benjamin spent his last night at home in the bedroom he and Aaron had shared growing up. He and Leah would be spending their honeymoon in New York City, then returning to the small apartment they would occupy in Hartford as Benjamin started his career working for his father-in-law. The Jewish population in Hartford was growing fast, nearing twenty thousand. Leah's father wanted to open another drug store in the part of town that was fast becoming the mecca for Jewish families. Benjamin was to be the manager and pharmacist.

"We were among the first to arrive at the Synagogue. Benjamin worried about being late. Mama was surprised she was to sit with the boys and me. 'They have no place for women to sit upstairs?' she said.

"This is a reformed synagogue, Mama. Everything is different in America. Here the men and women sit together and I think I like that much better."

"We had time to look around, taking in the experience of being in a real synagogue. Something we'd never seen before.

"The canopy was erected in front of the altar, bouquets of white flowers had been tied at each row of seats. We took our seats in the first row on the groom's side and waited as people began to arrive. So many people, so much finery. The boys and I wore yarmulkes for the first time. Mama and I had come so far from the village in the Pale, even I couldn't believe it.

"The organ music began. I'd never heard an organ before. Such a beautiful sound. Leah's mother was escorted to her seat in the front row on the bride's side. Benjamin and Aaron, his best man, stood under the canopy. Leah's sisters with young men at their sides came down the aisle. Then everyone stood as the bride, on her father's arm, began their slow walk to the canopy. Leah wore a white gown that just cleared her ankles, and a veil covering her face, training down her back to below her knees. What a wisp of a girl she was.

"I thought of Miriam's and my wedding, the joy of which was clouded by what I knew lay ahead for everyone we left behind. I reached for Mama's hand, knowing she was probably thinking of our wedding as well, no comparison to this fine event.

"Their vows over and the glass broken, the bride and groom started up the aisle to the shouts of 'Mazel Tov.'

"Family and friends were invited to a reception at the bride's home. We arrived along with many of the people we met at the engagement party. The dining room table was crowded with silver platters of food. Waiters carried trays of champagne glasses filled to the brim. What a joyous gathering, like nothing we had ever experienced. I think Mama and I both knew we would be seeing little of the bride and groom in the future. The farmhouse and our simple way of life could not compete with that.

"Food was devoured and the champagne flowed freely until it was time for the couple to cut the wedding cake. Leah's father toasted the couple and then pointed to me, catching me off guard. I had not prepared a speech. I thought for a moment, then raised my glass, 'To Leah and Benjamin, I wish you a long life and that you be as happy together as my Miriam and me. La Chaim.'

'Thanks, Papa,' Benjamin said, knowing how difficult it would be for me to speak in front of a crowd. 'We will be lucky indeed if we are as happy together as you and Mama.'

'You guys will miss your train,' someone in the rear shouted. With that, the bride and groom dashed upstairs to change. Dressed in their street clothes they ran down the stairs a short time later to a waiting car, brushing off the rice tossed their way. I heard the sounds of tin cans hitting the pavement as the car drove away. One more son gone from the nest."

Chapter 27

"Did Benjamin and Leah move far away, Grandpa?"
"No, They live in Hartford. Why do you ask, Maya?"
"Because they never come to visit."
"Yes, that is another long story, just not for today."
"What happened after they got married?"
"Well, now that we had a telephone, Benjamin, the good son, called us once a week."
"Don't stop now, Grandpa. I'm still trying to be patient waiting for the part where my parents get married."
"That will come a little later in the story, Maya."

"So Benjamin would telephone on Sunday. Our conversations were short. I didn't like this new contraption, but Mama seemed quite comfortable speaking into it.

'Everyone has a telephone now,' Mama said. 'Remember what you said, Papa. If we live in America, we have to act like Americans.'

"Though we spoke to Benjamin often, he and Leah didn't come to visit, nor were we invited to visit with them. I think his calls were not just to ask how things were, but to make up for his absence. I wondered why Mama never asked why there were no visits or invitations. No chance to see the granddaughters. After one of Benjamin's Sunday calls, watching Mama replace the receiver with a look of sadness reflected in her eyes, I could contain myself no longer. "Why do you never ask Benjamin to come to see you? How do you hold your tongue? It's only for you I say nothing, but it is not right.

'I do not ask because I know it is not of his doing. For such a wise man, Papa, sometimes you do not understand the boundaries of motherhood. When a son marries, his first duty is to his wife. I would be a fool to ask my son to choose between his wife and his mother. Benjamin knows. He's grateful I do not ask.'

"Irving finished what he called his undergraduate degree and was heading to law school, my son a lawyer. Only in America. He spent his summers helping at the farm and working part time at the general store. He would need the extra money for books. He dated Leah's sister, Sarah, once or twice, but nothing came of it. Maybe her family did not want two farmer's sons.

The day before he left to return to college, Irving had a long conversation with us about his name.

'What is wrong with your name,' I said.

'Nothing. I just think Richard Freeman sounds better.'

'Sounds better or sounds maybe not so Jewish?"

'Papa, I don't want to argue. I'm just saying from now on, my name is Richard, for whatever reason.'

"I was beginning to understand that I understood nothing. Was that what American boys did? Aaron took off and God knows where he was or what he was doing, Benjamin hasn't time for his family, and now Irving wanted to be Richard.

'I'll come home when I can,' Richard said. 'But I have to find a job to pay my expenses. I can't expect you to pay for more years of school.'

"So, one more chicken flew the coop. Well, we still had two boys at home, although I expected it was getting time for Jacob to leave us as well.

"Nineteen hundred and seventeen was the year no one would forget. The United States entered World War One. The war had already been going on for over two years in Europe. With three sons of draft age, Mama and I were worried sick.

"June fifth was draft registration day. Every male between the ages of twenty-one and thirty-one were required to register. It made no difference if a man was a citizen or an immigrant or even disabled.

"I felt it was the duty of our boys to fight for their country, if called, but the stories in the newspaper told an ugly picture and I didn't think much of the Army or any Army.

"One good event happened that year that made a difference in my life, the founding of the Federal Land Bank. For the first time, farmers like myself, could borrow money on the total value of their farm instead of just the bare land. A bank could lend money based on land and improvements at six percent. Five percent was interest, one percent principal for thirty years.

"A prime piece of bare land next to our farm was for sale. I took out a loan on the farm and bought the adjoining one hundred acres. I was now the second largest landowner in the area. Nothing for my sons or even my fancy daughter-in-law to be ashamed of, I thought. The biggest owner was the rich widow, Mrs. Hopkins. Her property was closer to town. For years I had leased pasture from her every summer to fatten my calves after they were weaned. With all the fancy milking equipment on the market, a small dairy farm like mine was having a hard time to compete. The Army had needed beef, so I'd turned to raising beef cattle instead. I bought young calves from the dairy farmers and was done with owning cows. I was happy to be rid of milking twice a day, but what would I do with all the extra time I would have?

"It was Mama's and my twenty-fifth wedding anniversary. It seemed like only yesterday she became my bride. I loved her every bit as much as the day we married. So much had happened in our lives. The years flew by much too fast.

"I hired a young Italian immigrant named Maria, to live in and help with the household chores. Our old helper had retired months before. We had more than enough money now so Mama didn't have to work. Maria had come to America from Italy two years earlier. She had no family as the sister she traveled with died, leaving the sixteen-year-old to fend for herself. Maria, a pretty little thing, seemed happy to have a home and work. She was a good cook and I was learning to like pasta, and to speak Italian.

"She had been with us for a few months when one summer afternoon, as Serge and I were busy at work in the horse barn, a fancy car drove down the road. I watched as it came to a halt in front of the house. A young man stepped out. As he removed his cap and goggles, I realized it was Aaron.

"Serge and I finished repairing the back wall of the barn that one of the horses had kicked out the night before. Then I walked back to the house to find Mama and Aaron sitting in the parlor talking and laughing. Mama was all smiles. Her first born son was home.

'Hello, Aaron,' I said. 'What brings you here?'

'Hello, Pops.'

"I recoiled at the word and the disrespectful way in which he spoke.

'I just dropped by for a visit and to tell you I got my draft notice. I'm being inducted next week.'

"The smile on Mama's face turned to one of fear. 'No Aaron, she said. 'Tell me, not the Army.'

'It's the Army all right, but don't worry, Mama, I'll find a way to stay in the States. This boy isn't going anywhere near France. I'm not fighting anyone, or taking a chance of getting shot, that's for sure.'

'How can you do that?' Mama said.

'Don't know yet, but believe me, I'll find a way. This boy isn't going anywhere outside the good old U.S.of A.'

"I knew he was right. No matter what it took, he would find a way to keep from doing his duty."

"After much coaxing from Mama, Aaron agreed to stay for dinner. He wanted to see his brothers.

"By six o'clock, Richard, Jacob, and Daniel were home and we settled down at the table. Aaron said hello to Serge and got only a sneer in return. He dominated the conversation commenting on how much the boys had grown, especially Daniel who was now fourteen and tall for his age. He talked about his adventures in the big city, while his brothers hung on every word.

"Aaron's conversation came to a halt as Maria appeared carrying a large salad bowl. 'Who's this lovely creature?'

'Maria, this is our eldest son, Aaron,' Mama said.

"Maria smiled, her cheeks reddened as she gave a small curtsy.

'What's she doing here, Mama?'

'She helps me with the house and the cooking, Aaron.'

'And she lives here. Alone?'

Mama nodded yes as I noticed Aaron taking in a full view of Maria, his eyes staying far too long on her breasts.

"Dinner was non-stop conversation. The boys wanted to know all about the nineteen-seventeen Cadillac roadster sitting in front of the house.

"All through dinner I watched, as Aaron kept staring at Maria. He kept trying to catch her eye. As Maria stood by Aaron's place to remove his dinner plate, I saw him reach over and pat her on her bottom. I would talk to him after dinner. No need to create a scene then.

"When dinner was over, we headed back to the parlor, leaving Maria to clean up and do the dishes. I saw Aaron whisper something in Maria's ear as he left the table to join us.

"The boys were eager to hear more about Aaron's adventures. He was happy to regale them with stories of his job as bartender and assistant manager of a nightclub in downtown Hartford.

'Won't they have to close if there's probation?' Jacob said.

'Doesn't matter what they do. I'll be away in the Army.'

"As it turned dark, Aaron said it was time for him to leave. He still had to drive back to town. We all saw him to the door and watched as he waved before he got into his car. I thought I saw someone in the passenger seat, but decided it must have been a shadow.

"Early the next morning, as I headed for the barn, Aaron's car was still parked in front of the house. Strange. I knew I saw him drive away last night. Maybe he had car trouble. They can keep those damn contraptions. Give me a horse and buggy any day.

"We had finished morning chores. Serge and I were headed back to the house for breakfast when I noticed the car was gone.

"Maria was singing to herself in Italian as she fried the fresh eggs I brought from the hen house. Mama was still in bed. No need for her to get up with the dawn now that we had Maria to fix breakfast. It made me happy to treat my Miriam as the princess I married. She had worked hard, given me five boys, and now the time had come for her to enjoy our good fortune. She still tended her rose garden, which had grown and matured over the years, producing beautiful, sweet-smelling flowers that graced our parlor from spring to fall.

"Richard went back to school in September, but I had not heard a word from Jacob about going to college when he graduated in the spring, so I decided to ask him about his plans. We were bringing in the remainder of the baled pasture grass to store in the barn for winter feed.

'Jacob,' I said, as we unloaded the last of the bales. 'Not one word from you about college. You have not decided?'

'Oh, I decided a long time ago, Papa. I didn't want to disappoint you by my decision not to go to college. I'm staying right here on the farm. It's where I belong, Papa. I hope you won't be too upset, but I've always known, since I was a little kid, that the farm's where I'm happy. I don't fit in anywhere else. I love this land, watching things grow, tending to the animals. I wouldn't be happy with some job in town."

"I couldn't believe what I heard. 'Disappointed? It was music to my ears. I couldn't have been happier. At least one of my sons appreciates and loves the land God has allowed us to sow. Jacob, someday this will all be yours, but I'm afraid I sealed your fate the day you were born.'

'What do you mean, Papa?'

'Aaron and Benjamin were born in the city and Irving, sorry, Richard was born with deep snow on the ground. But you, my son, arrived on a warm spring day. I took you from your mother's arms and carried you outside. Removing the blanket from your tiny feet I placed them on the ground and let the soil reach between your wee toes. When I stood to carry you back to the house, with every step, I told you that you would learn to love this land as I did. The dirt of the farm has been part of you from the day you were born.'

"I hugged Jacob, patting him on the back. 'I'm a happy man. At least one of my sons sees the nobility of being a farmer and will carry on after I die. You will always be richer than your brothers. No matter what happens, you will be the one who can always feed and house his family. Mark my words, even in America tragedy can happen.'

Chapter 28

"Wow, Grandpa, things are beginning to make sense. Irving is really Uncle Richard and my Dad always wanted to stay on the farm rather than go to college, but why doesn't anyone in the family ever talk about Uncle Aaron?

"I guess, Maya, every family has one black sheep. The one who is different from the rest of the flock. The outcast.

"Do I happen in the story pretty soon?"

"Not for a little while longer."

"Then please tell more of the story so we can get to me ."

"It was just before Thanksgiving, the feast we had learned about our first year on the farm and we've celebrated ever since. We had finished our turkey dinner when Mama said she needed to talk to me. I could tell by her look, something was troubling her.

'What do you want to talk about,' I said, as I walked toward the parlor.

'No, Papa, not the parlor. Let's talk in our bedroom. I don't want the boys to overhear.'

"I followed her to our room and sat down on the bed as she closed the door.

'Is everything all right with you, Mama?'

'With me, yes. With Maria, no.'

'I thought she was happy here.'

'She's pregnant.'

"I'd noticed she'd put on a bit of weight, but I thought it must be all the good food. I couldn't recall her having a boyfriend.

'Mama, how can she be pregnant? I've never seen her with a boy.'

'That's our problem, the father's not some boy. He's Aaron."

"I couldn't believe what I heard. How? Are you sure?'

"Oh yes, I'm sure. I had a hard time getting her to tell me the truth, but she told me about the last time Aaron was here. How he took her for a ride in his fancy car after dinner. He had a bottle of whiskey in the glove compartment. They parked down the road and at Aarons insistence she drank whiskey for the first time, After they had a few drinks Aaron began to kiss and fondle her. They came back to our house and he spent the night in her room.'

"I thought I saw someone in the car when he left that evening. I saw his car here in the morning, but I didn't give it a thought. Has she heard from him? What do we do now?

'What can we do? She will stay with us and have her baby. She has no family. We'll settle this when we hear from Aaron.'

"The more I thought about the situation, the madder I got. The madder I got, the louder my voice became until I was shouting. 'He may be our son, Mama, but he's no good, a bad seed. How dare he dishonor us that way in our own house?'

'Quiet. I don't want Jacob and Daniel to hear.'

"Well they'll find out sooner or later. They need to know how rotten their brother is." I lowered my voice and said, 'Have you heard from Aaron? Has he called or written you? Do you know where he is?'

"I don't think I've ever been so mad. If I could have gotten my hands on him I would have wrung his neck. 'We need to find him. He has to do the right thing by the girl and marry her.'

'I haven't heard from him, Papa, but maybe Benjamin knows where he is. I'll ask when he calls on Sunday.'

"When is this baby due?"

'In March.'

"Good, that gives us time to find Aaron. How is Maria handling this?"

'She's upset and embarrassed, feeling she's the one who brought shame to our house. No matter what I say, she blames herself.'

"I knew it was Benjamin when the phone rang on Sunday. I answered. Benjamin seemed surprised to hear my voice.

'Is everything all right, Papa?'

"Yes, and no. I need to speak with Aaron. Do you know where he is?"

'Yes, Papa, Why?'

"I will explain later. For now, I need to talk with him."

'Last I heard he was at Fort Belvoir in Virginia. Is Mama all right?'

"She's fine. You can ask her when I am through. So, how do I get in touch with him at where did you say? Fort Belvoir?"

'Well, if it's an emergency you should telegraph his commanding officer and ask him to have Aaron call home. Papa, please what's the problem?'

"Another time. I must speak with Aaron first. Here is Mama."

"I could hear Mama telling him everybody was well.

"Four or five evenings later Aaron called home. Mama called to me. 'It is Aaron.'

'I am coming. Let me speak to him,' I said as I took the phone from her hand, shaking I was so mad. 'Aaron,' I shouted. 'It's Papa. There is a problem here of your making. You have to fix it.'

'What are you talking about? What kind of a problem, Pops?'

'You remember, Maria?'

'Maria? You mean the kitchen help?'

'I mean the fine young lady that helps Mama, the one you got pregnant.'

"A long pause followed until Aaron spoke. 'That's nonsense, old man. What are you talking about?'

"I could feel my palms begin to sweat. 'I know you spent the night with her, here in my house. I know she's having your baby. You need to come home and marry the girl.'

"The laughter I heard from Aaron was sickening.

'You're crazy, old man. I'm not marrying her, even if it's mine. I didn't rape her. She was willing enough to go to bed with me and that's all it was. No big deal. She seemed happy enough when I left.'

'Well, it is a big deal now. Until you make this right, I want no part of you. Here, speak with your mother. Maybe she can talk some sense into you.'

"Mama held the phone away from her ear so I could hear what Aaron had to say.

'Hello, Mama, hope you're fine.'

'I'm not fine, Aaron, I'm sick at heart.'

'Why? What's wrong?'

'You know what's wrong. Maria is having your baby. She and the child she's carrying are your responsibility. The right thing for you to do is come home and marry her.'

'I already told the old man, no. When I marry, I promise you, it's going to be some real high class lady, not some dumb, illiterate, immigrant peasant girl.'

'You mean, not some illiterate immigrant peasant like me,' Mama said.

Aaron did not speak for several seconds. 'No, no, Mama,' he said. I didn't mean you. You're not at all like Maria. You have class.'

'I beg you, Aaron, please come home and do the right thing.'

'For the last time, Mama, I don't care what happens to her. Let her family deal with it.'

'If that's how you feel, then I'm with Papa. I should have listened to him years ago as far as you are concerned. From now on I want nothing more to do with you. You are dead to me. You have disgraced our family and brought shame upon us. God will deal with you in time, but for me, I don't want to see or hear from you again.'

"I watched as Miriam hung up the phone with tears in her eyes. It took several minutes for her to speak. Aaron's lack of quilt for what he had done, what lay ahead for Maria's weighing heavily on her mind

'I'll speak with Maria, Papa," she said, her words barely above a whisper. 'She will stay in our house and we will take care of her and our grandchild.'

As the weeks wore on and the evidence of Maria's pregnancy was obvious, I noticed Serge paying more attention to her, helping when he could with minor tasks like emptying garbage or bringing in firewood for the stove, staying after dinner to help with the dishes. I had no idea what they talked about or if Serge even spoke English. While his conversations with me were always about the farm, never about family, nothing that went on in our family seemed to get past him.

Chapter 29

I was old enough to understand all that Grandpa had to say about what happened to Maria.

"Did Maria have a boy or a girl, Grandpa? Did Uncle Aaron change his mind? You can't stop now. This is like the stories in the books I read."

"So, must I remind you again, child. Patience."

"And so, Maya, another winter arrived, each one easier than the last. The house was warm, we had electricity, a phone, a radio and a car to take us where we needed to go and the best improvement of them all, inside plumbing. Since so many people had automobiles, the roads were improving. A trip to Hartford took no time at all. The world was changing so fast I was having a hard time keeping up.

"While many Americans were beginning to lead a better life Europe was once again being torn apart by revolutions. With the end of the war in November of nineteen-eighteen, Germany was in desperate straits. New boundaries were being drawn, new countries carved out from parts of the old empires. Millions of people suffering, all signs of terrible things to come.

"There was still snow on the ground that March morning when Mama came running to tell me to fetch Mary Daniels. Maria was in labor.

"Serge and I went about our chores. I remembered how long first babies took to come into the world, but we checked in often to see how things were going. Mama fixed a simple meal for the family, then rushed back to be with Maria.

"I asked Serge if he would like to stay in the house for a while after supper, maybe wait for the baby to be born. He nodded yes, and as the hours dragged on we paced the floor together until we heard the muffled sound of a baby crying. Smiles on our faces waiting to hear if it was a boy or girl.

"Mama came rushing out of Maria's room shouting, 'Papa, quick go call the doctor. We can't stop the bleeding.'

"Serge and I drove as fast as the old Ford could go to town stopping at Dr. Fleming's house. He was waiting on the porch, black bag in hand. We had barely come to a stop at the farmhouse when Dr. Fleming stepped out and rushed up the steps as Mama opened the front door. 'Please Doctor, hurry. Nothing we do will stop the bleeding. Maria is very weak.'

"The color had drained from Serge's face. 'Sit.' I told him. 'I'll pour us a glass of Vodka.'

"It seemed like hours before Dr. Fleming opened the bedroom door. He shook his head. 'I tried everything possible, but she ruptured an artery. I'm so sorry, but the baby is fine. A strong, healthy, beautiful little girl.'

"Mary Harris had telephoned John to pick her up. She offered to see the doctor home. The sad, weary look on her face told of her heartbreak.

"I had never seen Serge look or act the way he did. He seemed a beaten man. He had always seemed so much in control of himself, but now he sat on the sofa with his head in his lap, his hands clasped in a tight fist when Mama entered the room carrying the baby she had wrapped in a blanket.

"Serge stood and walked toward Miriam. 'May I hold her?' he said.

Mama seemed surprised. Serge had never spoken anything but thank you to her before, but she placed the baby in his arms as tears began to form in his eyes. Serge rocked the baby to and fro in a manner that showed he knew all about babies. He asked if she had a name.

'No,' Mama said. 'Maria never had time to name her.'

'Then may I ask a favor,' Serge said in Russian. 'Please call her Sofia.'

'Sofia is a fine name,' Mama said. 'Yes, Serge, that's what we'll call her.'

"Serge held the baby girl a few moments more, brushing his lips on her forehead. 'Thank you. I must go now,' he said, as he placed the baby back in Mama's arms. 'Thank you both for everything.' Serge turned and left the room heading for the front door, tears streaming down his face.

'What are we going to do, Mama?'

'What can we do, Papa? We will raise her as if she's our own. Nobody but the boys and Mary Harris will know any different and they will understand when we explain the truth to them. Someday, when Sofia is older, we can tell her she's our granddaughter and not our daughter, but we'll cross that bridge later. For now we have a fine baby girl to raise.'

"The next morning Mama was up early tending to the baby, not the least upset to have another child to raise at her age, she had the little girl she had always wanted."

Chapter 30

"Wow, Grandpa, that's quite a story. So Aunt Sofia is not really my aunt, but my cousin? Our family is more complicated than I thought. Why hasn't my mother or father told me any of this?"

"I do not know, Maya. Maybe your father will be unhappy I am telling you. Maybe he will think you are too young, but someday you would find out, so why not now."

"That's silly, Grandpa. It's nineteen-forty and things are a lot different. Besides, I'm sixteen and I know all about the birds and the bees. Now, I can't wait to hear what happened next."

"I remember I headed to the barn, as usual, to start my morning routine. Serge was nowhere to be seen. I walked to the back of the barn where he had fashioned his sleeping quarters and called to him. No answer. Knocking produced no results so I slowly open the door. The only indication that anyone had lived there was the cot in the corner. Every bit of his personal belongings had been removed. My eye caught something resting in the middle of the cot. When I got closer I could see it was an envelope.

I opened the flap and a heavy gold locket fell out. Inside was a note in perfect Russian script addressed to me.

> *David my friend,*
> *Thank you for the many happy*
> *years I've spent with you and*
> *your family, the only home and*
> *family I've had since I left*
> *Russia. Once again my heart is*
> *broken. I can stay no longer. I*
> *must move on. Please give the*
> *locket to Sofia with my love.*

"I let the letter drop from my hand, feeling a real sense of loss. We had worked together all those years and I would miss him. Surprised. No, on second thought, maybe not surprised he would leave without a formal goodbye. There was an unspoken bond between us I never thought would be broken. I picked up the gold locket. On the front was the cross of the Russian Orthodox Church. I opened the clasp. Inside was a picture of a tall handsome man in a full Russian military uniform replete with gold braid, his chest full of metals. The officer was Serge. I knew he wasn't a peasant.

The picture told it all. He was upper class. Sitting beside Serge was a beautiful blond woman, elegantly dressed, her hair swept up on top of her head, jewels around her neck. She was holding the hand of a little girl, maybe three or four years old, wearing a fancy ribbon-trimmed white frock, high button shoes, and a matching ribbon in her curly blond locks.

"Somehow, I thought, the woman and the child must be dead. Something Serge had been unable to deal with, a mystery that would never be solved. He'd become fond of Maria. Her death more than he could cope with? What was the depth of their relationship? I would never know the answers. I slipped the locket in my pocket and went to work. No matter my sense of loss, the animals needed to be fed.

"It was hard to get used to the daily chores without Serge, not only his help, but the company he provided. Little by little, Jacob picked up the slack, taking on more responsibility. Daniel was at the university taking business courses. Sofia, now five, filled the void left by all the boys leaving home, but Jacob. Though I had noticed Jacob had been spending most evenings out of late. Mama and I knew that meant we would have another daughter-in-law before too long.

"Richard was in New York, a lawyer now, working for a big law firm. We did not see or hear much from him.

"What I had expected occurred on a Sunday evening. Jacob had been away for the weekend. Mama, Sofia, and I were finishing dinner when Jacob returned, followed by a small, pretty young girl wearing one of those new flapper-style dresses that made them look more like young boys with their flat chests. She wore fancy high heeled shoes, and silk stockings. Her hair was cut short in the new bob that seemed to be the craze. I liked women better with long hair.

'Mama, Papa,' Jacob said. 'I'd like you to meet Cora.'

'How nice. Come, Jacob. Bring Cora into the parlor,' Mama said.

"Yes, I thought, by the look on his face, she's the one Jacob is going to marry.

'Can I come too?' Sofia said as she smiled at Cora. 'She's really pretty. I like her shoes.'

"I thought Cora looked as if she would burst into tears at any moment and Jacob was a nervous wreck, beads of sweat on his forehead.

'Please, Cora. sit,' Mama said. We are happy to meet Jacob's friend.'

'She's not my friend, Mama,' Jacob blurted out. 'She's my wife.'

"No one said a word. Wife, I thought. How can that be?

'So, Jacob, you left yesterday a single man. How do you have a wife without a wedding?'

'We went to Hartford yesterday, Papa, and we were married by a justice of the peace.'

'And why would you do such a thing, Jacob?'
'It's a long story, Papa.'
"I noticed Cora was crying.
'So tell Mama and me the long story. We have all evening.'
'Well, Papa, I've been seeing Cora secretly for some time. Friday evening I went to Cora's house to ask her father for her hand in marriage and all hell broke loose. Her parents are immigrants from Poland as is she, and they're Catholic. It was like the old days at school, Papa, when all the Polish boys used to yell Jew at us and call us names, only this time I couldn't yell back because I didn't have my brothers to help. Her father forbid her to see me and threatened to lock her in her room or even kill her. I didn't know what would happen next, the man was acting insane. I thought he might really kill her because he kept pointing and me yelling Jew, Jew, Jew. Her brothers chased me from the house with a warning about what would happen if I returned. I hoped you wouldn't feel the same way about Cora, but we couldn't take a chance. We love each other.'
'Come child,' Mama said, as she rose from the sofa taking Cora in her arms. 'I remember what it was like to be in love and have a father say no.'
'What do you mean, you remember, Mama. Are we not still in love?'
'Of course we are still in love, Papa. I only meant I remember how frightening it felt to have your father reject the man you love.'
"I placed my hand on Jacob's shoulder. 'So, Jacob, Cora, Mama and I wish you both much happiness. You have our blessings. This is America. You marry who you wish. I say Mazel Tov, congratulations, and God Bless America.'
'Thank you, Papa. That's all very nice, but we need more than your blessings. We have no place to go and very little money. This is a big house. Can we stay and live here with you? Cora can help Mama and I'm still here to work the farm."
"How could I be any happier? 'Wonderful, I said. 'Don't you think so, Mama, our boy and his new wife here under our roof? I say as a wedding present, we buy new furniture for their bedroom and maybe build another bathroom upstairs.'
Sofia got up and put her arms around Jacob. 'I think it's a very good idea, Jacob. I don't want you to leave.' The evening ended cheerfully with everyone going off to bed. The newlyweds sharing Jacobs bedroom.
The room was dark as I returned from my nightly check of the animals. I started to undress, not wanting to awaken Miriam when I heard the sound of crying coming from the far corner of the bedroom. I turned on the nightstand lamp to find Mama sitting on her slipper chair in the corner of the room, tears in her eyes.
'Why do I find you sitting in the dark crying?'

'I am worried about Jacob.'

'What is to worry, Mama? He has a beautiful new wife and a roof over his head.'

"I heard Miriam sigh as she wiped the tears from her eyes. 'His wife is not Jewish,' she said. 'I worry will she make him a good home. To what God does she pray?'

"So, Mama, not to worry. I think there is only one God. How many different ways people find their way to him is of little importance."

'You may be right, Papa, but I think it will bring them many problems.'

'It probably will, but it is their problem to solve. They love each other, so they will find a way as long as we mind our own business.'

"I reached out my hand and eased Mama out of the chair and took her in my arms.

'Soon there will be children, God willing. We will not be two old people alone in this big house. There will be laughter, again, and babies for you to tend. We will be a family again. That is how I thought it was meant to be. In America, it seems the children cannot wait to leave home and move as far away as possible. We should be happy that at least one of our sons remains under our roof.'

'You should feel sorry for Cora's mother. Think of the tears she must be shedding tonight. She has lost a daughter over the silliness of how to worship God.'

"I kissed her gently. 'Go to bed, Mama. If Cora makes Jacob happy that should be all that matters.'

The new arrangement went well. Cora, your mother, was a shy, sweet child, a big help to Mama. She always said she never regretted marrying Jacob even if it meant giving up her family, because she was so happy with her new family.'

Chapter 31

"Finally, we're getting to my parents. They never talk much about themselves, and they never talk about mother's family. I never knew they didn't have a big wedding. I bet there are a lot more things I don't know. Right, Grandpa?"

"Yes, Maya, many things, I am sure."

"Mama was happy having babies in the house again. Billy, was born in nineteen hundred twenty-two and Maya, you were born two years later.

"We were one big happy family until tragedy struck the same year you were born. I had noticed Mama having trouble climbing the stairs, always seeming to be short of breath. She developed a cough that would not go away. She refused to see a doctor, saying she had had enough needles and doctors poking her before coming to America.

"I would listen no more as she seemed to be getting worse. One afternoon I was supposed to be taking her for a car ride, but took her to a doctor Benjamin recommended in Hartford.

"The doctor, after a thorough examination, prescribed some medicines, and said she was suffering from congestive heart failure, her heart having been weakened as a child by Scarlet Fever. He said she would probably be bedridden soon as the condition progressed. 'Let her live her days as she chooses,' he told me. 'It would not make any difference as there's nothing I can do to slow the outcome.'

"His words were like a dagger through my heart. I could not imagine life without my Miriam. Everything took second place to her.

"The weeks and months that followed saw Mama getting weaker and shorter of breath, as the doctor predicted, until she spent most of her days in bed, barely able to reach the bathroom, certainly not without help. Cora and Sofia were angels of mercy, tending to her every need. The boys, with the exception of Aaron, all came to visit, and toward the end, I stopped working leaving everything to Jacob, so I could spend all my time with her, telling her stories, reading the local news, remembering the old days.

"The warm spring sun shone through the bedroom windows, the time of the year when Mama's rose bushes were in full bloom. Every morning I would pick a fresh rose while the dew was still on it's petals, and place it at her bedside.

"As her time on earth grew shorter, I never left her bedside. I held her in my arms as she quietly slipped away. The light of my life was gone. Nothing else mattered.

"Despite the objections of the boys, especially Benjamin who thought she should be buried in the Jewish cemetery, I wanted her buried under the weeping willow that grew on the hill at the top boundary of the farm.

"Though he disagreed with my decision, Benjamin arranged for the Rabbi of his synagogue to come and hold the burial service at the farm. From the Rabbi's attitude, when he arrived, he was only doing Benjamin a favor. Benjamin, along with Leah's family, were important members of his congregation. Things did not start off well when the Rabbi's opening words to me were in Hebrew.

'This is America,' I said. 'You can pray in Hebrew, but here we speak English.'

"Benjamin gave me a look that said, easy Papa, as he beckoned his wife and daughters from the car. I watched as Leah approached, followed by their two teenage daughters.

'Well, Benjamin, I'm surprised you brought your family. This is the first time I've seen your wife since your wedding and I guess these are my granddaughters.'

'Please, not now Papa,' he said, a look of despair on his face.

'If not now, when? I don't suppose your family will be back until it's time to bury me.'

'Papa, please.'

'Can you not imagine how happy Mama would have been to know your beautiful daughters? But what, Leah, we didn't meet your standards? Just a poor uneducated pheasant farm family?'

"Leah gave me a dismissive look, turned and started to leave, but to her surprise, as well as mine, Benjamin raised his voice saying, 'You're staying.'

"The boys and I slowly carried Mama's coffin up the hill. I couldn't concentrate on the Rabbi's words. I looked at the wooden box containing her body and knew my life would never be the same. When I realized the service was over, I walked to her grave and threw the first spade full of dirt on her casket as custom dictated. One-by-one, the boys followed.

"I fenced off the area and planted moss. It would grow under the shade of the tree all summer and come back every spring with the thaw. I wanted her here at her home where she belonged. A cemetery seemed so cold and unfriendly. I needed to be able to visit her every day. I left enough room so when the time came, I could be buried next to her."

I asked my father about Grandma and Grandpa after I heard the part of the story about her dying. I wanted to know if Grandma and Grandpa were really in love all their lives?"

"Why would you ask such a question, Maya?"

"Well, Daddy, it's kind of the way he talks about her. His face lights up and his eyes seem so warm and loving."

"I can't believe you and your grandfather are having these kinds of conversations, but in love, yes, they were like two love birds. I can see them, now, sitting on the sofa in the parlor every evening, holding hands. Your grandmother never learned to read, so Papa would read her articles in the paper. He brought home books from the library and would read them to her. He could be a tough demanding character, always strict with us boys. The only signs of tenderness he ever showed was with Mama. He treated her like a princess."

"The story about her dying is so sad. I guess he still misses her."

"I'm sure he does, Maya. Your grandpa adored her. The light seemed to go out of his eyes after her death. He's never been the same. Long before any of us are up in the morning, though it's been years since she died, your grandfather picks a rose from her garden and walks up the hill to place it on her grave."

I wiped my tears on the sleeve of my sweater thinking what a beautiful thing to do. I hoped somebody would love me that much someday.

"So what other family secrets is your grandfather telling you," my father said.

"He told me all about you and Mommy getting married. It sounded so romantic, sort of like Romeo and Juliet."

"Sort of, only we didn't die."

"I laughed. "I'm glad you didn't die because I wouldn't be here. Is that why Mommy's family never visits? Just Aunt Paula once in a while?"

"It's a bit of bigoted nonsense we don't need to go into.

What else is Papa telling you?"

"Well, I finally learned the whole story about how my Aunt Sofia all of a sudden became my cousin Sofia."

"Enough. I think I should have a talk with my father about these story-telling sessions."

"Oh, please don't, Daddy. I'm the one who is begging him to tell me more, and isn't it important that somebody in this family knows all about our history?"

Chapter 32

"What was I like, Grandpa? Was I a brat like my brother Billy?"

"Billy was not a brat, Maya. He was just a very energetic boy. You, on the other hand, never stopped asking questions. Just like now. You had to know everything. Your brother tagged after your father, your mother was busy with the house, so you decided, even then, that I would be your question answerer. You followed me everywhere."

"So, I guess I was a pest even when I was little."

"No, far from it. I enjoyed your company as I do now."

"I'm not pestering, am I, if I ask what happened after Grandma died?"

"No, child, you're not pestering."

"Then please, tell me more, Grandpa."

"After my Miriam died, I was lost, Maya. With your father taking over a large part of the responsibilities of the farm, my work load lightened, leaving me more time to brood. Not until John Harris came by, one day, to tell me he was giving up his seat on the town council and had recommended me to take his place, that I found a new interest in life. A way to give back to the town for all the benefits I had received. John thought the town was growing so fast and changing in so many ways that it was important to have a farmer on the council. New businesses were coming to town buying up farms. The brand new modern schoolhouse was an sign of how many new people were settling here. The new, wider roads and faster automobiles were part of the reason. But imagine me, a part of the town government, now that I was a citizen of the United States of America.

"I attended the monthly meetings having studied the items on the agenda. When I spoke my mind, people listened. The other board members didn't always agree with me, but I got to say my piece and vote the way I pleased. What a wonderful country this is. God bless America.

"I kept busy. Trying to keep up with how fast the world was changing. Mr. Ford mass producing automobiles, people getting rich off the stock market, motion pictures that talked, women in short dresses with bobbed hair, and speakeasies with mobsters supplying bootlegged whiskey, gang shootings, almost too much for me to understand.

"Then, all the wealth, that was never anything but paper, came crashing down with the collapse of the stock market in October of nineteen twenty nine. The newspapers and the radio were full of stories about people standing in line for hours to take their savings out of banks as they began to fail. Millions of jobs were lost. Rich men, who had lost everything, jumped out of office building windows... the beginning of the great depression.

"Maybe being a farmer wasn't such an old fashioned idea after all. At least the farm could feed our family, which was increasing all of a sudden. First it was Richard and his bride, Helen, who arrived on our doorstep from New York, their car piled high with their belongings. Richard had lost his job. The law firm he worked for fired all but a few of their employees. He had lost all of his savings in the stock market. The two of them needed a place to stay until he could find work.

"Cora, Jacob, and I had a family meeting. I said, 'For my part, Richard and Helen can stay as long as they want, but it's up to you two. The extra work for Cora, and sharing the house is for you to decide.'

"Jacob turned toward Cora.

'I'm fine with it,' she said. 'It is Richard's home, too. He's family.'

"Richard and Helen were standing in the hall where we had left them. Jacob hugged his big brother and kissed his bride on the cheek.

'We're all exited to welcome you, Helen, and it will be good having you home again, Richard. It's been far too long since we spent time together.'

"Cora piped up, 'We want to know all about you.'

"Richard put his arm around his bride and said, 'We've been married less than a month. We were planning to visit before we got married, but the market crash changed everything. For all the years I've worked, I have nothing to show for it. It all went up in smoke with the crash.'

'Well, what is done is done. It is good to have you home, son, and Helen, welcome to our family, I hope you will be happy here. For me, I could not be any happier. See what a lucky man I am. I have three beautiful daughters, Cora, Sofia, and now Helen.'

"Helen put her arms around me and gave me a big hug.

'I was so worried about coming, but Richard was right. He said I'd be welcome even if I'm not Jewish. I know I'll be happy here. I grew up on a farm, so it's like coming home. Thank you all for being so kind.'

'Helen's from Ohio,' Richard said. 'But there was never any choice of where to go. Her parents are dead, their farm long gone. We worked at the same law firm. Helen was my secretary. We'd been seeing each other in secret for months. Company policy forbad employees to date, so if we were caught, it would have cost both of us our jobs.

'Things were so bad that when I got laid off I didn't even have enough money to pay my rent for more than another month. No way was I going to take off and leave Helen alone in New York. I asked her to marry me, even though I had no money, no job, and no place to live, she said yes. That's what I call true love.'

'Well we can be damn sure she didn't marry you for your money. Maybe it was your good looks,' Jacob said with a smile on his face.

'Let's not stand here in the hall. You both need to get settled before my kids come home from school,' Cora said as she started upstairs with Helen in tow.

"Jacob and I helped Richard unload the car carrying their things to the third floor, while Helen and Cora saw to getting the small bedroom ready.

"As the days passed, things seemed to be working out well. Cora and Helen were getting along famously. Helen was a big help with the house and the children, and Cora enjoyed the company. Richard was happy to be home around the things he was familiar with. He said it was like a vacation. He fished in the river, helping to put food on the table, and pitched in with the chores, and seemed to be enjoying getting dirty, sweaty, and tired. 'I never realized what a wonderful place this was to grow up, Papa, how lucky we were.'

"Daniel was the next to return home. Having recently graduated with a degree in accounting, he found no one willing to hire new graduates. In fact, no one was hiring. Instead the job loses were staggering. Daniel was happy to see Richard and meet Helen. He, too, seemed happy to be home.

"The dinner table was lively again, full of conversation and laughter, almost like old times, except for Mama being gone. I enjoyed having my boys home. My Miriam would be glad to see them taken care of, proud of what fine men they'd become. We were one big happy family, again. The young children were glad to have more people to pay attention to them. Maya, you were six and Billy eight. Your uncles had taken over most of your chores, leaving more time for mischief. You were the instigator, Maya, and Billy received the punishment when you were caught.

"Sometimes I felt sorry for Billy, Grandpa. Just not sorry enough to share his punishment."

"Sofia, now almost twelve attached herself to Helen, but all this peace and tranquility came to an end on a Sunday afternoon in June of nineteen hundred-thirty, as a flashy red convertible parked in front of the house.

"I watched from the window as Aaron got out of the car and walked toward the front door. It had been thirteen years since I'd seen or talked to him. I wondered where he thought he was going, dressed up like some city slicker in a tan, three-piece glen plaid suit, blue shirt, blue bow tie, wearing sunglasses. I noticed his mustache. I held my breath and answered the door.

'Hi, Pops, how's everything?'

'Everything's fine, Aaron. Why?'

'Well, I thought I'd come by for a visit and maybe stay for a couple of days.'

"I stood in the doorway blocking his entrance. 'I see. So how long is a couple of days?' I was sure he could sense the chill in my voice.

'Oh, come on, Pops. I need a place to stay for a little while. Let me in. Who counts days.'

'If it were only up to me, Aaron, I'd throw you the hell off the place this minute, but it's up to your brothers as well.'

'How about Mama? Doesn't she have anything to say? I know she'll be happy to have me home.'

'The last words I heard her say to you, years ago, was she never wanted to see you again. And she won't. Mama died two years ago.'

I watched as Aaron seemed taken aback. He shook his fist at me. 'Why didn't you tell me Mama was sick, old man?'

'And where was I supposed to look for you?'

'Benjamin. You could have asked Benjamin.'

'I did. He had given up on you, too. He said you had left Hartford and were off somewhere running bootlegged liquor from Canada. Just the kind of trash I'd expect you to be involved in.

'Well, you could at least have tried to find me.'

'I could have, but I didn't. You might as well come in. I'll call your brothers.'

"There were a lot of mixed and heated feelings as the boys discussed Aaron's return.

'It is up to you boys, but my vote is no. He is trouble. Always was and always will be,' I said.

"The decision was made. He could stay if he contributed to the workload. Anything short of cooperation on his part, and he was out. Fine with me. I figured it would not take long for him to wear out his welcome.

"Everyone gathered in the parlor as Richard was appointed the spokesman to set out the rules. In lawyer-like terms, Aaron was told he could use the smaller bedroom on the third floor and share the bathroom with me and Helen.

'No way. The room's too small, I have my girlfriend with me.'

'You didn't say anything about a girlfriend.' That was so like Aaron.

'Well, we've been together for some time. I couldn't just walk out on her. She's a great gal. You'll like her. She's a lot of fun. She's in show business. Give me a sec and I'll go get her. She's waiting in the car.'

"Aaron returned with a tall, leggy, bleached blond, with too much makeup and a bright purple sateen dress that left little to the imagination. So much for the fine lady he was holding out for. I think the new word was floozy.

'Guys, this is Trixie,' Aaron said, as he introduced her to everyone. 'I'll get our stuff. Show her around, then take her upstairs. She's been up since early this morning. I'm sure she'd like to rest.'

"Trixie ran her fingers through her hair, gave us a halfhearted smile and said not one word.

'Make sure she understands the rules,' Richard called after Aaron. 'Nobody gets a free ride.'

Chapter 33

I could barely remember the time when all my uncles came home, as Grandpa told more of his story. I remembered having so much fun with all the family. I liked having people pay attention to me. The uncles would play ball in the front field in the late afternoon after all the chores were done. Billy was allowed to play, but I could only watch. I was told I was too little to play. I remembered the time Uncle Richard took me fishing and I caught a mackerel we ate at dinner.

"Tell me more Grandpa."

"Well, as I expected, it did not take long for things to start going wrong.

"Trixie didn't show up for dinner that evening, until we were finishing our coffee.

'Sorry folks, I guess I overslept,' she said, not sounding sorry at all.

"She sat down waiting for someone to serve her. It was Cora who spoke up.

'There's stew on the stove. Help yourself.'

"Helen started to clear the dishes as Aaron, with a flourish, stood and handed each of us cigars he took from his breast pocket.

'The best Cuba has to offer,' Aaron said, as he bit off the tip of the cigar and lit it with a gold-colored lighter.

"Cora ordered us out of the house. 'If you men want to smoke, you can do it outside. Nobody wants the house to smell of stale cigar smoke,' she said.

"It was almost like old times. We sat on the front porch. A slight breeze came off the river. The weather was another warm humid June evening like so many in this part of Connecticut. I could hear the sound of crickets far off in the distance, and the croaking of frogs coming from the river. Fireflies flickered as they flew by. The slight aroma of cows filled the night air.

"The boys were enjoying trading tales of trouble they'd gotten into as kids. Richard remembered the time they tried smoking. How they had pulled down tobacco leaves drying in the barn, rolled them up to what looked like cigars and lit them. After a few puffs, Jacob remembered running outside and throwing up. Benjamin was the next one to get sick. Aaron laughed, 'I was dizzy for hours.'

'Yeah,' Jacob said. 'We never tried that again, and the time we tried to make hard cider didn't go so well, either, with all those bottles we'd filled with apple juice exploding in the cellar. What a mess. We had to clean the whole thing up before you found out, Papa. Good thing you didn't catch us or you would have had tanned our hides.'

'What makes you think I didn't know? You had learned your lesson the hard way, cleaned up your mess, and never tried it again. There was no use my saying anything.'

'How come you always thought I was too young to be part of the fun,' Daniel said.

'Because you were, little brother,' Richard replied as he patted Daniel on the head. 'Too bad Benjamin's not here. I guess he's the only one who chose the right profession. Folks need their medicine no matter what. Does he come to visit often? I haven't seen him since Mama died.'

"I shook my head. 'Benjamin keeps pretty much to himself.'

"The chatter and laughter was like music to my ears, my boys, enjoying being together again. Benjamin was missing a lot. I listened as Aaron went on and on about all the money he had made selling Canadian booze to the speakeasies, how life was great, and how he was living in the lap of luxury. 'That is,' he said, 'until the mob guys came gunning for me for cutting in on their territory.' He admitted he was kind of hiding out until things cooled down.

'Son of a bitch. Let me get this straight. You're not broke or out of a job, you're hiding out from a bunch of gangsters and putting everyone in this house in danger if they find you here. Are you crazy?' Richard said.

'Hell, what are you worried about. 'They'll never find me here. I changed my name a long time ago. The speaks are used to doing business with guys with Italian names. They're looking for Joey De Angelo, from New York's little Italy. That's why I brought Trixie along. They might try to find me through her.'

'Well," Jacob said. 'Big brother, whatever you name is, you'll never change will you? But this puts a different light on the situation. Your brothers are here because they couldn't find work and had responsibilities. Papa, Cora, and I told them welcome. This is your home, too. Stay until you get back on your feet, but you...you jackass, are rolling in money, or so you say. So here's the deal. You're going to pay for your room and board, and you and your girlfriend still have to pitch in with the work. If you're not happy with that arrangement, then get the hell off the farm. Nobody's happy you're here, anyway. Papa's right. You're nothing but trouble.'

"The evening was over. No one had anything else to say. I crushed out my cigar and headed for bed. Morning comes early on a farm. As I walked by the kitchen, I noticed Cora, Helen, and Sofia doing dishes. I asked were what's her name, Trixie, was.

'She ate and went upstairs, leaving her plate and dirty silverware at the table,' Helen said. 'Didn't even say thank you, just took out a long cigarette holder, lit up a cigarette, and went on her merry way.'

'We will see to that in the morning. If she and Aaron aren't down for breakfast with everybody else, clean up and make believe they don't exist.'

As I expected, Aaron showed up at ten, dressed for anything but work.

'Where's the coffee,' he said. 'I'm not much good until I've had my coffee.'

'As far as I am concerned you're not much good with or without your coffee, and Miss Trixie, is she up and pitching in, Aaron?" Richard said.

'I told you she's in show business. She's not used to getting up much before noon.'

'Well, since there is no performance scheduled for tonight, she'd better adjust her timetable to her present circumstances. She also needs to understand we share the bathroom. Locking us out for hours on end, and using up all the hot water hardly seems fair.'

"I knew it was only a matter of time before Aaron and his girlfriend became a problem. Rules and common decency meant nothing to him, nor it seemed to his girlfriend.

"The boys and their wives held another meeting several days later, and decided to tell Aaron and Trixie to leave. There was no need to ask my opinion. I did not want them here to begin with.

"The following morning, Jacob and Daniel helped load Aaron's car. The atmosphere was hostile. I arrived at the front door just in time to hear Jacob and Aaron shouting at one another in the driveway.

'Well, Jacob,' Aaron said, jabbing his index finger in Jacob's chest. 'I hope you're happy. If I get killed, it's on your hands.'

'Wrong. You're the guy who wanted to be the big shot bootlegger. I could care less what happens to you, any more than you ever cared what happened to us. I'm not the little kid you can threaten anymore. We made a deal and you wouldn't live up to it, like always. No one is ready to make excuses for you. You made your bed, now lie in it.'

'No, you're right. Mama's not here to take my side. She's gone and it's that horney old man's fault. He couldn't leave her alone. What was he thinking? She was too old to have another child. That's probably what killed her.'

'What the hell are you talking about?'

'You know damn well, Jacob, Sofia. A baby at Mama's age was crazy. He never could keep his filthy hands off her.'

'Ah, yes Sofia. Time somebody told you the truth. She's not Papa's, she's yours. Sofia is Maria's child. Mama and Papa raised her as their own.'

"There was dead silence. Aaron's shoulders drooped. I could see him processing what Jacob had just told him. Then he stood up straight and said. 'Why the hell should they look after her. She's Maria's problem not theirs.'

'You really are a despicable individual, aren't you? Maria died giving birth to Sofia. If the child was anybody's responsibility, she was yours, but responsibility is something you've never understood. Now get the hell off the farm and don't ever come back. I hope I never lay eyes on you again, and I'm sure I speak for the rest of your brothers.'

"I watched as Jacob turned and walked back to the house, leaving Aaron standing alongside his fancy roadster, dumbfounded. Goodbye and good riddance, I thought. Thank God the children were at school."

Chapter 34

"I sort of remember the uncle with the blond lady, but I didn't know that was Uncle Aaron. As I think back, I don't think I liked him very much. Eight or nine years is a long time to remember things when you're a kid."

"A very long time, Maya."

"There's a big dance tonight at the school gym, and I'm going with Tommy. He's really excited as he gets to drive us in his father's car. Want to see my party dress before we leave?"

"I would be so happy to see you all dressed up and to see young Tommy again. Is he old enough to drive?"

"Oh, yes. He's sixteen, going to be seventeen in two months. He's going to be a senior in high school. He has his license and everything."

"So, Miss Maya, run along. I'll be looking forward to seeing you in your finery tonight."

I couldn't believe Maya was the same age as my Miriam when I first told her I was going to marry her. I thought, how could Jacob and Cora be such modern parents that they would let her go off in a car alone with a boy, even Tommy who they had known for years. I admit I have trouble letting go of some of the past. Yes, my Miriam and I spent time alone together, but not with the permission of her parents. I guess I should not be surprised. Jacob keeps telling me I have to be willing to give Sophia more freedom. I could still hear my Miriam lecturing me about my demanding we leave old world customs behind and then not be willing to do so.

I was just fine with giving Sofia more freedom just as long as it did not have anything to do with boys. Was not letting her go off to college on her own, modern enough? Sofia was a good girl. I trusted her, but what happened to her mother was always in the back of my mind.

"Grandpa we're getting ready to leave."

I heard Maya call and started down the stairs. Tommy and Maya dressed in their party clothes, waited in the hallway for me. Tommy, with his blond hair slicked back, wearing a seersucker jacket and pants looked almost grown up. He must have grown a foot taller since the last time I saw him.

I caught a glimpse of Maya. She looked like an angel, so like my Miriam, with her hair piled on top of her head for the first time, in a green dress that made her hazel eyes sparkle. I breathed a sigh. She too seemed so grown up. I wondered how much longer she would be interested in stories of my past.

Jacob and Cora were standing in the hallway to see them off.

"Have a good time, kids. Drive carefully. Be home early, Tommy," I said.

With a, "Yes, Sir," they were gone.

I stopped short as I glanced at my son. It was not my place to speak as I did. It was Jacob's. Once again, I'd overstepped my role. I was not Maya's father. I was her grandfather.

Chapter 35

Sitting alone in my room, my mind drifted to events of the past. None of the happenings were part of my story. They were the story of the country and the world, things Maya would learn someday in a history class not from me.

Nineteen thirty-three was a banner year. Probation ended and Franklin Roosevelt was inaugurated president. As an American citizen, I was proud to vote for him. What a wonderful gift to be able to vote. Even women were allowed to vote, now.

Things were beginning to change in a hurry. Within one hundred days the New Deal was enacted, people were slowly beginning to find jobs, the bread lines were getting smaller, and everywhere you went the radio was playing, "Happy Days Are Here Again." Tennessee Valley Authority was born, Hoover Dam was completed, United Air Lines was flying Boeing passenger planes, and Douglas Aircraft built the DC1 for TWA. So many changes since I was a child. The horse and buggy days were over. This was Maya's world. But I did not want to be left behind.

Things were not so good elsewhere, according to the newspaper that came every morning to my mailbox. The days of rummaging through trash cans in Brooklyn for day-old papers was long gone. Russia was in the midst of what was the great famine and Adolph Hitler became Chancellor of Germany. His denouncing of the Jews became very popular. Someone had to be blamed for the state of the German economy and, as was often the case, the Jews became the perfect scapegoats. With the power given him by the passing of the enabling act and the death of President Hindenburg, Hitler became dictator in August 1934 and the world was about to enter a series of tragedies.

Hitler set about removing all Jews from positions of power and the Nazis began to round up tens of thousands of dissidents and Jews without adequate prisons to house them. And so Dachau was built, the first of the concentration camps.

I wrote to Harry begging him to come to America. He was the last of my family. I offered to send enough money to bring his whole family here, promising them a home with us on the farm. He declined my offer. He was too old, he said, a grandfather. The family was large. Many wouldn't consider leaving. He thanked me and wished me well, saying he had been through so many crises he was sure he could weather one more. I hoped he was right.

Things were changing on the farm, as well. Richard decided, with the economy beginning to pick up, it was time to open law offices in Hartford.

He had given up on New York, wanting to be closer to family. Daniel started an accounting practice in Trinity and was running for public office. The town was growing. The new golf course was bringing more people to the area. I was hoping Daniel would find a nice girl to marry and settle down.

Helen was anxious to leave the farm, to have a house of her own. The third floor bedroom was small and they were sharing a bathroom. Watching her with Billy and Maya, I knew she wanted a family of her own.

I was happy to see Richard, Helen, and Daniel spending a great deal of time with Benjamin, Leah, and their girls. I guess if you did something other than grub in the dirt, you were acceptable to Leah. Besides, I am sure she would never forgive me for my outburst at Mama's funeral, even if every word I said was true.

Sofia was maturing into a beautiful young lady. Tall, like her mother, with the same thick, dark-brown hair, piercing brown eyes and the fullest, longest eyelashes I had ever seen. She was a joy to me, a sweet child, smart and studious. Her beauty never failed to catch the eye's of the boys.

I had given her Serge's locket for her fifteenth birthday, telling her it was a gift from an old friend who was there at her birth. I didn't know how I was going to explain her birth. I kept putting it off thinking it was not the right time, maybe when she was older. The boys had been careful to keep the secret and treated Sofia like a little princess. She was their baby sister, no matter the accident of her beginning. I only wish my Miriam was there to see how she had grown.

The fortunes of the country were improving, but not necessarily the fortunes of the farm. We were beginning to struggle to have cash left over at the end of the year after paying taxes. In order to be prosperous, farms had to be bigger, more mechanized. The days of the small farm were coming to an end. Our farm still produced enough to feed and clothe the family, and pay for Sofia's college education, but we were beginning to dip into our cash reserves.

In the neighboring town of Hopkins, farmland was being bought up for new factories. With Germany invading Poland in nineteen thirty-nine, having already annexed Austria, World War Two was underway. Factories were beginning to churn out war materials.

Britain declared war on Germany followed by France, Australia, New Zealand, and Canada. I couldn't believe that America, the land of the free, didn't join in to save Poland, nor the other European countries as they fell, one-by-one. I never could understand how our government refused to allow Jews to immigrate and actually turned away a ship load of educated wealthy Jews from Germany, sealing their fate along with thousands of other Jews, to Hitler's ovens.

Part Two

Chapter 36

Things were changing so fast in my life. Tommy was graduating from high school. He'd been accepted to Yale and would be leaving at the end of summer. I was about to become a senior.

With school and parties, I had little time to spend with Grandpa. Our tea and cake sessions had just about come to an end.

One Saturday morning I was about to enter the kitchen, late for breakfast because I'd overslept, when I heard Daddy say, "Papa, I need to speak with you."

"So, Jacob," Grandpa said. "Speak."

"It's important. Can we go somewhere private?"

"What is so important that it is a secret?"

"I don't want to upset Cora, that's all."

"Speak. There's no one here but you and me, but it is not a good idea to be hiding things from Cora. So what is this all about?"

I knew I shouldn't listen, but if it was important enough to hide from my mother, maybe it was something I should know. So I stayed quiet, hidden from view in the hall.

"You know things aren't going too well on the farm," I heard Daddy say. Our income is way down. Even with the pasture we rent from Mrs. Hopkins, we can't compete with the price of the West's free-range cattle. Our profit is limited by the number of cows and calf's we can feed over the winter. Just like when you realized raising chickens to sell eggs was no longer profitable and gave it up years ago. The same mass production is killing us in the cattle business. We still have plenty of cash in the bank and the farm is free and clear, but, Papa, the cash won't last forever."

No wonder Daddy didn't want Mommy to hear any of this. I'd never heard any discussion of money before. That was scary stuff.

"I know what you are saying is true, Jacob." I choose, over the last few years, to ignore the problem hoping God would provide an answer, but seeing as I have not heard from him, what is your plan?"

"That's what I want to talk about, Papa. The defense plant in Hopkins is hiring. They're paying good wages. Sooner or later, we're going to be in this war, whether we like it or not. If you think you can run the farm by yourself again, I can add to our bank account by taking a factory job. It's the smart way to solve our problems, Papa, and it's the patriotic thing to do."

"Are you sure you want to do this, Jacob? I worked in a factory when we first came to America. Every morning when I walked into that building I felt as if I was descending into hell."

"Things are different now, Papa. There are labor laws to protect workers, and I'd be turning out something important for the country. If we're going to get into this mess, we need to have the best equipped Army in the world."

"I can still handle the farm alone. I am not that old and feeble, maybe just a little slower. Besides, I would feel useful again."

"Good, as long as you're sure. Then I'll look into applying for a job next week. I didn't want the kids to know money was tight. Maya will be ready for college next year and Billy needs to get his degree. They shouldn't need to concern themselves about my paying their way. I'll speak to Cora this evening. Thanks, Papa."

Wow, this was all new to me. Billy and I got just about everything we wanted, even the car Billy got as his high school graduation present. It never occurred to me there might be a problem with my going to college or that Billy might have to quit school. I'd never given money a thought. We seemed comfortable. I always had everything I needed. New clothes for the opening day of school, an allowance that I could spend on tickets for the Saturday afternoon movies. We had food on the table, a nice car. I guess part of growing up is facing reality, but I'd sure like to be a kid a little while longer.

"Hi, Daddy, Grandpa," I said, making believe I hadn't heard a word they said, as I entered the kitchen. "Sorry I'm late for breakfast."

Chapter 37

I thought about the changes that took place that year and the years that followed, and how Grandpa's story and mine had merged and become one. If I came for tea and cake on Sunday, the only free time Grandpa had now that he was in charge of the farm, we'd have conversations, not story telling.

I would sip my tea through a sugar cube remembering the first time I tried to drink tea that way and how silly it seemed. Now it was habit.

One Sunday, shortly after Daddy went to work in the defense plant, I started a conversation with Grandpa about the farm.

"I overheard part of your conversation with Daddy. I had no idea there was a money problem, Grandpa. The only problem anyone ever talked about was the draft and how everybody was concerned Billy might have to go into the Army. Is everything going to be okay now that Daddy's working at the defense plant?"

"Money is not for you to worry about, Maya. There is plenty for you and Billy to finish college and any emergency that might come up. Your daddy and I are just careful people when it comes to money. We only buy what we can afford to pay for in cash, and we put our money in the bank instead of the stock market. We remember nineteen twenty-nine, but believe me everything is fine."

"I believe you, Grandpa. If you tell me not to worry I won't. I promise I won't tell Billy what I overheard if he coes home for a visit. It's lonesome without him now that he's away at the University, and Tommy leaves for Yale in September. I won't have anyone to talk to or pal around with."

"Storrs isn't so far away nor is Yale, Maya. Billy comes home now and then for weekend visits, and next year you'll be at the university, as well."

"Maybe Billy will come home more often now that he has a new girlfriend. I'm glad he dropped Emily. I couldn't imagine having her as a sister-in-law."

"I see, a new girlfriend. All the more reason for young Billy to come home, and I am sure Tommy will be home weekends to see you. Everybody will be home for summer vacation. Tommy is a nice young man. He won't forget you. You two have been friends for a long time."

"I know he won't forget me. He keeps talking about getting married when he graduates. Grandpa, I don't want to think about getting married. I want Tommy and me to be just friends like we've always been. There are too many other things I want to do, and besides, I don't know if I like him that way."

"Not to worry, Maya. Tommy's graduation is four years away. You will have plenty of time before you have to think about marrying anybody."

I graduated from high school in the spring. Tommy invited me to the last fraternity dance of his school year. The dance was on a Saturday night in May, but New Haven was a long way away and it would mean spending the night. Tommy said he'd arrange for me to be a guest at the house of a friend of his family, and he'd drive me home on Sunday. Daddy wasn't keen about the plan, but Mommy said Tommy was trustworthy and I was a big girl, going off to college in the fall. I should go. It would give me a chance to see what college parties were like.

I already knew what Grandpa would say. "Young girls should not be allowed to go off on weekends with young boys."

I was really excited. I thought my senior prom dress was perfect for the occasion. The prom had been special even though my date had been a flop. Millard Young tried to kiss me after he'd slugged down a bunch of booze from the silver flask he'd borrowed from his father. He slobbered all over me. It was disgusting. I'm beginning to think boys can be so stupid.

I took the train to New Haven and Tommy picked me up at the station. I was so glad to see him. I really missed him. I could tell him anything, things I wouldn't tell my girlfriends. He seemed glad to see me, too, giving me a big hug and grabbing my overnight case.

We drove to the campus. I had no idea Yale was so beautiful. Tommy gave me a quick tour of the university, driving past Connecticut Hall, McClellen Hall, and Battell Chapel. We walked around campus and talked for hours, there was so much catching up to do, until it was time to get ready for the dance. Tommy introduced me to Dr. and Mrs. Howard, the friends of his parent's. They seemed really nice. Mrs. Howard showed me to their guest room, introducing me to their daughter, Jill, who would be going to the dance as well.

Tommy picked me up at seven. He was wearing a tuxedo. I'd never seen anybody, except in the movies, in a tuxedo before. He looked so grown up and very handsome, carrying a florist box containing an orchid. My first. He pinned it on my shoulder and we left for his fraternity house, a beautiful ivy covered brick building. Every light was on, music was blaring as the frat boys, all dressed in tuxedos, and their dates in gorgeous evening gowns, milled around. My dress looked cheap and juvenile compared to theirs. We walked inside. I'd never seen anything like that before.

All the furniture in the living room was pushed back against the wall. The rug had been rolled back to make a dance floor. The large dining room table was filled with trays of food, with a huge glass punch bowl and cups at one end. I noticed several of the guys spiking their punch with the contents of the flasks they had in the breast pockets of their jackets. The girls were drinking spiked punch as well.

Everything was very exciting, very grown up, magical. This sure wasn't anything like high school. I felt out of place, like a child at an adult party. The girls seemed very sophisticated. As I looked at their gowns, I realized they were unlike anything I'd seen before, except in magazines -- sleeveless with thin spaghetti straps that held up the dress while showing lots of skin and cleavage. I could see I needed to make some changes to my wardrobe before I left for college. Just because I lived on a farm in a small town didn't mean I had to look like a country bumpkin.

Everybody was nice to me. Tommy seemed to be very popular, which was no surprise. But somehow he seemed different, more grown up.

We danced and ate and danced some more, ending up on the back lawn with a few other couples. We found an empty bench in the corner under an old oak tree. I kicked off my shoes and wiggled my toes, not being used to dancing in high heels. Tommy sat next to me and held my hand, which seemed really strange. He said he was glad I came, then slipped his arm around me and kissed me. Not the slobbery kiss that Millard planted on me, but a long, kind of sexy kiss, my very first real kiss. It was kind of scary.

I didn't know what to do. We'd never made out like some of the other kids in school. I felt embarrassed, so I just stayed there in his arms waiting for what was to come next.

Tommy moved back a bit and looked at me saying, "Maya, I want you to have my fraternity pin."

"That's nice, Tommy, but why would you want to give me your pin?"

"Because it's a symbol."

"Of what?"

"Of a pre-engagement. It means you're my girl. We're going steady. That way I can be sure some guy isn't going to come along and date you while I'm here at Yale or when you're away at college." He kissed me again.

I jumped up. "We'd better be leaving," I said. I was confused. I wasn't sure how to handle all the kissing or what I thought might come next.

"I promised the Howards I wouldn't stay out too late, and we have a long drive back to Trinity in the morning."

"Okay. Sit down for just one second." He removed the fraternity pin from his tuxedo jacket and pinned it on my dress next to the orchid, which was a little worse for wear having been crushed between us on the dance floor. "There, it's official. You're my girl," he said and kissed me once more.

Tommy pulled his car into our driveway and I hopped out and reached for my case. "Want to come in for a while?" I said,

relieved when he said no, his folks were expecting him. He'd stop by tomorrow on his way back to school.

I didn't know what to do. Mommy had only dated Daddy and things were different then. Maybe I'd wait and talk to Sofia when I got to Storrs. She'd know what to do. She was more modern than Mommy. She had a job and I knew she had a boyfriend.

I ran upstairs to say hello to Grandpa and tell him what a good time I had. We had our usual long Sunday conversation about what was happening in the world. He was the only one who treated me as something other than a kid or just a girl.

Chapter 38

I enrolled at the University of Connecticut in the fall. For the first time I was on my own. No one to do my laundry, or cook my meals, or ask if I'd finished my homework.

I made a lot of new friends, dated a bunch of different guys, acquired a new wardrobe, and learned a lot of lessons that had nothing to do with a degree. With girls in my dorm helping, I experimented with makeup, smoked my first cigarette, and had my first drink. I learned a lot about boys and sex I never knew before, surprised at just how sheltered my life up to then had been. I was growing up, not an innocent kid any longer.

I don't know why I came downstairs so early that Sunday morning. Billy and I were both home for Christmas break. Daddy and Grandpa had their ears glued to the radio, their expressions grim.

"What's up with you two? You look as if the world has come to an end."

"In a way it has," Grandpa said. "The Japanese just bombed Pearl Harbor."

"Pearl Harbor? Where's that?"

"It's in Hawaii. It's our largest Naval base in the Pacific. The Japanese just sank or damaged eight ships, hundreds of airplanes and killed or wounded thousands of people according to the news reports," my father said.

"What does this mean, Grandpa?"

"It means war, child. How can this be happening again? I was lucky. Not one of my son's was lost, but over one hundred thousand families didn't share my luck. Have we learned nothing?"

"God, Daddy, if it's war does it mean Billy will be drafted, and Tommy, too?"

"Yes, Maya, I suppose it does," my father said. "My guess is every young man in the country will be drafted."

"And you, Daddy?" I could hardly deal with all the images that were going through my mind. "Will you be drafted, too?"

"No, I'm too old. They don't want me. Wars are only fought by young men."

The awful pictures of the war in Europe I'd seen in the Movietone newsreels at the movies began to replay in my head. I started to tear up. I was scared. The bombed out buildings, the dead and wounded in the streets. I thought of all the boys I knew. Could they be killed or wounded? Everything in my world was changing in an instant.

"The following day, we all listened to the radio with Grandpa to hear President Roosevelt declare war against Japan.

"I'm frightened, Grandpa. What's going to happen? What does all this mean? Are we going to be bombed like London?" Will the Japanese invade us?"

"I do not know, Maya. I only know, in the end we will win. God is on our side."

"I hope you're right, Grandpa."

"God bless America, I say it and I think it all the time. He has blessed America. I know God will help us." I prayed his help would have a better outcome than Uncle's village in Ukraine.

Days later, Germany declared war on us. I was bound and determined to do something to help the war effort, especially after Billy enlisted in the Navy the first of January, even before he was drafted. Time to grow up. Continuing my classes at the university seemed like a waste of time when I could be doing something to help the war effort, so I quit after finals in the spring. I could go back and get my degree when the war was over.

There was an opening in the office at the defense plant where my father worked. They advertised for someone to assist in the classified records department. My time at the university was a plus and I was hired. I started to volunteer three nights a week as a hostess at the USO canteen in Hartford, serving coffee and donuts, dancing with the GI's, or just being someone they could talk to. Two large bases had opened up nearby, an Army induction and basic training center, and an Air Force base that trained pilots and crews. I'd grown up in a hurry.

Tommy came home often. He'd received a deferment to finish medical school before serving time in the Army.

Things were busy at home. Everyone was doing their part in the war effort. Grandpa was in charge of the farm, which was focused on producing beef cattle for market. The Army was buying up all the available beef at any price, making the farm profitable again. Daddy worked overtime at the plant turning out airplane engine parts. Mommy volunteered for the Red Cross, leaving Grandpa to do the cooking when she was late getting home. No one complained. We all had a job to do

We had gas rationing, food stamps, limits on the number of shoes we could buy as the factories were busy making boots for the Army. Our lives and the lives of all around us had changed.

We saved tin cans and tin foil and bought war savings bonds. Eighteen dollars and seventy-five cents returned twenty five dollars in ten years.

I still had Tommy's frat pin tucked away in my dresser drawer. It had no relevance as I didn't have time for dating.

Standing behind the counter near closing time on a Tuesday evening, pouring coffee, a tall, dark-haired young man in an Air Force uniform approached. I noticed the gold bar on his shoulders, a second Lieutenant.

"I've been starring at you all night trying to get up the nerve to ask you to dance. It's almost closing time so it's now or never. May I have this dance?"

"Of course. I'd be happy to dance with you, soldier. My name is Maya, What's yours?"

"Hutch, William Charles Hutchison, Junior."

We stepped onto the crowded dance floor and he put his arm around me and found some room to dance. They were playing a slow tune, Glenn Miller's recording of Moonlight Serenade.

"Come here often?" he said.

"Yes, every Tuesday, Thursday, and Saturday."

We were practically standing still on the crowded dance floor when they dimmed the lights as the voice on the loud speaker announced the last dance.

"Damn, I should have asked you sooner. This evening is going to end way too soon."

With the last strains of See You In My Dreams, the lights came back up and the voice on the PA system said, "Goodnight, God bless, and many you all be safe."

Hutch asked if he could see me home.

"Thank you, but we're not allowed to leave with the servicemen. Besides, I don't live in town. I carpool with a couple of the other girls."

As we walked off the dance floor, he still had hold of my hand. "Thanks for the dance, Maya. Maybe I'll see you again." He turned and walked toward the door with the mob of other servicemen as the lights flickered, signaling the evening was over.

The house was dark, only the porch light on, as I walked up the steps and opened the front door. I tip-toed up the stairs to my room and got ready for bed, not wanting to wake anyone. My last thoughts, as I dropped off to sleep, were of the handsome Lieutenant.

Chapter 39

Grandpa and Daddy were already having breakfast when I came downstairs.

"You're late, Maya. You don't have much time to eat before it's time to leave for work."

"I know, Daddy. I got home late and had a hard time getting out of bed this morning."

"Maybe," Grandpa said, "you should not spend so much time at that canteen. You work hard all day and then rush out to dance all evening with men you don't know anything about."

"Grandpa, I'm surprised at you. You and Daddy are doing all you can for the war effort. The canteen is something special I can do. I just hope some girl in some USO is helping Billy to feel not quite so lonesome."

I arrived at the canteen Thursday evening and took my place at the coffee bar. I hadn't had time to take off my hat and coat when Hutch walked up. "Care to dance with a lonely soldier?"

I smiled as I stepped out from behind the counter. "I'm surprised to see you here again. Are you stationed nearby?"

He took my right hand in his, his left arm around my waist and we began to glide across the floor.

"You dance very well, soldier."

"Hutch, please."

"Alright, you dance very well, Hutch."

"I should even if it took four years of weekly dance lessons growing up."

I laughed. "You really went to dancing school? I thought that was only for girls."

"Well, not exactly dancing school, Miss Maya. The prep school I went to had mandatory dances every week with a nearby girls school, complete with a dancing instructor."

Thursday wasn't a night most servicemen had passes to be off base, so the dance floor wasn't crowded.

"I'm at the airbase for another month or so, before I ship out," Hutch said.

I felt very comfortable in his arms. Much as I protested that we weren't supposed to spend our time with only one serviceman, Hutch would cut in every time I danced with someone else. I never made it back to the coffee bar.

They dimmed the lights and we danced the last dance, my check against his as he held me tight. What was it about Hutch? Yes, he was handsome, but more than that, he was confidant, self-assured, with a sense of humor, and a twinkle in his eye. When the music ended and the lights flickered to announce the end of the evening, Hutch blew me a kiss and said, "See you Saturday, Maya."

Saturday was a repeat of Thursday. Against all the rules, I spent the entire evening with him. If we weren't dancing, we were sitting on one of the couches talking. The time flew by. The last dance was announced and the music started.

*'We'll meet again don't know where
don't know when, but I know we'll
meet again some sunny day,'*

The words of the song were ringing in my ears. I felt a lump in my throat. Hutch held me close. We barely moved. His body pressed close to mine so close I could feel his heart beat. A sensation of warmth engulfed my being. Was he feeling the same sense of sadness I was? I'd danced the last dance with lots of GI's before and never had this feeling. What made Hutch seem so special?

The music stopped, the flickering lights indicating the evening was about to end. Hutch smiled at me, his arm still around my waist. "I have Sunday off," he said. "Come to town and meet me. We could spend the day together, just the two of us, without any of the rules."

The invitation took me by surprise, I thought for a moment. Tommy wasn't due home this weekend. I wanted to say yes, but I was confused, conflicted. I really didn't know him. He'd be leaving soon. They all shipped out sooner or later. Much as I wanted to see him again why would I want to get involved?

"Please say yes, Maya. I don't know how much longer I'll be here."

Something reminded me of Grandpa talking to Grandma. Was it the tone of his voice, the look in his eye? I felt as if I could hear Grandpa telling me his story, how he wasn't going to let silly rules stand in his way.

"Alright," I said. "I'd like that. I can take the bus to town and meet you in the afternoon."

"Make it noon. We can go someplace nice for lunch. I'll be at the bus station waiting for you."

The lights flickered. It was closing time. Hutch smiled, "Boy, this evening went by much too fast."

The P.A. system kept announcing, "Goodnight, gentlemen. Good luck and stay safe." Slowly Hutch headed for the exit. "See you tomorrow."

After helping with the clean-up, I looked for Carol. She was driving that night. She beckoned to me as she waited at the door with Jean.

"Hurry, Maya. My feet are killing me. I can't count the number of times I got stepped on tonight."

We walked out into the warm summer air. Jean rushed to sit in the front, so I climbed into the back seat and we were on our way home.

"I watched you spend the whole night with that nice looking officer," Carol said. "You know that's against the rules."

"What could I do? Every time I danced with someone else he cut in?"

"Well, Maya, you could have said no."

"Yes, Jean, I suppose I could."

Both the girls laughed. Of course I could have said no, but I didn't want to.

They dropped me off at my front door. "I'll see you both on Tuesday. It's my turn to drive. I'll try to be on time."

I stared out the window as the bus pulled into the depot and spied Hutch waiting for me. The apprehension I'd felt disappeared the moment he smiled. He reached out his hand as I stepped down, giving me an unexpected kiss on the cheek.

"I was so afraid you wouldn't come. Let's go. One of the guys recommended a nice place to eat not too far from here."

We walked a couple of blocks to a small café. After being seated at a window table, the waiter arrived handing us menus and asked if we cared for a drink. Hutch ordered a beer, asking if I'd join him.

"I'm not much of a drinker. Iced tea will be fine."

We talked all through lunch. Getting to know one another was so much easier without the noise and distraction of the canteen. Hutch told me he was from Denver, Colorado. His father was the president of a local bank, his family had lived there long before Colorado became a state.

I asked if he had brothers and sisters, and where he went to school? All the usual questions, no different than those he asked of me.

We'd finished lunch, and lingered at the table until it was obvious the waiter wanted us to leave. "Where to now?" Hutch said, as we walked out onto the sun filled street.

"Its been a really nice afternoon, but I should be heading for home. I'm expected for dinner. We eat early on Sunday's."

"There's still plenty of time before I have to be back to the base." He paused. "I know what. I'll keep you company on the bus. That way we can have more time together."

We boarded the bus and talked all the way to Trinity. He was so easy to be with. I felt sorry when the bus stopped, but relieved when Hutch insisted on seeing me home.

We walked through the village with Hutch speaking of its charm, so different from Denver. We passed the pasture we leased from Mrs. Hopkins. "Those are our cattle grazing," I said.

"Really. My family got its start raising cattle. We still own and operate a cattle ranch in Weld County. I used to spend my summers there when I was a kid."

When we reached my driveway, I realized I couldn't just leave Hutch there to walk back to the bus stop. "Would you like to come in for a while?" I guessed that was his plan all along.

"I could use a drink of something cold."

As I walked up the steps with Hutch following, I noticed Grandpa sitting in a rocking chair on the porch.

"I see you have a friend, Maya," he said with a twinkle in his eye.

"Yes, Grandpa. This is Hutch."

"Hutch, like in rabbit hutch."

"No, silly, it's a nickname. His name is William."

"Nickname, that is a new word for me. So, what does it mean?"

"Its when you call someone something other than their real name."

"Like Tommy for Thomas?" Grandpa said.

Sly old fox. He knew exactly what he was doing. "Yes, Grandpa, that's exactly right. I'm going to get us something cold to drink. Can I bring something out for you?"

"There is cold cider in the icebox. Have a seat young man. Tell me about yourself."

"There's not much to tell, Sir. I'm in the Air Force stationed at the base just outside of Hartford, learning to be a navigator on a B-seventeen bomber."

By the time I returned opening the screen door, juggling a tray full of glasses, I heard Hutch say, "It's my job to find the target and then to bring us home or find someplace safe to land if we can't make it back to our base, and when we're under attack I man one of the machine guns."

Sitting on our front porch talking to Grandpa, I could see how comfortable Hutch was. Sometime later, my parents drove up and I made more introductions. Hutch was invited to stay for supper, which he accepted.

I went inside to help my mother. While Daddy had talked for years about an addition to the house it still was without a dining room. Our oversized kitchen had been the site of family meals even before my father was born. It had such a warm comfortable feeling, I doubt we would have used a dining room even if we had one.

I set the long rectangular oak table with colorful mats and found ironed napkins to match. I took down mother's best dishes as she eyed me with suspicion. All the while keeping one ear attuned to what was happening on the porch. I heard Hutch telling my father his family ranch ran twelve hundred head of cattle on both their land and on open range for part of the season. From the sound of things, they seemed to be getting along.

Dinner went well. Hutch answered all the questions put to him. He handled much of the conversation with humor. Though dinner was long over, we remained at the table until looking at his watch, Hutch said, "I really should be leaving. I have to be back to the base on time."

He thanked my mother for the wonderful meal, telling her how much he enjoyed home cooked food instead of Army chow, and how much he enjoyed being a part of a family again, if only for one evening. He shook hands with my father and Grandpa, and started for the front door.

"Drive him to the bus stop, Maya," Grandpa said. "You cannot expect him to walk."

Daddy nodded, reached in his pocket and handed me the car keys.

"I'll be right back," I said, as we scurried out the door.

I parked at the bus stop. "I'll wait with you until the bus comes."

"This has been a wonderful day, Maya. I hope you enjoyed yourself as much as I did. It was kind of your family to invite me for dinner."

"It really was a nice day, but I admit I was nervous as you were given the third degree. Embarrassed by all the personal questions you were asked."

"You can't blame your folks for being careful. They don't know anything about me. For all they know, I made up the whole story."

I stared at him, a worried look on my face.

"Come on, Maya, I'm teasing. Everything I said was true."

I could see the lights of the bus in the distance. We walked to the turn out as the bus came to a stop. Hutch took me in his arms and kissed me. Not a friendly kiss, but one filled with passion. Tingles went down my spine. I'd never been kissed like that before.

"I'll see you on Tuesday. I have your telephone number. I'll call you tomorrow." He waved as he boarded the bus.

I got back in the car, still feeling the tingling sensation. I hadn't been kissed by a lot of boys, but none of their kisses made me feel the way Hutch's did.

Chapter 40

By the time I got home, the dishes were done and everyone was sitting on the porch. Daddy was smoking his pipe and Grandpa lit one of the foul smelling Russian cigarettes he liked.

"He seems like a very nice young man," Mommy said.

"Very polite. Seems smart. You two seemed to be getting along well, but what about Tommy?" Grandpa said.

"This has nothing to do with Tommy. Hutch will be leaving in a week or two and I'll probably never see him again."

"No, child," Grandpa said. "I saw the way he looked at you. You will see him again."

All day Monday, I wished the time to pass in a hurry, wanting it to be Tuesday. I'd hurried home after work Tuesday to change clothes. I wanted to look my best, even putting on a pair of my hoarded silk stockings. I combed my hair, re-did my makeup, and ran out the door, shouting goodbye to everyone. I'd promised to pick up the girls.

I put out trays of donuts, sugar and cream for the coffee, all the time watching the front door. The hours passed by, but Hutch never appeared.

"Looking for you friend?" Carol said. "He might be someplace else. Some of the girls are talking about the new bar that opened up last week with a bunch of hot hostesses and no rules. They seem to be attracting a huge crowd of GI's."

That didn't seem like Hutch, but the crowd did seem a little thin that night. How well did I really know him?

I dropped the girls off and headed for home. They kidded me all the way about my no-show. I tried hard to hold back the tears.

Climbing the stairs to my room, careful not to wake anyone, I felt let down. I had been so sure he felt the same way I did. I closed the door before turning on the light. Then noticed the note on my bed, it was in my mother's handwriting.

Hutch called to say
He's been confined to base.
He'll try to call you tomorrow evening.

I let out a big sigh of relief. Hutch had an excuse.

We didn't get to talk very long when he called. He said there was a long line of airmen behind him waiting to use the phone. They were shipping out to the desert to do practice bombing runs and would probably get leave before they went overseas. Saying he'd write as soon as he could, he hung up as I started to sing quietly under my breath,

"We'll meet again, don't know where don't know when, but I know we'll meet again some sunny day."

I received a couple of letters a week telling me what he was doing. They all ended with "Miss you."

Tommy was home most weekends. He'd be ready for his internship at the Hartford hospital in January. I was glad to see him, as were my parents. I tried hard not to make comparisons. Tommy and Hutch were so different and my feelings toward them were, too.

Winter arrived early. The snow made it harder to keep my schedule at the canteen. At the end of November I received a letter from Hutch saying he had leave coming in December. He'd planned on spending Christmas with his family in Denver. "If I fly out for a visit," the letter read, "could I stay at the farm for a few days? I don't want to ship out without seeing you again."

I was excited at the thought of seeing him, but nervous. What was I going to tell my parents? How could I explain our relationship when I couldn't define it for myself? What was I going to tell Tommy? I waited until we'd finished dinner to ask Grandpa if he had a minute. I really needed to talk to him.

"Maya, I always have time for you. What would you like to talk to me about?"

"Not here, Grandpa. Let's go to the parlor."

Grandpa followed after me. I sat on the sofa and he sat next to me.

"So, what's so important we have to have a private talk?"

I told him about the letter from Hutch. "What should I do?"

Grandpa thought for a moment, and then said, "Do you want to see him?"

"Oh, yes. That's the problem, I really want to see him, but what will I tell Tommy? I don't want to hurt him. You know how I feel about him."

"So you have two young men interested in you and you don't know what to do. Maya, you don't have to choose between them. Not yet anyway. Has either asked you to choose? I cannot tell you what to do except to follow your heart."

"That's not exactly what I wanted to hear."

"Have you talked to your mother, yet?"

"Not for advice, besides I haven't made up my mind to invite Hutch."

"Child, girls usually ask their mothers for advice of the heart, not their old grandfathers. Maybe you should talk to her."

"Maybe she won't want him here and that will decide it for me." All kinds of thoughts ran through my head. No, she'll be okay with him staying here if that's what I want, and I guess that's what I want. "Thanks, Grandpa. You've been a big help."

I rushed off to find my mother.

Chapter 41

Light snow fell as I drove to the Army's Bradley Field. Hutch had hitched a ride on an Air Force plane. He called to say he'd landed and would be waiting at the entrance to the field.

My heart pounded with excitement as I approached the gate and saw Hutch exit the sentry's station. He opened the car door, reached across the seat, and kissed me on the cheek, then slammed the door behind him as I turned the car around and headed for the farm.

"I can't begin to tell you how great it is to see you, Maya. I've been looking forward to this since they told us we'd have leave for Christmas. This is sure better than writing letters." Hutch starred at me for a moment before he said, "You look even prettier than I remember."

"It's good to see you, too, but I can't believe you'd come all this way just to see me. Won't your folks be disappointed that you're not spending all your leave at home?"

"I already told them all about the wonderful girl I met in Hartford. They might not be happy, but they understand."

I stopped in front of the house and was about to open the car door as Hutch reached over and put his arm around me. "Let's stay here for a little while longer," he said. "I don't want to share you. Our time together is too short to waste a minute of it."

The three days Hutch spent with us were wonderful. He was so much fun to be with. I felt so comfortable with him. We talked for hours getting to really know each other better. We talked about what we'd do after the war was over. I spoke of finishing my education. Hutch said he'd be expected to return to Denver to begin his career in banking. His degree in Economics was geared to his role as the next in line to run the family's bank.

In the evenings, after dinner, we'd took the car and parked someplace quiet and secluded still talking, but more often engaging in some serious making out, my first experience with wanting to be kissed.

The last night, before he was to leave, Grandpa insisted that we accompany him to Mrs. Hopkins yearly gala, her famous Christmas party. This would be her last grand event as she'd sold her estate, the property now deeded to a real estate developer. She was moving to town.

I was surprised I hadn't seen much of Grandpa. I thought he'd be more interested in spending time with Hutch and me. Instead, he'd spent most of the day shut up in the old tobacco barn. I'd finished getting ready for the formal event. The pale peach chiffon gown I wore to a sorority rush party, my first expensive purchase, was perfect for the occasion. I was about to go downstairs when I heard Daddy and Grandpa in a heated conversation in the front hall.

"Papa, I don't think this is a very good idea."

"Son, just this once. I do not care what you think."

"But, the sled. Really. I haven't seen that old thing since I was a kid, and Clipper, Papa that old horse hasn't been out of his pasture in years. God knows how old he is."

"Jacob, old Clipper will be fine. He doesn't have far to go and he'll have a rest before we start for home."

"Have you given any thought to the traffic? The road is a lot busier than the old days when Serge would take us for sleigh rides."

"Well, then the cars will just have to look out for me. Now, if you will let me pass, Clipper is harnessed and waiting, already hooked up to the sleigh in the barn. Tell Maya, I'm ready to leave."

"Watch out you don't freeze to death out there, you could catch cold and die of pneumonia."

"I do not plan on doing either. It could be very late before we reach home, No need to wait up for us."

I started down the stairs, holding up the hem of my gown so I wouldn't trip. Hutch walked to the bottom of the stairs. He'd had been waiting for me in the parlor.

"Wow, Maya, you look like a dream come to life. This is the first time I've seen you all dressed up. My God you're beautiful." I watched him smile as he looked me up and down. "You take my breath away.

"From the conversation I just overheard, I think your Grandfather has something special in store for us."

"Have a good time kids," my father said as we headed for the front door. "Maya, look after your Grandfather. I hope he knows what he's doing. For God's sake don't let him drink too much."

Hutch opened the door. Stepping out into the cold night air. I stopped and stood in amazement at the sight before me. I'd never seen the old sleigh before, although I remember Grandpa telling me all about it in one of his stories. There it stood, its polished wood, its metal frame, gleaming in the moonlight with old Clipper looking better than I'd seen him in years. The old horse had been beautifully groomed, his mane pulled, the hair shaved from his ears, and his whiskers gone. Grandpa had added silver bells to his freshly cleaned and oiled harness.

"Climb aboard your carriage, children. You will find a fur blanket on the seat to keep you warm." Grandpa turned to run his fingers through the reins."

Hutch had his arm tight around me, the fur blanket covering us, and as if by magic, we began to glide over the light snow. I felt like a fairy princess, in the arms of her prince charming, on my way to the ball.

The only sound was coming from Clipper's breath and the sleigh bells. The lighted candles in the carriage lamps, on either side of the sleigh, cast a heavenly glow. The cold night air smelled sweet with the scents of wood burning fireplaces. We reached the main road, turned right and headed for Mrs. Hopkins' estate as cars drove around us. A few honking, but most giving us a thumbs up.

"This really is something special. I can't imagine the hours he spent polishing and cleaning. What it must have taken to put the whole rig together. No wonder you're so fond of your grandfather," Hutch said. "He's quite a guy."

"I know, but he's also an old softy when it comes to romance. He wanted to make this last night special for both of us. I think he's very fond of you."

We could see lights ahead as we approached the house, cars parked on either side of the main road. With a flick of the rains the old horse picked up his head and pranced down the long driveway as guests turned at the sound of the sleigh bells. It seemed every room in the house was lit up. A group of people walking to the front door stopped in their tracks as we approached, not sure the spectacle they were seeing was for real. We stopped at a spot on the driveway close to a clump of trees. Grandpa stepped down and tied Clipper's reins to one of the trees answering my question even before I asked.

"He is not going anywhere. Spread the blanket over the seat in case it snows so you won't be riding home sitting on wet snow."

We walked up the six wide brick steps to the front door of the imposing red-brick manor. I'd never been that close to the house before, nor had I been able to see much of anything but the four large brick chimneys from the road. We stepped inside to a warm greeting by Mrs. Hopkins.

"Caroline," Grandpa said. "May I present my granddaughter, Maya, and her friend, Lieutenant Hutchinson?"

I sized up our hostess. In her seventies, I guessed, and handsome in an elegant way. Her jewelry alone must have cost a fortune. I watched as she reached out her hand to Grandpa.

"David, I'm so glad you came. I was afraid you wouldn't. And how nice you brought your granddaughter." She turned toward me and said, "Your grandfather and I have been good friends for many years, almost too many to count. When I was much younger, I had quite a crush on him. He was a very good looking man, still is, but he was so happily married I didn't stand a chance. Come in, leave you coats in the hallway, have a glass of champagne and join the party."

We entered the massive hallway that led to the ballroom where most everyone seemed to be gathered.

"This is quite a place," Hutch said as we looked around. A huge Christmas tree dominated the end of the room, every branch trimmed with twinkling lights and silver-colored glass ornaments tied on with red ribbons. Christmas music came from somewhere. The Large fireplace was aglow. The sweet smell of burning wood filled the air. The room was crowded with people dressed in expensive formal attire. I recognized the Governor of the State and the Mayor of Hartford.

Hutch took two glass of champagne off a tray as a waiter walked by, handing one to me.

"Here's to a memorable evening. Just one of many, I hope."

Hutch and I roamed through the many spacious rooms downstairs looking at the various paintings, pictures, and awards that filled the walls. Trays of canapés were offered by servers, as guests greeted us with smiles, a few stopped to make conversation. Hutch, in his uniform, was attracting a great deal of attention in the older crowd. I didn't see anyone from Trinity.

Hutch had just returned from his search for more champagne and had just handed me a glass when I glanced up to see Tommy and his parents enter the room. My heart skipped a beat. Tommy saw me and headed in my direction.

"You didn't say anything about coming to Mrs. Hopkins' party, Maya." He looked at Hutch with a quizzical expression.

I could feel my cheeks redden as I said, "Tommy, this is our house guest, William Hutchinson." I could feel my stomach begin to churn.

Hutch put out his hand. "Everybody calls me Hutch."

"I don't remember you saying anything about a house guest either, Maya." Turning toward Hutch he said, in a dismissive manner. "When will you be leaving?"

"Tomorrow. I'm heading home to Denver for Christmas."

Tommy started to carry on a conversation with Hutch, ignoring me in the process. He had no intention of leaving us alone. The situation was getting complicated. Awkward. Time to leave.

I excused myself and went looking for Grandpa. He appeared to be having a good time, champagne glass in hand, deep in conversation with a couple of men I didn't recognize.

"Grandpa, can I interrupt for a minute? I think it's time to leave for home."

"It is still early, Maya. Is there a problem?"

"Yes, Grandpa. It's Tommy."

"I see. Well, do the best you can," he said with a twinkle in his eye. "We will leave in a while." He turned his back and continued his conversation. He wasn't in a hurry. He was going to leave me to deal with the situation.

I returned to see them still talking. Much to my surprise, Tommy seemed rude. Hutch was taking it all in with a smile. He seemed to have figured out the whole thing."

"Tom, here, tells me you've been friends since grammar school. That he gave you his fraternity pin."

"Yes," was all I could think of to say.

"Tom told me he has a deferment, which is why he's not in uniform." Hutch's attitude was equally dismissive.

I hoped the verbal jabs didn't turn to blows. The whole thing was getting ugly and that was probably my fault for not telling Tommy, Hutch was visiting.

Hard as I tried, I couldn't break up the sparring match, nor could I move on. I sighed a sigh of relief as Grandpa appeared on the scene. "Hello, Tommy," he said. "I see you have met Maya's friend."

I shot him a look, pleading for him to say we should leave. But he still didn't seem to be in any hurry. I wanted to disappear. I was so embarrassed, but Grandpa knew what he was doing. He continued to engage Tommy in conversation asking about his parents, discussing the weather. It seemed like an eternity before Grandpa said, "Okay, kids, it is past my bedtime. Time to go. Good to see you, Tommy. Say hello to your parents. Come children. We need to say goodbye to our hostess."

Hutch reached for my hand. "Nice to have met you, Tom." We followed Grandpa to the door.

Grandpa untied Clipper and climbed up on the driver's seat as we hopped into the sleigh. Hutch covered us with the blanket as the old horse turned and slowly headed down the driveway.

"I'm so sorry."

"Sorry for what? Certainly not that Tom is mad about you? I can understand that. If the situation were reversed, I doubt I'd have been as much of a gentleman."

Hutch put his arm around me and kissed me sweetly on the lips. "You were with me. That's all that matters."

We rode the rest of the way without saying a word. I sat huddled up against Hutch listening to the sound of Clipper's hoofs hitting the pavement, and Grandpa humming a tune I'd never heard before as snow flakes gently fell.

When we arrived home, Grandpa opened the doors to the tobacco barn and led Clipper inside. He unhitched the harness, saying goodnight as he led the old horse back to his stall leaving us alone in the dark empty barn with only the moonlight casting a few shadows.

"I'm sorry to be leaving tomorrow. I wish I could spend all my leave with you, but I do have family. It's been wonderful being here. You're folks have been so kind. The way you looked coming down the staircase and tonight's sleigh ride are something I'll remember forever."

He took me in his arms. "Maya, I don't know what your situation is with Tommy, you can sort that out on your own time. I only know I love you. I knew you were the one from that very first night at the canteen. When the war's over, and I make it back in one piece, there's something important I want to ask you, but for now, just promise you'll wait for me."

I could hear Grandpa saying the same thing to Grandma as he left for the Army.

"I'll wait for you, I promise," was all I could say. The long kiss that followed awakened feelings I'd never experienced before, but I knew taking this one step further would be a mistake.

"I'm so scared," I whispered, as I clung to him. "Scared something might happen to you. Do you know where you'll be sent?"

"My best guess in somewhere in eastern England. All our training points to bombing raids over Germany."

"It sounds so dangerous. I hate to even think about it. I'll be worried about you every second until you're back. Promise you'll stay safe."

"Don't worry, we're well trained. Our crew is first rate. We're flying great planes, and besides I've got you to come home to. I'll fly my twenty-five missions and be home. It'll be a piece of cake."

With the fur blanket protecting us against the cold night air, we stayed wrapped in each other's arms until the break of dawn. Talking was no longer necessary. With so little time left before he was gone, we wanted to spend every second together. We tried to be quiet as we entered the house not wishing to wake anyone. Shoes in hand we climbed the creaking stairs hoping the old treads didn't give us away.

The drive to the airport was in silence for the most part, both of us lost in our thoughts. We no longer had time for idle chatter. I offered to come in with him as I stopped in front of the airport entrance, but he said no.

He hugged me tight and whispered, "Just keep your promise and wait for me."

"Promise me you'll come home. I promise I'll be waiting." I couldn't stop the tears.

"I'll write," and then he was gone.

Tommy stopped by Sunday morning saying he wanted to talk to me.
"Sure, Tommy, what do you want to talk about?"

"Don't be cute, Maya. You know damn well what I want to talk about. I thought you were my girl."

"Oh, Tommy, not now. I don't know what to say. I didn't plan it this way. I like you both in different ways. It's so confusing. How can I explain it when I haven't even sorted it out in my own mind."

"Well, I'm not giving you up to some uniform. You've always been my girl and always will be. As soon as my internship is over, I'm going to join Dad's practice in Trinity, and then I plan on marrying you. So you can forget all about Mr. Air Force."

"Tommy, I'm not ready to marry anyone until the war is over. I'm needed at my job and at the canteen. There's no time to think about weddings now."

"Okay. If that's what you want I'll wait until the wars over, but we'll be seeing a lot more of each other when I return to Trinity. Your friend is gone. I'm still here."

Chapter 42

Sofia came home for Christmas, accompanied by her boyfriend, Archibald McGovern, Archie for short, an assistant professor of English at the same university where Sofia was employed.

The whole family liked him at once. He was funny, and smart. Tall, with a slightly receding forehead and horn-rimmed glasses, looking as if he could use another fifty pounds. His tweed sport coat and bow tie completed the picture of what I thought all professors should look like.

I watched them together. They seemed a lot like Hutch and me, self-conscious and nervous around the family, but off by themselves the attraction was obvious.

We were invited to Uncle Richard and Aunt Helen's house for dinner on Christmas Eve, their two young boys eager for Santa Claus' arrival. Grandpa was just fine with the idea of Santa Claus as we'd had Christmas at the farm ever since I could remember.

After the boys were sent to bed, and all the adults had opened their presents, Sofia said she had an announcement to make. I think we all guessed what she was about to say. Everyone looked giddy, except Grandpa. The color had drained from his face as he heard Sofia tell of her forthcoming marriage to Archie.

There were hugs and congratulations until Sofia looked at Grandpa. "Papa, aren't you going to wish us happiness?"

Archie spoke up before Grandpa could say a word. "I had every intention, Sir, of asking you for Sofia's hand in marriage, but it seems she jumped the gun. I do hope you will forgive her and give us your blessing."

I saw the forced smile on Grandpa's face as he said, "Yes, of course, children. You have more than my blessing. You have my best wishes."

Sofia rushed to Grandpa's arms. "Thank you, Papa," she said. "Archie will be a wonderful son, you will see."

Everyone had questions. When? Where?

Archie said they would be traveling to Boston to spend New Year's with his parents, and would like to be married during spring break.

The women in our family loved the thought of a wedding. My mother and Aunt Helen were huddled in a corner already discussing wedding plans with Sofia. The look exchanged between my father and Grandpa said something was amiss.

When we arrived back at the farm, I heard Grandpa tell Sofia he would like to talk with her alone before she and Archie left for Boston in the morning.

I awoke to hear Sofia and Archie talking as they walked down the stairs. I grabbed my robe and slipped out of my room, anxious to overhear what Grandpa had to say to Sofia. I knew that was none of my business, but it might be the same discussion he'd have with me before I married.

I stood in the hallway, hidden from view, as Grandpa and Sofia talked about the trip to Boston. Then Grandpa said, "Sofia, there is something I need to discuss with you. Something you need to know before you marry. God, forgive me, something I should have told you years ago, but could not find the courage." I heard him sigh, "I wish Mama were here. She could do this so much better than me."

"This sounds serious, Papa. What is it you need to discuss?"

"Well, I do not know where to begin, so I will just say it is about your birth."

My God, I thought as I overheard the conversation. Sofia doesn't know.

"What about my birth, Papa?"

"I am not your father, Sofia."

"I don't understand. What do you mean, you're not my father."

"No more than Mama was your mother."

Silence filled the room. I knew I should leave, but I stood glued to the spot waiting to hear the rest.

"Papa, I don't understand."

I could hear the concern in Sofia's voice.

"Let me have a moment, child, to gather my thoughts and I will tell you the whole story."

Again, silence. The suspense was killing me.

"Your mother, Maria, was a lovely young girl, almost eighteen when you were born, an Italian immigrant who lived with us as a helper for Mama. She was beautiful just like you, the same dark hair and brown eyes, the longest lashes I had ever seen, and your same sweet smile. Well, I am sorry to say, she became pregnant. Mama and Mary Harris were with her when she gave birth to you. Mama was the one who cleaned you, wrapped you in a blanket and held you tight."

"This woman, Maria, who you say is my mother, where is she? Did she just run off and leave me?"

"No, Sofia, despite the doctor's attempts to save her, she died in childbirth. That was when Mama and I decided to raise you and love you as our own."

I hoped no one would come down stairs and catch me eavesdropping. It seemed like ages before Sofia spoke, her voice shaking.

"If Maria was my mother, who was my father, Papa?"

"You do not need to know."

"No, you're wrong, I do need to know. It's my life. Now I need all the answers."

"I am much too ashamed to tell you. Trust me, you will be happier not knowing."

"I don't want to be happier, Papa. I couldn't be anymore unhappy than I am right now. I insist you tell me. I have a right to know."

Again, there was a long moment of silence before Grandpa spoke.

"You are right, child. No matter the shame he brought to our family, you have a right to know. I am ashamed to say your father is my eldest son, Aaron. I am your grandfather."

"You mean that arrogant disrespectful man who was here with the blond showgirl? He's my father?"

I heard no sound. Then in almost a whisper, Sofia said, "Do my brother's know?"

"Yes."

"And they've kept the secret all these years, Papa?"

"There was no secret to keep. In their eyes you are their baby sister. I hope you can forgive me for not telling you years ago. I long ago gave up thinking of you as my granddaughter. You have always been my most precious child. Can you forgive me?"

"There's nothing to forgive, Papa. You'll always be my father. I think I love you even more now that I know the truth. What about Archie? What do I tell him?"

"Ah, Sofia, that is up to you, but love cannot grow when it is clouded in secrets."

I tiptoed upstairs before I got caught, thinking what a wise man my grandfather was.

Chapter 43

The war dragged on. I was overwhelmed by work at the factory. We were now operating round the clock, my counterpart working the night shift. I still managed my three nights at the canteen. Thank God I was so busy I didn't have time to consider the future.

Hutch wrote often. He'd been gone a year. His letters spoke of longing for the war to be over, wishing to spend time with me. They said little of what he was doing. Often there were heavy black lines drawn through his words. Something had been censored.

The evenings I was home, I listened with Daddy and Grandpa to Edward R. Murrow's broadcasts from London and worried myself sick thinking about Hutch, while counting my blessings that the war had not come to our shores.

Tommy was working full time in his dad's office, his deferment continued as he and his father were the only physicians for miles around. I saw him when I had time. He was back to being his old sweet self and never mentioned Hutch.

December's snow had begun in earnest. Christmas was only days away. I thought of the wonderful sleigh ride and wondered when the damn war would end. The predictions had been it would be over by Christmas, then the Battle of the Bulge occurred and the war continued to drag on.

I could count on at least two letters a week from Hutch. I saved every one reading them over and over again. Each letter reminding me of how much I missed him. Then in February, the letters stopped coming. I hoped against hope that nothing had happened.

At dinner one evening, mother mentioned she hadn't seen any mail from Hutch lately. She checked the mailbox, daily, watching for word from Billy who was serving aboard a destroyer in the Pacific.

As each day passed my fears grew. I was worried sick. "It's not like Hutch to stop writing without a good reason," I said.

"Maybe he's found himself a pretty English girl in one of the British canteens," Daddy said with a smile on his face.

"Not funny, Daddy. Not funny at all." I left the table before they could see me cry.

Several nights later, I was in my room when I heard the phone ring. Mother called, "Maya, it's for you."

"Who is it?"

"I don't know, dear. It's a woman asking for you."

I picked up the phone.

"Maya?"

"Yes, who is this?"

"Thank God I found you. I'm Anne Hutchison, William's mother. I've been trying to reach you, but I didn't know your last name. William only spoke of you as Maya."

It took a moment as I tried to understand why Hutch's mother would be calling me. My heart was racing. I had a strange feeling in the pit of my stomach as I said, "Is he all right?"

"No, dear, I'm afraid he's been wounded."

Wounded. What an ugly word. No wonder his letters stopped. "How is he? How can I reach him?"

"He was flown by air ambulance to Walter Reed hospital in Washington D.C. a week ago having received a serious wound to his left leg. I flew out two days ago from Denver to see him. That's the reason I'm calling. He's terribly depressed, not his usual happy optimistic self. I can't seem to reach him no matter how hard I try. He barely speaks to me. I was hoping you might spend a few days visiting with him at the hospital. I'm sure seeing you would make a world of difference."

"Tell me, please, will he be all right?"

"It's not a life threating injury, dear, but the outcome is touch and go."

"I'm sorry. I'm not thinking straight. Of course I'll come. I'll leave first thing tomorrow morning. Tell him I'm on my way and thank you for going to the trouble of finding me, Mrs. Hutchinson."

"Don't thank me. I'm selfishly doing whatever I can to help my son recover. I don't think they allow visitors outside of family members so I'll tell them his sister is coming to visit. I'm looking forward to meeting you tomorrow at the hospital. William spoke so highly of you."

I heard the click as the call ended. I stood with the phone in my hand, a million thoughts running through my mind. "Daddy," I shouted. "Can you drive me to the train station tomorrow morning?"

My father walked into the kitchen as I was putting the receiver back on its cradle.

"The train station? Where are you going?"

"Hutch has been wounded. He's in the hospital in Washington D.C. That was his mother on the phone. I've got to go and see him." The tears started running down my cheeks. "Oh, Daddy, I'm so scared."

He put his arms around me. "Dry your tears, Maya. I hear the military hospitals are doing wonderful things these days. Going to see him is the right thing to do. I'll drive you to the station before work. Do you need any money?"

I waited for my father downstairs. I'd been up for hours imagining all sorts of awful things, wondering if I was strong enough to deal with whatever the problem was.

Grandpa was having breakfast. I poured a cup of coffee and sat next to him.

"I'm sorry to hear about your young man being wounded. I know he will be glad to see you. Stay as long as you are needed."

"I'm not sure I can handle this."

"Of course you can. You are far stronger, more grown up than you think. Give him my best. Remember, he needs you to be strong for him. No tears."

"Come on, Maya," my father said as he entered the kitchen. "Let's go. I don't want to be late for work."

"Grandpa," I shouted as I headed for the door. "If Tommy calls, tell him I'm out of town. Just don't tell him where or he'll be really upset. I can't deal with that now. Thanks, bye."

It took almost eight hours to reach Washington D.C.'s Union Station. I worried every mile of the way trying to hold my emotions in check. I caught a cab to the hospital. I entered the old red brick building and walked past the guard to the front desk. "I'm here to see my brother, Lieutenant William Hutchinson."

The clerk, a WAC, flipped thorough a Rolodex file. "Second floor east. Stop at the nurses station," she said, as she pointed toward the staircase. "Visiting hours are almost over."

I thanked her and headed for the stairs. When I reached the nurses station, I was told to wait while they checked on the patient.

I paced the hallway until a nurse and a handsome middle-aged women approached. I knew at once she was Hutch's mother. He resembled her.

"Maya," she said as she embraced me. "I'm so glad you came. The nurse says it's all right if you visit as long as you don't tire him. Follow me."

As we reached a set of double doors leading to the ward, she said, "I didn't tell him you were coming, afraid he would resist. I'll leave you two alone. Stay as long as you wish. I'll be in the visitor's room. He's in the fourth bed on the left," she said, as she took my suitcase. "I'll keep this for you."

I took a deep breath, ran my fingers through my hair and opened the door. I tried not to stare at the men lying in beds as I walked down the aisle. I wanted to cry at what I saw. Some of the curtains separating the beds were closed. As I reached bed four I saw him, his leg in a cast suspended in air by a pulley. His eyes were closed. I walked up to the bed and whispered, "May I have this dance?"

Hutch opened his eyes, a look of surprise on his face. "Maya, is that really you? How did you get here? How did you know where I was?"

"Your mother called me last night. I had to come and see you. I left home by train this morning."

"Step back and let me look at you. You cut your hair."

"Yes. Do you like it?"

"Yeah, it's different, but I think I like it. How long are you going to stay?"

"As long as you like. Tell me what happened. Do you know how long you'll be here?"

"I don't want to talk about me. I want to hear about you. Are you still going to the canteen?"

"Yes, but with a new set of rules."

"What new rules?"

"Well, no more dancing with service men. I just smile and serve coffee and donuts."

"I like the new rules, but why?"

"Oh, I was afraid I'd meet another handsome, sweet taking airman, and I can only promise to wait for one man at a time."

"I was afraid to ask if you'd kept your promise."

"Shame on you, Hutch. I always keep my promises." I saw a smile cross his face. "Tell me when you feel tired. The nurse told me you need your rest."

"That's all I do is rest. They keep me pretty well doped up. Do you think you could spare a kiss? I'm pretty scruffy. I haven't shaved in days and can't remember the last time I had a shower."

"You look awfully good to me,' I said, as I bent to kiss him on the cheek. He grabbed me, holding me in his arms. "I wasn't sure I'd ever see you again." Tears were filling his eyes.

I pulled up a chair and sat next to his bed, holding is his hand in mine. "Please tell me what happened."

"You don't really what to hear. Besides it's not important. I made it. I beat the odds."

"Please, Hutch. I need to know. I won't stop asking until you tell me. You can ask my Grandfather. I can be pretty persistent.

"If you insist, but there's not much to tell. We were part of a strategic bombing raid over a factory in Germany when the aircraft in our group were attacked by scores of German fighter's. They pretty well shot up our plane. We lost a left engine making it impossible to reach our home base before we ran out of fuel. I caught a bullet to my left leg. The bombardier managed to slow the bleeding and propped me up long enough to plot an alternative landing spot. I tried to man my gun and succeeded for a while until I guess I passed out. The pilot did the rest. We landed safely."

"But you're going to be alright?"

"They managed to remove most of the bullet fragments at the field hospital in England, but the bone is pretty well shattered. My flying days are over."

"But it's going to be okay after they take off the cast, right?"

"At the moment, the casts only purpose is to hold everything in place until the operation day after tomorrow. They're going to try to insert a metal plate and some screws to hold what's left of the bone together."

I tried not to show any concern, but the words 'to try to' swirled around in my head. I didn't know what to say.

The silence was horrible, until Hutch said, "You still seeing Tommy?"

"Well seeing, sort of in a way, yes. We still live in the same town. He's taking care of patients in his father's office. I know he wants to ask me to marry him, but I told him I wouldn't listen until the war was over."

I could see Hutch was having trouble keeping his eyes open, "It's time I go. I left your mother waiting in the lounge. Take a nap and I'll be back."

"You promise?"

"Yes, but not tonight. I'll be here early in the morning. I promise. Remember I always keep my promises."

"I can't tell you what it means to have you here. See you tomorrow."

I kissed his forehead and left. I found his mother waiting for me.

"How was he, dear?"

"Happy to see me. We just chatted. I did promise to come back tomorrow, so I need to find a place to stay."

"There are no hotel rooms available in this whole town. It's only through a friend of my husbands I have a hotel room. You're staying with me."

"Oh, I can't impose."

"Nonsense. Besides, I want to get to know you. Now, lets take a taxi back to my hotel and have a cocktail and dinner. We've lots to talk about."

Chapter 44

I called home to let everyone know I was okay. Grandpa answered the phone even though I knew he hated the contraption, as he called it. He asked how Hutch was and I related the events of the day.

"Grandpa, they're going to operate on Hutch day after tomorrow. I have to stay until then."

"Of course you do. Be brave. Call and let us know what happens. Tell your young man I will ask God to make him well. I'm not sure God listen's to me, but I will ask anyway. What harm can it do."

I returned to Walter Reed the next morning. Hutch was shaved, his hair combed, and wearing a fresh hospital gown. He looked one hundred percent better than the day before.

We spent the morning making small talk. We talked about my job. He asked about my family, how Grandpa was doing. He spoke about the crew, the guys he flew with. They'd flown over thirty-seven bombing raids together, more than the twenty-five required. They either volunteered or were volunteered for extra missions as they were running short of experienced crews. Some guys had flown fifty or more missions.

"I miss the guys, Maya. It's hard to explain the feelings we have for each other. We're like brothers. I'm worried about my replacement. Worried it might be some young newly graduated navigator with no combat experience. It's one thing to navigate in a school room, another all together when you were getting shot at or flying through flack."

I asked what was next and he said all things being equal, he'd probably be assigned to teach. He planned to put in a request for duty at the airbase outside of Hartford. "I bet you can guess why," he said.

"No, I don't mean what's next in the military. What's next when the war's over? They say it won't be long, now."

"That's funny you should ask, Maya. I've been lying here thinking about the future. A lot depends on what happens with my leg, but if everything goes well, my plans have changed."

"What plans are you talking about?"

"Before I went overseas, remember, I said I expected to become a banker like my father. I always imagined I'd live in a big house in Denver just like my folks, be a big wheel in the community, and associate with the cream of Denver's society. Well, somehow that doesn't appeal to me, anymore. War can change your perspective. I'll let my brother reap all the banker's rewards. I'm not the same guy I was before I went overseas, before I saw what war was like first hand. I see things differently now.

The big house, being a big wheel, all seems so superficial. I want something entirely different."

"That's interesting. If not a banker what do you want to do?"

"Well, the nights I wasn't thinking about you, I did a lot of soul searching. Hank, the ranch manager, is getting on in years. I think I'd like to take over his job. I know I don't want the big city anymore. I want someplace quiet, away from all the pointless social games. All the meaningless trappings I grew up with. I've always loved our ranch. It's the prettiest part of the country you'll ever see. Warm summers, mild winters, with trees and mountains and cattle grazing green pasture as far as your eye can see.

"I want to write a book about the heroic men that make up the bomber crews. I can see myself writing at the ranch. It's peaceful, none of the distractions of the city. I could never find time to write in Denver. I'd be constantly drawn in too many directions. The social demands of a banker.

"It all sounds wonderful, but what does it have to do with the operation?"

"That's a long story I don't want to talk about now, but Maya, could you be happy living on a ranch a long way from any town, no close neighbors?"

"Why do you ask?"

"Because you're the most important part of my plan. Don't answer now. Let's see what happens in the next few weeks."

Hutch started to change the subject just as his mother came and saved the day. The nurse had said it was time to leave. The surgeon was expected for a pre-op consultation.

Chapter 45

The surgery was scheduled for ten o'clock in the morning. I promised I'd be there before they took him to the operating room.

When I arrived the privacy curtains were pulled closed around his bed. I peeked in. He seemed to be sleeping. As I walked over to his bed, Hutch opened his eyes and smiled at me. "I'm a little punchy from the pills they gave me a while ago, but I've been waiting for you. Will you be here when I wake up?"

"If you want me to, I'll be here. I promise." He seemed so fragile, unlike the way I was used to seeing him. He'd always been so confident, self-assured, outgoing, and upbeat.

He reached for my hand and held it tight as the orderlies came to wheel him away. "Pray for me, Maya. So much of our future depends on this operation."

His hand pulled away from mine as they wheeled him down the aisle. His mother was waiting at the doorway to see him. I was amazed she would allow us so much time together.

As the gurney disappeared through a set of doors at the end of the hall, Hutch's mother suggested we go for a walk. The fresh air felt good, even warm with the sun high in the sky -- February's false spring, the few warm days before winter returned.

"Mrs. Hutchinson, I know you and Hutch are not telling me everything. You're both holding something back. There's no way Hutch would be depressed by the prospect of repairing a broken leg. I need to know what's happening. What you're keeping from me."

She looked at me and after a moment said, "Yes, Maya, I have been holding back. I haven't told you what will happen if this operation doesn't go well. But somehow I know you're strong enough to deal with the facts." She took a deep breath before she said, "If the metal plate can't give support to the undamaged bone, the plan is to amputate his leg below the knee."

I couldn't breathe. I couldn't speak. I moved to a nearby bench and sat. I thought I was going to faint. Hutch's mother sat beside me and put her arm around me.

"Now you understand why I tried so hard to find you. He needed you being here. Needed something to hold on to."

"How can you possibly be so brave?"

"This has nothing to do with bravery, dear. A mother knows her children, Maya, and I know how strong William is. No matter what happens, he'll get through this. I love all my children equally. They make their father and me very proud. I know they will all succeed in life, but of all of them, given the right set of circumstances, William has the ability to do great things, to achieve more than most."

We sat for a while, both of us deep in thought. There was nothing I could say. Mrs. Hutchinson broke the silence. "I'd always hoped that William would marry someone from among our friends. As you can imagine, he's always been very popular with the young ladies, but if he chooses you and you agree, I will be pleased. Your very different from the girls he grew up with, but you bring him something he needs and that's good enough for me. I'm sure his father will feel the same way."

We returned to the hospital in the late afternoon to await whatever news the surgeon had to deliver. As the hours dragged on, I found it harder and harder to hold on to my emotions. Afternoon turned into evening and still no word, until almost eight o'clock when a tired, drawn looking doctor appeared.

"Mrs. Hutchinson," he asked.

Hutch's mother nodded, yes.

"Well, Ma'am, it's too soon to be positive, but I'm optimistic we've saved the leg. He might have a slight limp as one leg is going to be a bit shorter than the other, but if he heals well, and baring any unforeseen complications, I think we're out of the woods."

For the first time, I saw Hutch's mother breakdown. With a sigh of relief, the tears she must have been holding back for days came streaming down her cheeks as she tried to thank him.

"Can we see him?" I said.

"Not now. He's still in recovery. Come back in the morning. He'll be sedated, but he'll know you're here."

We left the hospital, arm in arm. Words were not important.

Chapter 46

I was packed and ready to leave after my hospital visit. Much as I wanted to extend my stay I had to return home. There was still a war going on and my job was important. I'd phoned home to say I'd be arriving in the early evening and would call when I was at the station.

When we reached the hospital, Mrs. Hutchinson told me to go first. She was planning to stay for a few more days and would have plenty of time to visit with her son after I left.

I pushed the curtain aside just enough to walk through. "Hutch," I said as I approached his bed. "I'm here, as I promised."

He opened his eyes and in almost a whisper said, "Marry me."

"Hutch, let's talk about that when you're better."

"I'm having a hard time staying awake or making a lot of sense, but I'm alert enough to tell you I love you. I need you. Marry me." Then he seemed to drift off, as if he'd waited with all his strength to say the words and once said he was free to sleep.

I had to go if I was going to catch my train. I asked his mother to explain why I had to leave, and thanked her for everything as I walked out the door.

From the tone of Hutch's letters, I'd known for a long time this was going to happen sooner or later. He was going to ask me to marry him, but I'd tried to put it out of my mind. There were too many things to deal with, but that escape was gone. Hutch's words had forced me to face facts. I would need to give him an answer.

Chapter 47

I arrived home exhausted. The events of the last few days were catching up with me. I had little to say to the family, promising details later, and went to my room.

The following evening, I knocked on Grandpa's door. "May I come in?"

"Of course. It has been a long time since we've had visits in my room. I am sorry I have no cake to offer."

"I don't need cake, Grandpa, I need advice."

"As I told you before, the kind of advice you are seeking should come from your mother."

"She can't help me, nor can my father. Think about it, Grandpa. Daddy has lived in the same house his whole life. Mommy's parents didn't come to this country until she was ten. Her ideas of love and marriage are still old world."

"That may be true, but she is still a woman."

Yes, but Mommy's ideas of marriage are different from my friends or mine. She's content to clean and cook and never disagree with Daddy. She moved a mile down the road when she married and hasn't been out of Trinity more than a dozen times in her whole life. My parents are wonderful people, but they have no world experience, not like you have. They've never had to deal with the kind of decisions I will have to make. Besides I can't talk to them the way I talk to you. They still treat me like a child."

"So, Maya, what is it that's troubling you?"

I told Grandpa all about my time in Washington and Hutch's proposal. Not sure if Hutch was aware of what he was saying.

"So, child, what do you want me to say?"

"What do I do about Tommy? To be fair, I promised to listen to his proposal when the war was over."

"The war is over for Hutch, and it never began for Tommy, so talk to him. Listen to what he has to say. Not every young woman has two fine men wanting to marry her, but it is not fair to keep them both hanging on. It has got to be one or the other, or who knows, maybe neither. You do some serious thinking and then we will talk again."

That evening I received a call from Hutch's mother telling me how well he was doing. So well that she felt free to leave in the morning for Denver. "He's still confined to bed. He said to tell you he'd write, and call as soon as they let him reach a phone."

"Thank you for calling. I've thought of nothing else but how he was doing."

"He said to tell you he meant what he said when he proposed."

I was happy and confused all at the same time. Grandpa was right. I had to make a decision.

"Thank you, Mrs. Hutchinson for everything. Tell Hutch I'll write to him, that I plan on visiting him again, soon."

"I'll tell him. I want you to know I approve. He needs you and as I said before, that's good enough for me."

"Thank you, and thanks again for being so kind."

"No thanks necessary. I just want to see my son happy."

I waited for Tommy at the park on Saturday afternoon promising a picnic lunch and some time to talk. He arrived right on time at noon carrying a bottle of wine.

"It's been a while since we've spent time together, Maya. Of late, it seems you've been too busy for me. But whatever the reason, I'm happy to see you. You look great by the way. I like the new hairdo?"

I led him to a blanket I'd spread on the grass under the shade of an ancient oak tree by the lake. It was a quiet spot off the beaten path. Tommy sat and opened the wine as I handed him paper cups from the picnic basket and put the wrapped sandwiches on paper plates.

"When I spoke with your grandfather, earlier in the week, he said you were visiting Hutch at Walter Reed. I assume that means he was wounded."

I really didn't want to talk about Hutch. I asked Tommy how his practice was going, anything to change the subject, but he wouldn't let it go.

"What kind of wound?"

"They put a metal plate and some screws in his leg where a bullet had shattered a bone."

"That sounds serious. Probably going to give him trouble his whole life."

As I sipped my wine, I asked about his parents, but no matter what I said, the conversation always came back to Hutch.

"How'd you find out he was injured?"

"His mother called me. Tommy can we please stop talking about Hutch?"

"Here, have some more wine, Maya. You seem really up tight. You know, I'm not stupid. This picnic is all about telling me he asked you to marry him, right? So why the charade?"

"I'm sorry, Tommy, this isn't going well."

"No, not well at all. Have you said yes?"

"I haven't said anything."

"Then, if you're waiting for me to ask you to marry me, you know that's always been my plan. You just weren't ready to hear me out. If you want a formal proposal, then Maya, will you marry me?"

I didn't know what to say. What was I thinking? The picnic was a really stupid idea.

"Look, Maya," Tommy said, as he poured more wine in his cup. "We've known each other since we were kids. I know your every mood, your every quirk, like when you bite your lower lip when you're deep in thought. I know blue is your favorite color, chocolate your favorite ice cream flavor. I know you better than you know yourself. We've been good friends. We get along well with each other. In my book, that's a prerequisite for a good marriage."

Tommy scooted over toward me and took my hand in his. "It's meant to be. In a few years, when my father retires, the whole practice will be mine. We'll build a nice house in town. You'll be near your family, near your Grandfather for the many years he has left. I may not be the most exciting guy in the world, but you know all about me. You know how I feel about you. I'll devote my life to seeing you're well taken care of."

I nodded. What could I say? Everything Tommy said was true.

"Your friend, Hutch, what do you really know about him? You've seen each other a few times and exchanged a bunch of letters, hardly enough to base your entire future on. Besides, where did you say he was from?"

"Colorado."

"That's way across the country. All your friends and family are here. Who knows, he might not look so interesting out of uniform. Romance lasts only so long, and medically speaking, I'd be worried about his health, not only the leg, but they're finding in some of the airmen, all the hours they spent at high altitudes is having an effect on their brain function. Look Maya, I don't expect your answer now. I'll give you a day or two to think it over, but I can't wait in limbo forever. I've been more than patient as it is."

"I know, Tommy. You're right. I can't believe how patient and understanding you've been. That's one of the things I love about you."

"Just remember, Maya, I'm the known factor. The steady guy you've known your whole life. You have no idea what you'd be letting yourself in for with the other guy. You'll have plenty to think about later, so for now let's enjoy the lunch, the wine and the afternoon.

Chapter 48

I found Grandpa at the barn grooming old Clipper. I sat on a bale of hay and watched like I used to do when I was a kid. "Tomorrow's Sunday, Grandpa. Can we have tea and cake in the afternoon? I still remember all the afternoons you'd tell me stories. I've missed our story time."

"Tea and cake it is. Like old times."

"Yes, like old times. I have some things to figure out before we meet. Thank you, Grandpa. See you tomorrow." I walked off making a mental list of all the things I wanted to talk to Grandpa about. Better yet, I thought, I'll make a real list. That way I won't forget anything.

Sunday afternoon I knocked on Grandpa's door and heard the familiar sound of, "Come in," just like I'd heard for so many years while growing up.

"So, Maya, you want to have a tea party," he said as he put aside the Sunday newspaper. "What shall we talk about? You have already heard all my stories."

"Don't tease me, Grandpa. Its only the biggest decision I've ever had to make in my life."

"Sit. I will pour the tea."

I watched as Grandpa went through the tea ritual I'd seen him perform so many times. If I married Hutch, our time together would come to an end. I took the glass from his suntanned hand, the skin drawn tight, the veins raised, brown spots of old age clearly visible. Where to begin?

"Tommy asked me to marry him yesterday and he said some things I hadn't thought about before."

"So what things might that be?"

"Well, how he knows all about me just as I know all about him. That marrying him would assure I remained near you, my parents, my friends, and the rest of our family. He was confident he could support me, and whatever family we had, in style. He said I know nothing about Hutch. It's all true, Grandpa. Hutch and I only spent a few days and a years' worth of letters getting to know one another."

"So."

"I know what Tommy says makes sense. Tommy is safe. A doctor makes a good living and Hutch has some crazy idea about running his family's cattle ranch, instead of joining his father as part of the family bank. Who knows if the ranch is a successful enterprise or not. I know enough about farming, and I'm sure the same holds true for ranching, to know it's not an easy life. It can be full of hard work and hard times."

"All you say is true, Maya."

"Grandpa, I've never even considered his possible health problems, which Tommy seems to think could be serious." I took a deep breath, trying to work up courage before I said, "Grandpa, can I ask you a very personal question, one I wouldn't dare ask my parents?"

"Ask."

"I know you and Grandma loved each other, but was there passion in that love?"

"Ah, what an interesting question, Maya." Grandpa took a long time to answer. "Truthfully, and I will answer only because it is an important question, yes, there was great passion to the very end."

"Did you speak a lot of love?"

"Why would we speak of love, child? What would have been the need? We lived our love every day."

I let his words sink in as I reached for the list in my pocket, careful as I unfolded it.

"What have you there, Maya?"

"Oh, it's a list of things I wanted to ask you."

"Child, that's not how you make a decision about love, marriage, and your future. Maybe if you were buying a refrigerator a list would help. But love, you listen only to your heart. That's where the answer lies. Not on items checked off a list. Your heart will give you the right answer."

"But don't you see, Grandpa, that's the problem. My heart is with Hutch. I get goose bumps when he kisses me. I'm excited and happy just to be with him. Tommy is comfortable, like an old shoe. He's always been my best friend, but they're no fireworks when he kisses me. Are goose bumps enough?"

I took a sip of my tea, lukewarm. Pushing the glass aside I said, "Did Grandma regret leaving her family behind?"

"Of course she did, but her life was bound up with me and later with her children, as well. In the beginning, coming to America was a difficult adjustment for her, as was the farm, but she came to love this place as I do. Just like I told you in my story."

"I'm worried about being so far away."

Grandpa laughed harder than I'd ever heard him. "Child, its Colorado, part of the United States. It's not an ocean away, not a foreign land with a foreign language. Your grandmother did not have a telephone, or an automobile. She could not fly across the country for a visit with family. She did quite well. You will do better."

I threw my arms around him. I loved him so dearly. "Thank you, Grandpa. You make everything seem so simple. I'll write to Hutch tonight and tell him how much I love him and my answer is yes, a thousand times yes. I'll deal with Tommy later.

Chapter 49

I made one more trip to see Hutch before he was discharged from the hospital. I took the early train planning on coming home the same day. I found Hutch in a large room, full of servicemen, some in wheel chairs, some in various stages of recovery, just hanging out. There was a card game going on in one corner. A dart game against the back wall.

It took a minute to spot Hutch. He was sitting in a chair dressed in pajamas and a bathrobe, a pair of crutches by his side. I heard a few low whistles as I walked toward him.

Leaning on his crutches, he stood and kissed me to the sound of more whistles.

"Quiet, you guys. Give the lady a little respect. She's my finance."

"Look at you, up and standing. You look so much better than the last time I saw you. How do you feel?"

"I feel great, now that you're here. What a surprise. You never wrote you were coming. Let's find a place away from all these guys where we can talk."

We found a quiet corner and pulled a couple of chairs close together.

"I got your letter with your answer. I let out such a yelp when I read it, my nurse ran over thinking there was something wrong. Nothing else mattered after that. You were mine."

Hutch reached over and took my hand. "I expect to be released in a few weeks. I don't want to wait to get married. I need you by my side. It shouldn't be to long before I'm discharged. There are plenty of guys who plan to stay in the Air Force when the war's over, so they won't need a gimp. Besides, I waited long enough to ask you to marry me. I don't want to be without you for even a day. I've thought of nothing else since I've been here."

"I must admit I've been scared thinking about moving so far away, driving my Grandfather crazy with questions, seeking his advice, but seeing you puts my fears to rest. All I want is to be with you. I don't care where we live. I've had enough of letter writing. If you're to be released soon, how does the first part of May sound for a wedding?"

"Sounds great, the sooner the better. I'll probably be sent home on leave for a few weeks and continue my rehab at Fitzsimmons Hospital in Denver before I report to my new assignment. Can you make all the plans without me?"

"My mother and Aunt Helen will be thrilled to be wedding planners again. But don't you have some idea of the kind of a wedding you want."

"Sure...short, sweet, and soon. Hell, I don't care about the details, I just want us to be married. Anything is okay with me."

"What about your mother? Shouldn't she be included in our plans?"

"Leave her out of it. Her ideas are far more extravagant than anything you or I would want. Just do what makes you happy. The only thing I need to know is when and where to show up."

We talked and laughed. I felt an excitement I'd not felt before. This was the man I was to marry. All my worries had gone up in smoke. I hated to leave, but it was time. The nurses and orderlies were readying everyone for dinner and I had a train to catch. We kissed goodbye. Hutch promised to telephone now that his new crutches allowed him freedom.

I settled in my seat on the train happier than any time I could remember. I was going to be Mrs. William Hutchinson very soon.

Hutch was discharged from the hospital the first part of April. The wound had healed well. He was doing the exercises his doctor prescribed. He would be reporting to Barksdale Field in Louisiana on limited duty. Hutch phoned almost every day and we set our wedding for the sixth of May.

I wanted to be married at the farm. Mother was Catholic, but I hadn't attended her church since I was a toddler. My father was Jewish, but he didn't attend services, and Hutch and his family were Episcopalians. The farm seemed the only neutral ground.

The weather in May should be perfect for an outdoor afternoon wedding. The house was way too small to hold everyone. The only thing casting a shadow on the whole affair was a conversation I walked in on between my parents. I knew the wedding was costing a lot of money, but they both assured me it's what they wanted. Never having had a real wedding themselves, they seemed to think it was important.

I was about to enter the kitchen when I heard Daddy saying, "Cora, stop worrying. Everything will be fine as long as I can keep my job at the factory. The war with Germany can't go on much longer, but who knows how long it will take to defeat Japan? It's only if they close the factory that we've got problems."

"What will we do if that happens, Jacob?"

"I figure if we sell off the hundred acres on the other side of the house, it should bring a good price. We'll be fine for a lot of years. The kids will be gone. Developers are snapping up land betting there will be a building boom when the troops return from overseas."

I raised my voice, something I'd never done to my parents before, as I walked into the room, "You can't do that, Daddy. It will break Grandpa's heart if you sell off some of the land. You know he loves every inch of the farm. Think how hard he worked to buy that land. The farm is his whole life. I can do without the fancy wedding if that's the problem."

"Maya, this is really none of your business, but your wedding is not a problem. Your mother and I are just trying to look ahead."

"Daddy, the land will always be valuable." I tried to lower my voice. Please, promise me you won't sell anything until after Grandpa dies. Promise me, please."

"I'll think about it. Besides, as long as the factory is open there's no problem." Now don't worry. You and your mother just go ahead with the wedding plans as if this conversation never took place. Was there something you wanted?"

"Yes. I wanted to ask if Grandma's old trunk is still in the attic."

"Probably. I don't remember anyone taking it down. Why?"

"I need something borrowed, something old, and something blue to wear at the wedding. I thought I'd see if there was anything in the trunk I could use."

"Well, be careful if you go up there. It's been years since anyone's been in the attic. Take a flashlight with you. The light bulbs have probably burned out."

I climbed to the third floor. All the bedroom doors were closed, their occupants moved on ages ago. Reaching for the cord hanging from the ceiling, I pulled as hard as I could. It took several tries before the steps dropped down. A rush of warm air hit me in the face. I climbed into the attic, its musty smell filling my nostrils. The attic was shaded in grey. The windows, clouded with grime let in only a little light. The sills covered by a layer of dust. Dead flies and cobwebs were everywhere.

I turned on the flashlight and scanned the area. An old crib and highchair stood in one corner, odd pieces of furniture stood stacked against the far wall. Then I saw the trunk hidden behind an old sofa, it was a lot bigger than I'd expected, but then Grandpa did say it had held down comforters, pillows and all Grandma's stuff.

I tried to dust off the top with some old newspapers I found, but it didn't help much. The trunk top was heavy. The hinges squeaked as I propped it open. I wondered what treasures I'd find inside. A sense of excitement came over me. This was really my grandmother's trunk. The one from Grandpa's stories. It was still in good condition after all the years it had been stored in the attic, having once traveled across the ocean. With care, I sorted through picture albums tucked in one corner, alongside letters tied together with ribbon, written in some foreign language. Odds and ends of baby clothes, a comforter and at the bottom of the trunk something wrapped in reams of tissue paper. It felt heavy as I carefully lifted it out. Lowering the top, I sat on the trunk and peeled back a corner of the tissue paper to see what it was protecting. I gasped as I realized it must be grandma's wedding gown. I hurried down the attic steps, the gown tucked under my arm, and rushed to my bedroom to unwrap my treasure.

As I peeled back the layers of tissue, I was amazed to see the condition the gown was in. The seed pearls were still stitched in place. The gown itself had not yellowed with age, though it smelled a little musty. I grabbed a hanger from the closet and hung it on the back of the closet door. The gown looked as if it might just fit. I ran downstairs to find my mother.

Mother carefully examined the dress. She was sure the stale smell could be removed, but she worried it might begin to disintegrate exposed to the air. "You'd better ask your grandfather if it's alright with him if you wear the gown, but wouldn't you rather have something new. Something of your own?"

I knew Grandpa wouldn't mind, and as I expected, he was overjoyed as he reminded me it was really my great grandmother's wedding gown. I'd be the third bride to wear the dress. The gown was like a thread that tied me to my grandmother. I hoped it would bring me the love and devotion that it brought her.

Chapter 50

The days flew by until it was almost May sixth. I was rushing to get the last details completed. Hutch was arriving Friday afternoon from Louisiana, his parents and sister, were arriving Friday evening. They'd invited our family for dinner at the Banker's Club in downtown Hartford on Saturday.

I still had to pack and get everything done before the ceremony on Sunday.

Mommy and I had been busy shopping for my trousseau. Now we both needed special dresses for Saturday night, which meant another rushed trip to Hartford. We went from shop to shop, but there wasn't much of a selection. Women's fashions weren't a high priority during the war. There were restrictions on the amount of material that could be used.

Mommy found a grey crepe dress that fell a discrete distance below her knees. It had a peplum and shoulder pads. She thought it was a little extreme, but I convinced her it was perfect, just the right look for her. I still hadn't found anything appropriate.

Our last stop was at G. Fox and Company on Main Street. As luck would have it, I found my dream outfit. I tried on the navy, light wool, slim skirt with a high-cinched waist. Two rows of small brass buttons graced the short double-breasted jacket of the same material. A white silk blouse went beneath the jacket. I viewed my image in the dressing room mirror. Wow. I loved the look. Only the price, twenty-two dollars and ninety-five cents, was way more than I'd expected to spend. I tried on the few less expensive dresses they had in size two, but only the navy blue outfit would do. I wanted to look my very best to meet Hutch's father and sister for the first time.

We arrived home from our shopping trip just in time for me to pick up Hutch at Bradley Field. I watched as he walked toward me, the crutches having been replaced by a cane. I noticed a slight limp as he hurried toward me. He put down his suitcase case grabbed me in his arms and with passion kissed me. We hurried to the car. I couldn't stop talking, I was so excited to see him.

"Slow down, sweetheart. I'm not going anywhere."

"I can't. There's so much to tell you."

"You've got the rest of our lives to tell me. Let me look at you. God, you get more beautiful every day. I can't wait until Sunday."

"Neither can I. And may I say you look very distinguished with your cane."

"I was hoping you'd say sexy, but I guess distinguished will have to do. I'm staying at the hotel in Hartford with my folks. Why don't we drive there and wait for them."

I was on my way home after dark. I left before Hutch's parents arrived. I was too nervous to spend time with them and I still had a million things to do at home. Saturday evening would be time enough to visit with them.

We were to arrive at the Banker's Club at seven. It would be a rush even if Daddy got home from the factory on time. He was still working a six-day week.

The Banker's Club was on the top floor of the tallest building in town. I'd read about parties held there in the society column, never expecting to visit the place myself. As we rode up in the elevator, Daddy remarked he hoped they'd let him in the door. The club was restricted. Jews were not allowed to be members in many such clubs, nor buy homes in so called restricted neighborhoods.

The elevator doors opened revealing a large foyer with a spectacular view of downtown Hartford. A printed sign on a metal stand indicated Hutchinson party in the executive suite with an arrow pointing left.

The doors of the suite were open, the room set with a long U shaped table draped in a white cloth, with white candles and large floral arrangements. Mr. and Mrs. Hutchinson were standing just inside the door with their daughter Elizabeth, Hutch's sister. Hutch was standing by their side.

He walked toward me, took my hand and introduced me to his father, William. I'd forgotten Hutch was a junior. His father greeted me with a smile and a kiss on the cheek. He was a tall, greying, impressive looking man. I noticed the tailoring and material of his suit. Daddy and Grandpa's suits looked shabby by comparison. Mrs. Hutchinson, Patricia, kissed me as well, saying how glad she was to see me again, especially on such a happy occasion. She looked lovely. The high-necked, long sleeved pastel pink gown with its pleated skirt looked like it was right out of Vogue. I met Elizabeth, who seemed rather aloof. The green lace gown she wore matched the color of her eyes, and looked very expensive.

I suddenly felt out of place. My navy blue outfit seemed too casual for the event. The Hutchinson women were wearing what I would call fancy cocktail gowns. It was obvious Trinity was not Denver and I was not high society.

Introductions over, Hutch took me by the hand leading me to the balcony, and pushed open the French doors. As soon as we stepped outside, he reached for me, holding me in his arms.

"I missed you all day. I could hardly wait for evening. One more night then I'm never letting you out of my sight again. He stepped back a bit and said, "You look like a million bucks."

"I feel so out of place. Your mother and sister look so elegant."

"Don't pay any attention to them. You suit me just fine."

"I think we'd better go back inside. I don't want to abandon my family."

I stood with Hutch in the receiving line as the rest of my family arrived. The Hutchinson's greeted my uncles and their wives, Sofia and Archie, although it seemed more like a duty they were preforming because it was the socially accepted thing to do.

Dinner was special. The food and service was unlike anything I'd experienced. A different wine with every course. A whole new world was opening up. I wasn't sure how I'd fit in.

Mr. Hutchinson tried to engage my father in conversation. I felt sorry for Daddy. He wasn't much of a conversationalist at best, certainly not up on world affairs or economics. He was, after all, a farmer turned factory employee. I shouldn't have been surprised when Grandpa voiced his opinion. He and Mr. Hutchinson carried on a long conversation about what we could expect from Russia when the war was over.

I watched as the two men engaged in world politics, loving that Grandpa stood his ground, not the least bit cowed by the banker. I knew he felt being a large landowner gave him status if not wealth. My uncles, all educated men, seemed quite comfortable partaking in the discussions.

The evening ended with everyone looking forward to tomorrow. No one more than me.

Chapter 51

I awoke early. Who could sleep the night before their wedding? I needed a cup of coffee. I found Grandpa sitting at the table.

"Good morning, Maya. Ready for the big day?"

"Ready, but concerned about going off and leaving you and my parents behind. You're my support system. How will I get along without you? I've never really been on my own before."

"You will do just fine my little sparrow. You are ready to leave the nest, to test your wings. You and your husband will build a life together. Like the sparrow tests its wings and finds it can fly, the more you test yourself the stronger you will become."

"I'm sure your right, but there are just so many if's that worry me."

"So, don't you suppose your groom is worried as well? Be happy, stop looking for things to worry about."

"But I won't be able to have tea and cake anymore. I'll miss you so much, Grandpa," I said as I threw my arms around him. "What will I do if I need to discuss something with you?"

"You will send me a letter, child. I'm sure brides throughout the ages felt concerns just like you do. They managed and so will you."

"I love you, Grandpa. I'll miss you."

"Not as much as I will miss you. Now finish your coffee and run along. Get ready for the most important day of your life."

The wedding went off without a hitch thanks to my Mother and Aunt Helen's attention to detail. The weather cooperated, a perfect May afternoon, warm, windless, the fields green and too early for pesky flies. The guests were seated in white high-backed chairs set in rows on the freshly mowed field in front of the house. Everyone came dressed in their summer finery.

A green felt runner led from the front door, down the steps, ending at the flower covered canopy, my nod to Jewish tradition. I was half Jewish, half Catholic, about to be married by a Methodist minister to an Episcopalian. God Bless America, as my grandfather would say.

We exchanged our vows with Hutch's mother, father, and sister in attendance. His younger brother, Phillip, was on a ship somewhere in the Pacific, as was my brother, Billy. Three of my uncles and their families, Sofia and her husband, Tommy and his parents, and all my friends were there as well.

Grandpa escorted Mother to her seat just before my father walked me down the aisle to the sound of the wedding march. I heard Grandpa gasp as I passed by dressed in the beautiful gown my Grandmother was married in and wearing the bracelet Grandpa had given her all those years ago. Tears filled Grandpa's eyes, the words, my Miriam, were on his lips.

The ceremony concluded just as we had planned. Hutch kissed his bride as a glass was placed under his foot to be broken, the final nod to Jewish tradition I hoped would bring with it the same happiness my grandparents had enjoyed. This was hardly the wedding Hutch's parents had expected their son to be a part of, but they were understanding, though I felt they were a little uncomfortable throughout the ceremony, which was absent of the usual religious content.

The late afternoon reception was held at one of the newer hotels in town. My parents outdid themselves. Everything was perfect. We slipped away, early, to catch a train for New York where we would honeymoon for two days before Hutch had to return to duty.

I felt a sense of unease during the train ride. Excited, of course that I was now Mrs. William Hutchinson, but nervous thinking about our first night together. I wanted to please Hutch. Wanted everything to be perfect, but I had no idea what would be expected of me. There were so many things I didn't know. Things I couldn't ask Grandpa. Things I never discussed with my mother. She never mentioned our wedding night even when she helped me choose a nightgown as part of my trousseau. She seemed uncomfortable with anything related to sex. The book I checked out of the library was clinical. It detailed things I already knew, not what I needed to know.

Hutch took my hand in his. "Honey, you seem a million miles away. What are you thinking?"

"Nothing important. Maybe just a little overwhelmed."

I'm sure every bride is positive she made the right choice. If I allowed myself to admit the truth, I knew from the very first moment when Hutch asked me to dance that night in the canteen, he was the one.

Our wedding night was the first time I saw the extent of his injury. The long scar was still slightly red and angry looking. I couldn't imagine the pain he'd gone through, or know the pain he would continue to suffer, but this night was all about making love to each other.

Happily my fears were for naught. When Hutch took me in his arms telling me how long he'd dreamed of this moment I knew I should have realized he'd be the perfect lover. The joy I felt in that beautiful flush of passion, as our two souls became one, will stay with me forever. Nothing else in the world matters except Hutch.

We had a whole day to explore New York before it was time to leave for the air base. Hutch was surprised that number one on my list of things to see was Ellis Island, but he was happy to humor me as long as I promised another night of lovemaking. Why would I find that a problem? I promised. Reminding him once again I always keep my promises.

"Then promise me you'll throw away the damn nightgown."

The next morning, the eighth of May, found us in the middle of downtown New York as the city went crazy with the announcement of Germany's surrender. Masses of people crowded onto the streets to express their sheer joy at the first signs of the war's end. Peace was now in sight. There was hugging, kissing, singing, dancing in the streets, flag waving by more people than I'd seen in one place in my whole life. Hutch was laughing with tears of joy in his eyes, knowing his buddies would be safe. The bombing of Germany was over.

Chapter 52

A cramped studio apartment outside the airbase in Bossier, Louisiana, awaited us. We weren't there a full month before Hutch was discharged from the Army. They wouldn't be training a lot of new airman. He'd heard there was a plan to quickly end the war with Japan.

We returned to Denver to stay in the large brick house belonging to Hutch's family, much grander than my house, for sure, and even grander than I had expected. I realized Hutch's family must be well off, but he never let on about the kind of wealth he grew up with. Hutch's mother was delighted to have her son home and wanted to hold a reception in our honor. She insisted upon taking me shopping. She wanted to purchase the perfect dress for me to wear for the party. It was obvious my clothes were inadequate for the occasion. She didn't want to be embarrassed in front of her friends and family.

I met all of the extended family, the friends, and the business associates of Hutch's father, wearing a one-of-a-kind designer gown in pale green silk, from Denver's finest woman's shop, that showed off every curve in my body. It cost more than I earned in months at the plant. My hair had been newly styled, and I had my first manicure at the upscale beauty salon patronized by Hutch's mother and sister.

Hutch's friends and family were all very welcoming, although I did get a few chilly greetings from several of the young single females.

Hutch never left my side, telling me to relax. "You're the most beautiful female here. Check out the glances from my male friends. They're damn envious, but truth be told I like the real you better than my mother's creation."

We talked for days about our future as Hutch showed me the sights of Denver. Hutch was more determined than ever to settle on the family cattle ranch. His father was disappointed. He always expected his son to join him at the bank his grandfather had founded before the turn of the century. Hutch and his father engaged in many heated discussions that turned into arguments in his father's library. They went at it for days.

I overheard his father say how foolish it was to throw away his education, his chance for a well-paying, prestigious position to chase after some childhood fantasy about being a cattle rancher. "You have a wife now, William. You need to concern yourself with providing for her and the children I expect will be in your future. The ranch is hardly the place I would expect you to take your bride."

His mother pleaded with me to talk some sense into Hutch after both she and his father had failed.

The talks continued, sometimes becoming shouting matches, as Hutch wouldn't give an inch. The family gave in to what he wanted. Coming to an agreement. If, after five years, Hutch still wanted to remain on the ranch, and if he succeeded in making the ranch a profitable enterprise, his father would deed the property to him free and clear.

The die was cast. A few days later we set off for the ranch, our new home, in a new 250 Ford truck. The truck bed piled high with our belongings. In a way, I was glad to be leaving. Maybe after a while, I would learn to fit into Denver's high society, but for now, I felt uncomfortable and ill at ease with the Hutchinson's life style.

Once we were underway, I couldn't help but ask Hutch the question that had been bothering me ever since our arrival in Denver. "Hutch I'm confused. Why me?"

"What do you mean, why me?"

"Well, with all the beautiful, wealthy, sophisticated young women you grew up with, why would you pick me? I can't begin to compete with their looks and charm, or their dowry."

"Sweetheart, you've got them beat in every way. That first night at the canteen, I couldn't keep my eyes off of you. You were the prettiest girl I'd ever seen. More important, you seemed real, and the Sunday I spent with you and you're family, I could see how you were brought up. Your family was unpretentious, down to earth hardworking people. They welcomed me into their home, never once trying to impress me with how much money they had or how important they were like some of my father's friends. Nor were they interested in my station in life. Those party girls I grew up with were fun to drink with and fool around with, but they're a bunch of phonies. Proper pedigrees, but no perception of what life is really about. I never thought about marrying any one of them. It's you I fell in love with, you I wanted, and you I was lucky enough to marry."

All during the drive, Hutch kept telling me how beautiful the ranch was, how peaceful. "It's just like heaven on earth."

My first view of the countryside was breathtaking with its vast expanses of open land, pastures, trees, meandering streams, and mountains, without a house or town for miles, so different from Connecticut. I asked about the mountains, and was told they were the *Sangre de Cristo* range, part of the Rocky Mountains. When we reached the eastern plains, Hutch said, "It's just a little further to the ranch."

We'd driven about two hours before turning off the main highway. We drove along a fenced dirt road stopping in front of double gates straddling a cattle guard with the Double H brand in large metal letters arched over the entrance,

As we drove down the gravel road, I expected to see a farmhouse at the end, like home. But no house came into view. Off to the left, was a log cabin, and beyond, a long wooden structure Hutch said was the bunkhouse. There were pens and shoots, a large horse barn and fenced areas all around.

"Here we are," Hutch said, as he parked in front of the log cabin.

"Where's the house, Hutch?"

"The cabin is ours for the near future. Hank, the foreman has lived here forever, but he's game to stay in the bunkhouse until he retires. It may need some fixing up, but we'll be fine. I promise you later I'll show you the perfect place to build our house, but just look around. Have you ever seen anything prettier in your whole life?

This was hardly what I'd expected from the glowing description Hutch had laid out. I realized what his father meant when he questioned bringing his new bride to the ranch.

"I've got great plans for the future, sweetheart. This is going to be a showplace before I'm through, trust me."

The look on Hutch's face, the gleam in his eye, reminded me of Grandpa telling me about his dream of one day owning a farm.

I stepped up onto the wide, well-worn, wooden planks that made up the porch and followed Hutch into the log cabin. The room was dark. I saw only a few small windows to let in the sunshine. The smell of stale tobacco and beer was overwhelming telling me no woman had ever lived here. Hutch saw the expression on my face.

"Honey, we can fix this up, and I promise it's only temporary. We'll figure out what we need for a few days and go shopping in town. Just wait till tomorrow. We'll take a couple of horses and I'll show you the ranch, all thirty-six hundred acres of it. Then you'll see what I mean."

I walked through the living room thinking the antlered deer head over the fireplace had to go. The bedroom and bathroom were every bit as off putting as the living room. I made mental notes, as I went along -- new bed, new shower curtain, cleaning supplies. The refrigerator had been emptied, but the freezer was full of packages marked deer, rabbit, beef. After looking around, I understood why Hutch suggested we leave the beautiful silver and crystal wedding presents at his mother's house for safekeeping.

Driving to the nearest big town, well over thirty miles away, we started to purchase the things on our list, but the stores closed before we'd finished. We stayed the night at the local hotel, which must have been at least a hundred years old. We headed back to the ranch the following morning, the truck bed full of our newly purchased items. Hutch unloaded all the packages, while I put the food in the refrigerator. We set up the new box springs and mattress and made the bed with the beautiful linens we'd received as wedding presents. Satisfied with our accomplishments, we flopped down on the old leather sofa to catch our breath.

No more than five minutes had passed when Hutch was up, itching to go. "Let's pack a lunch," he said. "Then I'll saddle up a couple of horses. I can't wait to show you the ranch."

He was like a kid with a new toy. Instead of starting the massive cleanup job the cabin was in need of, I found myself putting on a pair of Hutch's jeans, several sizes too big, rolling up the cuffs, and putting on my tennis shoes. I soon learned that tennis shoes were a no no.

We rode for about fifteen minutes before we came upon the first sighting of cattle, deep in tall grass. All but the babies carried the double H brand on their hips. Hutch was talking a mile a minute. There it was again, the same expression on his face that hit home. The same look, the pride of ownership Grandpa got when he spoke of the farm. I was just beginning to understand his love for the ranch. It represented some special need for him. Would I be living a modern day version of my Grandparent's story?

Stopping by one of the creeks that ran through the property, Hutch hobbled the horses so they could graze and not run off, then took our lunch out of his saddlebags. He placed the beer to cool in the water on the edge of the creek, and we sat on the grass while he told me more of his plans.

"I hope you're not too disappointed in the cabin. I have to admit I had no idea it was so primitive. I haven't been to the ranch since I was a kid and spent summers here. Maybe I romanticized it a bit, but all I could think of during the war was getting back to you and bringing you here. The life I led in Denver, before I went overseas, had no relevance once I watched my buddy's' planes shot down or explode in mid-air. Life took on a whole new meaning when the guy I joked with, played poker with the night before, was carried off a plane, his body riddled with bullet holes, or when I tried to stop the bleeding and ease the pain of one of my crew hoping to keep him alive until we landed, that's when I began to think about what I wanted out of life and Maya, this is it."

I watched as pain registered on Hutch's face when he mounted his horse, he made no mention of his leg. As we rode back to the cabin, Hutch pointed out improvements he wanted to make. He led the way to a treed-rise overlooking the creek. "This is where we'll build our house. Feel the slight breeze? The trees will provide shade and we can see across acres of pasture. I promise you, in a few years, I'll build you the house of your dreams. Look at this like an adventure, sweetheart. If adventures were easy, everyone would be an adventurer. If we take the chance and work hard, we can reap the rewards. All I need to know is that you're with me."

I was beginning to feel better. It might be a little rough in the beginning, but I knew he'd make good on his promise. "I love the site. It'll be perfect for our house."

We arrived back at the barn just in time to see four riders approaching. As they came closer, Hutch said it was Hank, the foreman, and three cowboys Hutch didn't know.

"Well, if it ain't little Hutch," Hank said. "All growed up, home from the war, married and everything. Hutch introduced me. Hank dismounted and took the reins of my horse. "Welcome Ma'am. I'll put the mare up for you."

He turned toward Hutch and said, "How long you and the misses planning on visitin'?"

"I thought my father made it clear, Hank. Maya and I are here to stay. I plan on taking over the management of the ranch, with you running it, for as long as you want to stay."

I noticed a disturbed look on Hank's face. Hutch continued. "I've been working on plans for some big improvements."

Hank didn't respond, just turned and introduced us to the three cowboys, Tex, Chet, and Buzz who was holding on to Hank's horse.

I could see I hadn't made much of an impression in my borrowed jeans and tennis shoes as I climbed down off the saddle.

That night, as Hutch made love to me, I began to feel at home. If my grandmother could handle tougher circumstances, I'd be fine. I had the man I loved beside me.

As time went by, I found I had a lot to learn about the hardships two green horns would encounter in the cattle business.

Before I dropped off to sleep, still aglow from our love making, I said, "I've been thinking about our new house. You have to promise me something."

"I'll promise you anything you want sweetheart."

"Just promise me a rose garden."

Hutch rolled over on his back. "I'd have promised you the moon if that's what you wanted, but I must admit you're a funny little thing. I'd imagine after an evening of amazing sex, you'd say, I love you my darling, or you're a perfect lover, not promise me a rose garden."

"I do love you, my darling, and you are the perfect lover, but a rose garden is important. I'll explain on another day, but for now, goodnight and sweet dreams." I rolled over on my side as Hutch snuggled up to me, his arm resting around my waist. This must be heaven.

Chapter 53

Our days were busy. Hank left after a month. He'd been in charge for so long, he found it hard to take orders or even suggestions from Hutch. Thank heaven the three hands stayed on.

I scrubbed every bit of the cabin, adding curtains and pillows, and a few new pieces of furniture. It made a cozy nest for the two of us.

I was working harder than I ever had. We scrimped and saved every penny, knowing that we had to keep the ranch in the black. I added Levi's, boots, and warm jackets to my wardrobe. While the winters were what the locals called mild, though not nearly as harsh as Connecticut, there was still plenty of snow and freezing nights. The cabin had no heat, only the fireplace to keep us warm.

Hutch was bound and determined to master every aspect of the operation of the ranch. He worked long hours alongside the ranch hands coming home so tired most nights he had trouble staying awake through dinner. He'd kiss me goodnight and fall exhausted into bed. I could see his leg was bothering him, though he never complained.

Winter made no difference in the routine. The cattle still had to be checked. If the ground was frozen, the pasture dead or dying, the hay we grew in the summer had to be trucked to different locations on the ranch for the cattle to feed on. Since Hutch left early every morning, I would spent my days alone, waiting for his return only to find him too tired to be much company in the evening. I was getting discouraged.

I wrote to Grandpa often telling him how much I missed him and missed having someone to talk to about my feelings. How I wasn't sure I could handle five years under our present circumstances. I was lonesome and a little homesick, tired of spending the long days alone with little to occupy my time.

Grandpa wrote back, his letters on lined paper with carefully written script. I opened the envelope and started to read what he'd written.

Dear Maya,

> *I miss you as well, but your wedding picture in the parlor fills me with happiness, you in Mama's beautiful gown standing beside your handsome husband in his dress uniform. I am disturbed when you say you have no one to talk to about you feelings. Child, you are married to the one person in the world who holds your happiness above his*

> own. Your husband is wise beyond his years. He learned much from his war experiences having nothing to do with killing. Talk to him. Speak of your feelings. Trust him as your friend as well as your lover.

I read his letter hoping I could bring myself to tell Hutch how difficult the adjustment was for me. I realized how ill equipped I was to deal with my new responsibilities and how lonesome It was when he and the hands were off tending the cattle. The nights they didn't return camping out somewhere in the far reaches of the ranch were the worst.

Time passed and I said nothing. I never could find the right time. Hutch seemed so happy even though at times the deck seemed stacked against him. I wrote to Grandpa telling him again I wasn't sure I could make five years under the present circumstances. I didn't know life could be so hard. I felt the whole world was against Hutch's succeeding and I really needed an Olga.

About two weeks later, I saw an envelope in our mailbox. David Freeman in the upper left hand corner, his return address in his careful script told me it was an answer from Grandpa.

Having torn open the flap, I pulled out the letter surprised by the first sentence which read,

> Do you love your husband, yes or no? If the answer is no, then pack your things and come home. If the answer is yes then quit your whining. Hutch told you about his dream. He does not care if the whole world is against him as long as you are with him.

I could feel the tears start to run down my cheeks. I missed Grandpa so much. He always put me on the right path. I read on.

> Your grandmother had never had a chore before she married me. Not only did she survive the ocean voyage, she carried two babies up and down three flights of stairs and had no bathroom. I watched, in despair, as her beautiful hands reddened from scrubbing clothes, her nails cracked and broken. She never complained. She loved me and believed in my promise to her. If she could withstand five years in an attic with two babies, you can stand the same five years. As for an Olga, you have one. Her name is Cora and she is your mother. Pick up the phone and ask for her help. So stop your complaining, stop acting like a spoiled

child. Become the strong woman, the loving wife I know you can be, dear Maya. Help your husband. He needs your love and support. You are smart. Be brave. You can do it. Make his dream your dream. Work with him and all will be well.

I put the letter away, dried my tears, and ran outside, I needed to find Hutch. I had been acting like a spoiled child. As I headed toward the barn, I saw his truck come down the road. He stopped and I got in.

"What's up, sweetheart?"

"I need to talk to you. We have some things to discuss."

"Sure. I know just the place for a long talk." He started the engine and drove to an area of the ranch I hadn't seen before. Opening the truck door, he grabbed a blanket from the back and motioned me to follow.

We walked to a small secluded glen hidden by a copes of pine trees alongside the creek. He laid the blanket on the deep grass and stretched out. "Come sit by me. Now what is it you want to talk about?"

"I wanted to tell you how much I love you."

"I've never doubted that, but it does seem things have gotten a little off track. We haven't had much time for each other in a while. I admit I've been working hard coming home tired, but you've been rather aloof, lately."

"That's what I want to talk about. I've had a lot of things I had to think through about us."

"And?"

"And I've finally got everything sorted out."

Hutch rolled over on his side reaching for my hand, his lips brushing my fingers.

"I know I want what you want. If you tell me you plan to grow oranges in Tanzania, I'll be there helping you plant the trees. I know how much the ranch means to you and I'm going to be here by your side for as long as it takes to make your dreams come true. They're my dreams, too."

"That's music to my ears. I've been worried that you weren't happy here. I'd give it all up, Maya, before I chanced losing you. But what brought about the sudden change?"

"I received an answer to a letter I'd written Grandpa. He's such a wise old man and he knows me so well. He made me see things in a different light."

"I've missed you," Hutch said, as he began to unbutton my blouse. "I promise to put things in a better perspective, to be a better husband. Then he whispered, "Thank God for Grandpa."

As he lay on top of me and kissed me.

"Not here, Hutch."

"What better place?"

I had never experienced anything to equal that afternoon's love making. The sweet smell of the grass, the ripple of water flowing along the creek, the sound of cattle in the distance, I felt as if we'd bonded with the land beneath us. Our land.

All our troubles melted away that afternoon. Never again would there be anything but joy between us. No problem we couldn't resolve. I didn't think it was possible to love anyone as I loved Hutch. As Grandpa would say, we lived our love.

While the going was hard at times and there were days when the cards seemed stacked against us, we never faced the uncertainty that my grandfather did. There was never a mortgage payment to make, never a concern that failure would throw us out on the street penniless with no place to go. Yes, failure would be hard for Hutch to live with, his father would gladly welcome him back and a prominent place in the bank would be his.

Every day I gained greater respect for the hurdles my Grandfather had to overcome to keep a roof over his family's head, food on the table, and provide for the needs of a wife and five boys. My problems paled by comparison.

From that day on, I wrote to Grandpa once a week, filling my letters with happenings at the ranch and sending pictures. He loved the picture of me in my Levi's, boots, vest, winter jacket and Stetson. He answered every one. I was becoming a pretty good ranch hand. Instead of being left home alone, I took Grandpa's advice and rode along to check the herd or drove the truck carrying supplies, camping out if we rode too far to make it back home before dark. The hands didn't seem to mind my coming along. I think they preferred my cooking.

Grandpa especially liked my letter in the spring telling him how I helped with the ear tagging, shots, branding, and the castrating of the calves.

The event was quite a production, unlike anything I'd ever seen before. I grew up with a small dairy herd not a thousand head of beef cattle. Our neighbor, Jim Holliday and his ranch hands came to help. They branded the young stock on the left hip with the H bar H that had been the ranch's brand since the 1890s. After receiving inoculations, the youngsters were turned loose and the hungry, dirty bunch of men, their job finished, grabbed cold beer out of a tub of ice, waiting for Hutch to barbeque steaks and rocky mountain oysters as Annie Holliday and I brought out enough food to feed an army. We did the same ritual the following week at the Holliday's ranch.

Tommy was right. There were a lot of things about Hutch I didn't know. Contrary to what Tommy suggested, what I was learning about my husband was how very special he was.

Once I started to follow Grandpa's suggestions, our life couldn't have been happier. I talked to him about my feelings and he listened, making things right when he could.

Hutch was so excited that summer when, after the many discussions we had about starting our family, I became pregnant. I wrote to Grandpa with the news as soon as I was sure, and his answer was full of joy.

Then came the phone call from my father telling me Grandpa was in the hospital and it didn't look good. "If you want to say goodbye, Maya, you'd better hurry home."

"What happened, Daddy?'

"Yesterday morning, when your grandfather didn't show up for breakfast I checked his room, but he wasn't there. I thought he might have gotten a late start delivering his morning rose to your grandmother's grave, so I went looking for him. I found him lying on the ground almost at the top of the hill, the rose still clutched in his hand. He'd suffered a massive stroke. We honored his wishes, Maya, so he isn't on any life support system. The Doctor's say it's just a matter of time. There's nothing more they can do."

I tried to speak through the tears. "We'll fly out today. I don't know what I'll do without him, Daddy."

"I know baby, we all thought he was indestructible. Call and I'll pick you up at the airport."

Hutch and I flew home on the next fight, but we were too late. Grandpa died just hours before we arrived. Maybe that was a blessing. I would always remember him as the strong, proud man who shaped my childhood and served as my role model. How lucky I was. Every kid should have a grandfather like mine.

The funeral was to be the next day at the farm. Grandpa's wishes were to be buried in the plot next to Grandma's.

Early in the afternoon, the hearse arrived. It stopped short of the hill, and Benjamin, Richard, Daniel, Sofia's husband Archie, Hutch, and my father carried the coffin up the hill and lowered it into the grave.

The Rabbi started to speak, but his words were lost to me for I was in a different place. Once again, the little girl with a sugar cube clinched between her front teeth listening awestruck to her beloved grandfather's tales.

I was brought back to reality, as Hutch put his arm around me whispering, "Are you alright, sweetheart."

The simple service Grandpa would have wanted was over. He'd spend eternity where he wished to be, on his land, next to his beloved Miriam.

When it was my turn, Hutch helped me place a small amount of dirt on the shovel and drop in onto the coffin as I cried my heart out. So much of my childhood was tied up in him. I knew more about my grandfather then his own sons. He was the one I went to for advice. I dearly loved him and now he was gone.

We walked back to the house to find it overflowing with people. All the family was gathered in the parlor. I shouldn't have been surprised by the large number of friends and neighbors who dropped by to pay their respects to my Grandpa, the Jewish immigrant, who vehemently proclaimed he'd immigrated from the Ukraine, but he wasn't a Russian. My Grandfather who had gained the love and respect of the whole community.

I spent as much time as I could with the family. It had been almost three years since I'd left home. Everyone expressed great excitement about the baby I was carrying. I glanced at my watch--almost time to leave for the airport. I needed to find Hutch. I found him on the front porch deep in conversation with a group of men I didn't know.

"Hutch," I said. "Can I drag you away? It's almost time to leave and we have one last thing to do before we go."

"Sure," he said, as he excused himself and followed me out the door. I stopped by the rose garden and borrowed Hutch's Swiss Army knife to cut two perfect red roses and started toward the hill.

"Where are you going, Sweetheart?"

"To Grandpa's grave."

"We were just there. I don't want you getting tired walking up that steep hill, again."

"Please, I'm not tired. There is one last thing I need to do. I can rest on the plane." Hutch knew better than to argue when I made up my mind.

I opened the gate in the picket fence and handed Hutch one of the red roses. "This is for you to leave for my Grandpa. We owe him a great debt."

"How so?"

"If it weren't for his guidance, I might not have had the courage to listen to my heart. I might have taken the safe choice rather than saying yes to you."

I watched as Hutch dropped the rose atop the casket.

"If it weren't for Grandpa telling me wonderful stories about his and Grandma's journey to America, his love of the land, and all of my grandmother's struggles adapting to farm life, I might never have understood your needs or my role as your wife. Nor would I have recognized or understood the true meaning of love."

I put my rose on my grandmother's grave and heard Hutch say, "Thank you old man. She's all that matters in my life."

We walked down the hill hand-in-hand as I said, "If it's a boy can we name him David?"

Chapter 54

David was born four months later, And Janey two years after that. I thought of my Grandpa and his life story often as we struggled those first years of our marriage, scrimping, saving every penny we could to make the necessary improvements on the ranch. Grandpa's stories helped me get through the hard times and relish the good ones. Our cabin had been small for the two of us, but now two babies had been added to the overcrowded space.

Hutch's mother begged him to return to Denver and join his father and brother at the bank. She was upset with our living conditions, especially now that our household included two young children.

"William, what are you thinking?" she said. "You're not providing the proper conditions under which I expect my grandchildren to be raised. That is not how you were brought up."

When that didn't work, she tried pressuring me. I didn't need anyone to tell me Hutch was working hard, had lost weight, nor did I doubt for a moment his determination to make his dream come true. Something had changed him during the war. The ranch was his salvation. Far be it for me to challenge his reasons or his dream. I was happy just being with him. His dreams had become my dreams. Maybe someday his mother would understand.

The five years passed and true to his word, Hutch's father deeded the ranch to him. His brother would receive the bank.

We'd saved every penny of the quarterly dividends Hutch's stock in the bank provided, and with our debt-free ownership of the ranch, we could take out a loan to build our house -- two stories, five bedrooms and four bathrooms, more perfect than I'd dreamed, along with the beautiful rose garden Hutch planted for me once he'd heard the story.

I cried tears of joy when Hutch handed me the first blossom repeating Grandpa's utterance that every rose was a symbol of his love for me.

My mother sent an article from the local newspaper announcing Tommy's engagement to the Trinity elementary school's kindergarten teacher. We received an invitation to the wedding and over the years announcements of the birth of their two daughters. I hoped Tommy was happy. His friendship was such an important part of my growing up.

Hutch finished the book, which he first spoke of the day of my visit to Walter Reed Hospital. The true story was published, remaining on the New York Times best-selling non-fiction list for years.

My parents came for a visit. I know they were overwhelmed with what they saw. Mother loved the house, especially the kitchen. Daddy gained new respect for Hutch when he saw the extent of the land, the number of cattle, and the complexity of the operation.

"This place makes the farm seem like child's play," Daddy said at dinner, having spent the whole day riding around the ranch with Hutch.

I never asked if they'd sold part of the farm. I didn't want to know.

The ranch prospered way beyond our wildest dreams. All the hard work paid off, and our family increased by two, Christopher and Molly. We figured as long as we had already produced the two smartest and handsomest children in the world, we should have two more.

Hutch served on the county council and held an influential position in the Cattleman's Association. He'd read book upon book as well as every article he could get his hands on always looking for ways to improve the production. He wrote letters to Senators and Congressman and testified before committees regarding protection of the rights of ranchers and the need to continue their ability to lease land from the government's bureau of land management

We spent every Thanksgiving and Christmas with Hutch's family in Denver. Hutch's mother had mellowed some now that we had a proper house in which to raise our family, although she abhorred, that we lived in the middle of nowhere. His brother, Philip, was now vice president of the bank. He and his wife Glenda, the only child of a wealthy Colorado mining family, lived in a lovely house in the most fashionable section of Denver, as pretentious as his parents, with a full staff. They moved in the upper reaches of Denver society. I asked Hutch if he ever regretted his choice, although I knew the answer, I never regretted it. We had wonderful friends and neighbors, honest down to earth, hardworking people. None of the phony airs of sophistication of some the people Hutch grew up with.

Our kids had a special place to grow up. They had farm chores just as I did as a kid. They were learning responsibility, and independence unlike Phillip's children, who had everything handed to them on a silver platter.

Each year on the Fourth of July, the whole family came to the ranch for a barbeque and swim party. Philip's children as well as Hutch's sister Elizabeth's children, loved coming to the ranch. As they grew older, they came for summer visits without their parents. They enjoyed the freedom the ranch allowed. The cousins were very close, but our kids were never interested in spending much time with them in Denver, uncomfortable with Denver's structured society.

Hutch was writing another book about the problems family ranchers and farmers were having competing with the large corporate enterprises.

He still kept in touch with his old Air Force buddies. They still planned a reunion every other year. They have little in common after all these years, except their wartime experiences. They'd laugh and joke and drink a little too much at their get-togethers, but it's the only time they speak of their war time experiences. War is something they don't seem to talk about at home.

Now in our forties, we'd never had a real vacation until the kids offered to run the ranch with the help of our foreman, while we went to Hawaii to celebrate our anniversary. They did all the planning, made hotel reservations, purchased first class airplane tickets, made lists of places to visit, all on their father's credit card, of course.

We spent two glorious weeks sleeping late and eating well. Our days consisted of sitting on deck chairs in the sand on beautiful Waikiki beach, swimming in the ocean, and appreciating our good fortune. The long scar on Hutch's left leg was still evident. He would limp when he was overly tired or stood too long. I knew it still bothered him when it was cold. If I asked if he was in pain, the answer was always the same, "What's a little discomfort. I made it home," he'd say. "I was the one out of three who did. I beat the odds." He told me the saying among the Pilots was any one who made it back from their first mission was living on borrowed time.

The Air Force awarded Hutch the Silver Star for navigating the plane to a safe landing area, despite being wounded, when it was evident they couldn't make it back to base, thereby saving the crew. The whole time even though he was in severe pain and bleeding heavily from his wound, he succeeded in downing two German fighter planes before passing out.

We took long walks on the beach after dark, enjoying the carefree existence, and made love every night like a couple of newlyweds.

On our last evening before heading home, we went for a long walk along a secluded portion of beach. The only sound was from the waves as they crashed on shore, the only light from the moon and the stars. I was thinking back over the years we'd spent together, still feeling the glow from the champagne we drank earlier at our anniversary dinner.

Hutch took my hand as we slowly ambled further down the beach. "I've been thinking what a lucky guy I am. Marrying you was the smartest, most rewarding thing I've ever done. Nothing I've accomplished would have happened without your help, nor would it have meant a thing without you. You're the sweetest, prettiest girl I ever met, but you're the only one who would have stood by me in those early days at the ranch."

Hutch stopped and turned toward me. "I loved you with my whole being the day we married, but that can't compare with the way I love you now. Are you happy, Maya? No regrets?"

"I've never been happier than I am this very minute. I'm so proud of you. I look at you and can't believe your mine."

Hutch slipped his arm around my waist, that same twinkle in his eye. "Let's head back to our room. I'm in the mood to show you just how much I love you."

His touch still sent tingles down my spine.

We were ready to go home. Nice as Hawaii was, nothing was as special as our ranch.

Sofia and Archie's daughter, Donna, was to be married in the spring. The whole family was invited. I hadn't been home since Grandpa's funeral, and thought we should all attend. When the invitation arrived, it seemed the wedding would take place in Providence. Archie was now a full professor at Brown as was the father of the groom. I was relieved. I had no desire to see the farm again. I wanted to remember everything just as it was. I couldn't bear to think of Grandpa's bedroom other than how I remembered it, nor, did I want to know if any part of the land had been sold.

I'd taken one of the most memorable parts of my childhood with me the day of Grandpa's funeral, my grandparents wedding picture and had it restored, matted, and framed. It hangs in our bedroom as a reminder that love conquers hardship.

Sofia and Archie's daughter's wedding was such a special time. Hutch looked so distinguished in the well-tailored business suit he seldom wore. The weathered look of a rancher and the slight limp added to the mystic. My sons' concessions to suits and ties were dress boots. They insisted cattlemen never wore anything but boots. Our beautiful daughters, Janey and Molly were well turned out in new dresses, and if I say so myself, I'm aging well.

We were invited to a family dinner, the night before the ceremony, to meet the bride and groom and the groom's family. I received a warm greeting from Uncle Benjamin as we entered the banquet room at the hotel. He'd been to our wedding, but I'd only spoken with him once at Grandpa's funeral. His wife, Leah, looked as if she wished to be anywhere but where she was. Her daughters and grandchildren also looked down their noses at the group. Uncle Benjamin was some bigwig in Hartford's Jewish community and I guess, in her mind, we didn't measure up.

I met Uncle Daniel's wife, Deborah, for the first time and liked her immediately. She was outgoing, very pretty and seemed the perfect match for shy, reserved Daniel. She had been a war widow with two young children when Uncle Daniel married her. They now had two children of their own and Daniel headed a successful investment company.

Uncle Richard's law firm was large and well regarded in Hartford. He and Aunt Helen looked wonderful. Helen and I still correspond now and then. Their sons were now married men. My parent's, of course, were glad to see us, but the most joyous greeting came from Sofia. She kept telling me how wonderful it was to see me and how happy she was that we brought our children.

Hutch seemed quite at home in the crowd. He had a way of relating to people that I've never mastered.

I was so glad we made the effort. The wedding was lovely as was the reception, but most of all, seeing my family together for such a happy occasion was special, probably not to happen again.

My brother, Billy, sent his regrets. He'd married a girl he met during the war when his ship was in dry dock in Bremerton. He stayed on in Washington after he was discharged from the Navy and was in the construction business in Seattle. As the distance between Seattle and Denver isn't that great, we see them and their two children from time to time.

When we said our goodbye, I looked around the room and wished that Grandpa could have been there. How proud he'd be to see how successful his family was. He came to this country with a few pennies in his pocket and a dream he pursued until he made it come true. He set an example for his sons to follow. Only one failed to live up to his standards.

Had Grandpa stayed in Russia all the family would probably be dead by now, as the number of Jew's slaughtered in the war alone numbered over six million.

Chapter 55

There had been talk in political circles of asking Hutch to run for an open senate seat, but he turned them down saying he wouldn't be happy spending so much time in Washington, away from home and family.

Our kids were growing up so fast it scared me. Our eldest son David was interested in staying in the cattle business. He'd entered Texas A.& M. We hope Chris will do the same. We looked forward to the time we could turn some of the responsibilities over to the boys. Although we have a good crew, we'd love more time to ourselves.

Things were changing in the cattle business. Most of the time, the ranch hands checked on the herd with motorized vehicles. The only time they used horses was to round up the strays in the hills or to bring in the calves for branding, or for shipping steers to the feedlot. Hutch had been researching and visiting feedlot operations and was thinking of duplicating what he'd seen on a portion of the ranch. We could fatten our steers for market as well as those of the other local producers. He thought it could be a very profitable enterprise.

Janey is to be married next July to a young lawyer she met when he was in law school at the University of Colorado, and attended one of the Hutchinson's fabulous Christmas parties. He's a fine young man who'll make a wonderful addition to our family. Janey will be moving to Denver. I offered her the wedding dress I was married in, explaining how it had been handed down through the generations. She declined. Kids nowadays have little interest in tradition. I guess I should be thankful the wedding won't be love beads and tee shirts emblazoned with "Make love not war."

Maybe Molly will be interested in the dress when it's her turn to marry. She loves ranch life so I'm sure she'll wed one of our neighbor's sons and stay close to home. Her daddy bought her a lovely quarter horse mare she's been taking to local horseshows getting ready for the fall's world-class event in Denver.

The Vietnam War is escalating. Having two sons of draft age, Hutch is worried sick.

"Once you've seen war up close, you never want your son's to experience what you've been through, to see what you've seen," he said one evening as we watched the news. Time would tell.

There's a new ground swell for Hutch to run for governor. This time he hasn't said no, only maybe. As his mother once told me, he was bound for greatness. Imagine me, the wife of the governor of the state. I smiled, knowing what my Grandpa would say if he were here. "God Bless America."

CPSIA information can be obtained
at www.ICGtesting.com
Printed in the USA
LVOW11s1011250318
571079LV00003B/210/P